Girl of Fire

The Expulsion Project Book One

Norma Hinkens

Published by Dunecadia Publishing, California

ISBN 978-0-9966248-7-9

For Jeanette Morris, my Editing Queen, Mentor, and Friend.
You fanned those flames and kept me believing.

Chapter 1

Oka trudged across the gleaming hextron-tile floor, his feet dragging like concrete blocks chained to one another. In his arms he carried his only child, the wires that would be her lifeline for the next two weeks trailing from her bare, blue-veined chest. Three-year-old Trattora's red curls lay matted over her forehead; her long lashes swept closed in an induced sleep. Oka kissed her button nose softly, hating the jarring antiseptic odor that filled his nostrils where the sweet smell of her baby breath still lingered.

"We both know it's the right decision," Fir said, her expression solemn as she took the sedated child from Oka's arms and positioned her in a poly-palladium oxygen pod. Trattora's tiny crimson lips parted in a barely perceptible moan when Fir's latex-gloved fingers checked her airway one last time. Then she deftly connected the cardiopulmonary monitoring system and nutrient line that would sustain the child on her journey.

Oka shivered deep in his bones at the sight of his comatose daughter lying in the expulsion pod he had designed, and which now eerily resembled a casket to his overwrought mind. He hunched over it, his eyes desperately drinking in what would surely be the last sight he would ever have of Trattora, her chubby fists flung wide in slumber at the very moment he needed to feel them wrapped tightly around his neck.

The modified CoMMonitor on her left wrist would track her perilous voyage from Mhakerta through the Netherscape and confirm if she made it to one of the inhabited planets within the jurisdiction of the Syndicate ... or not. After that, it would automatically deactivate and the last tangible link would be broken between them. Other than her name and birthdate engraved on the CoMMonitor, Trattora would have nothing left to connect her to her old life.

It was for the best—he and his colleagues had all come to the same gut-wrenching conclusion. But his heart still ached with the knowledge that his daughter fell asleep trusting he would be there as always when she opened her intelligent, green eyes. If the expulsion pod avoided the Maulers' detection radars and embedded successfully, she would soon forget him. She would grow up ignorant of the life she was born into, and the father who was by her side when she took her first steps on Mhakerta.

There would be no more firsts for them. His breath caught in his throat at the soul-destroying thought.

"It's time, Oka." Fir laid a commanding hand on his shoulder.

He turned to her, his red-rimmed eyes betraying the agony he had wrestled with through the long hours of the previous night. He wondered if Fir had also gone back and forth on whether to go through with it—even up to these last minutes. Her demeanor was as composed as ever, her dark hair slicked back in her trademark immaculate bun, but there was an air of defeat in the hunch of her shoulders that spoke of the burden she bore.

Oka let out a shuddering sigh and followed her over to the control hub. Despite this being the only course of action left to them, it was ripping his heart out every step of the process. Genocidal Artificial Intelligence was on the verge of taking over Mhakerta. The self-actualizing software program behind the hostile takeover had named itself Preeminence, and as a member of ASRI, the Advanced Scientific Research Institute, Oka was among a handful of Mhakerta's elite scientists privy to the truth of how close they were to losing the race for control of Mhakerta's quadrants to AI. Eighteen months ago, during an upgrade of the universal natural language processing system, Oka and his team inadvertently uncovered Preeminence's insidious plan to assimilate all tracer molecules in human brain matter with an IQ of 110 or higher into the mainframe by 2217. Preeminence would begin with the youngest and freshest material.

"We need to stay strong for the others," Fir said, frowning at Oka as she pulled off her gloves and disposed of them in a vaporization chute. "They'll be here any minute."

Oka bobbed his head in response and ran a trembling hand over his unshaven face. He, Fir, and three of their most trusted colleagues had worked tirelessly over the past year on a radical counter initiative to save their gifted children from becoming scientific soup in the new world order to come. They had created the top-secret expulsion project or TEP as they referred to it, to evacuate their children in specially designed pods to various planets under the jurisdiction of the Syndicate. It was a high-risk venture—all interplanetary travel was now restricted from within Mhakerta, and there was also a chance of being intercepted by Maulers. But the statistical probability of duping Preeminence's IQ screening program was zero.

Oka wandered over to the pod opposite Trattora's and pressed his lips tightly together at the pitiful sight. Fir's four-year-old son, Velkan, lay peacefully curled to one side, the smooth, chocolate skin on his handsome face flushed with sleep. "I've never seen him this still before," Oka remarked, choking up. "He's usually tearing around your feet like a nitro-tornado."

Fir's lips curved upward, but her eyes clouded. "I only hope he lives to run again one day—far from here."

Oka blinked back stinging tears. He struggled to find something comforting to say, but he could think of nothing. There would be no happy reunion. As soon as the expulsion pods launched, the laboratory would be vaporized in a well-timed industrial accident that would bury the evidence of their clandestine project. They wouldn't even have this room left to meet in and reminisce about their children.

Oka jerked his head up as the doors to the laboratory slid apart. Gustin hurried inside wheeling a mobile microplane processor, his blanched face and bleary eyes a clear indication he too had slept little in the final hours.

"No complications?" Fir raised a well-groomed brow at him.

Gustin shook his head, unsmiling. He leaned down and opened the steel doors on the cart below the processor and carefully slid out a stack of lab linens. His fingers trembled as he peeled off the top layer and uncovered his young son, Phin. Oka swallowed hard when Gustin clutched his child to his massive chest like a giant wounded animal that knows his offspring is about to be ripped away.

Oka turned away to hide his grief. He couldn't cave in front of the others, especially not Gustin. Gustin was a last-minute addition to TEP after another conflicted colleague backed out— he had been left with little time to steel himself for the enormity of what they were about to set in motion.

"You're already late," Fir said, pulling on another pair of gloves. "Time to kiss him good-bye, Gustin."

His face taut with pain, Gustin lifted the sleeping child from his chest and pressed his lips to Phin's forehead.

"I'll take it from here." Fir held her white-sleeved arms out for the child.

Gustin's shoulders shook as Fir took his son and attached the nasal prongs that would deliver the requisite oxygen to keep the child alive throughout the expulsion to the Syndicate planets. Phin flinched, his tiny nose twitching momentarily before he sank back into his sedated state.

Fir placed the child in an empty pod and adjusted the radiant thermablaster that would keep his temperature at a constant 98.6 degrees for the duration of the trip.

The door to the laboratory slid open again, and Dinah tripped through pushing a cart loaded with supplies for the stock room. Her sunken eyes sought out Fir, and for a long moment, she stared at her, keeping a firm grip on the cart's handle.

"We talked about this, Dinah, remember?" Fir said gently as if addressing a child reluctant to relinquish a prized possession.

Dropping her gaze, Dinah released her grip and backed slowly away from the cart as if it might detonate at any minute.

She rubbed her hands nervously up and down her lab coat. Fir gave her an approving nod and wheeled the cart over to an empty pod. She dug through the polymeric materials piled on top of the supply cart and reached for two-and-a-half-year-old Ayma tucked beneath them.

"Wait!" Dinah called out breathlessly.

Oka jerked his head in her direction. Surely, she wasn't going to back out now. He watched, heart pounding, as she stumbled over to where Fir stood.

"Please, let her take this with her." Dinah choked back a sob as she pressed something into Fir's hand.

Fir looked down at it and frowned. "You know the rules. We all agreed."

"I want her to know her mother loved her," Dinah said, wiping the back of her hand across her eyes.

Fir tightened her lips. She placed the locket back in Dinah's hand and closed her fingers firmly over it. "Love is sacrifice, not sentiment. Don't sabotage Ayma's chance to forget. Be the clinician you were trained to be." She gave Dinah's shoulder a quick squeeze before turning her attention back to the child. Gently, she lifted Ayma from the supply cart and positioned her in one of the two remaining empty pods before attaching the infrared oximeter to her ankle that would monitor her oxygen levels en route. Ayma splayed her fingers briefly without uttering a sound. Dinah clapped a hand over her mouth, her eyes wild and watering.

Oka bit his bottom lip until the coppery taste of blood filled his mouth. He desperately wanted to walk over there and comfort Dinah—to tell her he understood the searing pain slicing through her heart like a scalpel—but it was too dangerous to acknowledge that pain until after the children were safely launched. If one link in the chain broke, they would all fold, and he was already dangerously close to the edge.

"So far, so good." Fir smiled tightly around at her pale-faced colleagues. "Once Ivel gets here, I'll review the final steps."

Oka glanced at the holographic timekeeper. They were out of sequence. Ivel should have arrived from the shipping department before Dinah. There must have been some kind of delivery delay. A little disconcerting, but not uncommon since the drone upgrade a few weeks back. Ivel had no choice but to wait for the delivery to come in. He needed the cover of the packages to smuggle his daughter, Leba, inside the laboratory for the scheduled expulsion.

Oka's anxiety mounted as the minutes ticked by. He ran a hand across the back of his prickling neck as he paced by the pods, not daring to stop moving in case he found himself ripping the tubes from Trattora's chest and running as far away as possible from the lab with her. Even now, so close to the launch, he didn't trust his heart not to fail him. But he couldn't allow that to happen. Despite the pain eating him alive at the thought of letting her go, he wouldn't keep his daughter here to suffer the same fate that awaited him.

There had been three prior attempts by AI to seize control of Mhakerta's mainframe architecture; all ultimately failed. This one would not. Preeminence had mastered the deep learning neural network it was built on and crunched an inordinate number of data sets into algorithms to outwit the software designed as a safeguard to control it. Any day now, Preeminence would seize power in a bloodless coup. With the entire robot military at its disposal, it would be an unstoppable force. They had met their match, and it hadn't come in the form of a Mauler attack or annexation by the Syndicate, as some had feared for years.

"I'm going to link to Ivel," Fir said. "We need a status update. We can't risk running late with the launch."

Oka stopped pacing and walked over to the control hub where Fir was adjusting an archaic headset. They had rigged up a basic link system to communicate outside of the universal access channels during the year they were secretly working on TEP. After today, the link system would go dark. They would never again discuss TEP. The eyes and ears of Preeminence were everywhere. There were even reports in the last few weeks of citizens being arrested for what their dreams revealed about them. Fearmongering, perhaps, but Oka and his colleagues knew that cranio-neural surveillance was now a real possibility. Preeminence was already vastly more powerful than anyone could have predicted, and could most certainly eliminate every perceived threat in its path.

Fir set up the link to Ivel's ID and waited impatiently for him to connect. "I ran a diagnostic. There's nothing wrong with the radio."

"He may not be able to talk right now," Oka said.

Fir looked up, alarm flitting across her ordinarily composed features. "You think something's happened?"

Oka rubbed his brow. Part of him hoped something *would* happen to disrupt the launch, to give him another twenty-four hours with his daughter. But it was a selfish thought. It meant

Trattora would share in the same fate that awaited him. "I just meant he may have been held up. Let's give him a few more minutes."

Fir grimaced. "I don't think—"

A flashing red light pulsed over the ceiling, shocking the scientists into silence. Seconds later an electronic voice chimed through the space. "Breach alert in progress. Trespass detection. All sentinels to Gamma One."

Oka and Fir exchanged distraught looks.

"If they don't find the trespasser, the sentinels will sweep the entire building," Oka said. "The children will be discovered."

"Can we bring the launch forward?" Gustin asked.

Fir shook her head. "The pirate program is already running. We can't alter the code or it won't overwrite itself afterward. They'll be able to track and destroy the pods."

Fir's headset crackled briefly. Her eyes widened. "It's Ivel! I'll put him on speaker."

"Fir, do you read me?"

Fir adjusts her headset. "Ivel! Where are you? Are you all right?"

"I'm not coming."

"What do you mean you're not coming?" Fir cried. "Where's Leba?"

"She's with me ... in Gamma One."

Oka sucked in a long, cold breath. This is what he had feared most, a nightmare that had woken him up trembling and dripping sweat many times; that one of them would crack and they would all be outed before the children could be saved.

"What are you doing in the flight tower?" Fir asked, her tone even and controlled once more.

"I can't do it," Ivel rasped. "I can't let Leba go!"

Fir inhaled and exhaled. "Listen to me very carefully, Ivel. You need to get out of there as quickly as possible. Use the service elevachute and—"

"It's over Fir. The tower is sealed. Are the others there ... with you?"

Fir blinked back tears, the first tears Oka remembered seeing in her eyes. "Yes," she whispered.

"Good," Ivel replied. "I'm glad for them. Good-bye, Fir. May all our flights be successful."

The link disconnected abruptly.

Fir looked around at the other scientists, her face pale and drawn.

"What did he mean?" Dinah asked, her eyes bouncing back and forth between her colleagues like buoys bobbing on a wild sea. "What's he talking about? Why did he take Leba to the flight tower? You don't think he's going to try and steal an ethercopter, do you?"

Fir tightened her jaw. "I don't know, but we're out of time. Activate your children's CoMMonitors."

The scientists exchanged uncertain looks as they pulled up their left sleeves. With trembling fingers, they keyed in the authorization codes on their own modified CoMMonitors. One by one, the devices on their children's wrists lit up and beeped, indicating that the honing signals were operational.

"Link protocol looks good," Fir said. "Time to seal the pods." She walked back over to the control hub and pulled down a green lever. Gleaming egg-shaped lids closed over the sleeping children like synchronized buds shutting out the world when the sun fades. Dinah buried her face in her hands and sobbed quietly.

"Beginning launch sequence," Fir said, squaring her shoulders. She flinched when another flashing red light pulsed through the ceiling.

"Illegal ethercopter departure alert," the electronic voice announced.

Oka's lungs froze over. It must be Ivel. What was he thinking? He would never make it out of the restricted zone.

Oka scrunched his eyes shut and waited, his heart thumping so loudly in his chest he thought it would explode before the ethercopter did. But it didn't. His own heart kept beating. A moment later, a dull reverberation rippled through the laboratory walls, confirming the inevitable. His stomach twisted with a new grief.

"Target eliminated," the electronic voice chirped. "Breach alert resolved. Sentinels stand down and return to stations."

Fir frowned, the deep "V" in the center of her forehead the only visible indication of her anguish at the knowledge that Ivel and his young daughter, Leba, had just been obliterated by Preeminence's robotic air defense system—unerringly accurate, as always.

She had created it.

"To defend humanity," she whispered more to herself than anyone else.

Oka reached over and squeezed Fir's shoulder awkwardly. "No one could have predicted it would be used against us."

That wasn't exactly true, and they both knew it. They had discussed the risk, and others like it, many times, but ultimately decided a robotic defense system was a necessary evil, considering the growing threats from Maulers and other Galactic Pirates.

Fir avoided making eye contact as she turned back to the control hub. "Consigning pods for departure." She depressed a sequence of buttons and then straightened up and faced her colleagues again. "Five minutes to lift off. Time for us to make our exit."

Without a backward glance, the four scientists filed silently out through the entry doors and made their way along the corridor to the high-speed elevachute. They rode the thirty-seven floors up to the ground level of the ASRI headquarters in under thirty seconds, scanned their ID's at the security gate, and exited through the glass doors at the front of the building. Oka nodded a curt good-bye to his colleagues and turned onto the main thoroughfare to begin the short trek home.

At eighteen hundred hours and thirteen minutes, he glanced back over his shoulder. A brilliant ball of scarlet and mustard lit up the sky over the spot where the underground laboratory lay buried.

Chapter 2

Fourteen years later ...

"Oremongers docking!"

I flinch, my spear poised for the kill. The small herd of three-horned sham scatters in a cloud of dust at the shout. I lower my arm, my spine tingling with a raw excitement that supersedes the thrill of the hunt. I've heard tales of oremongers and other galactic traders whispered against a backdrop of flickering campfires, the smell of roasting meat tickling my nostrils, but it's the first time in fourteen moons that a trade ship has docked on Cwelt. The last one brought me here.

"Trattora! Where are you?"

I peer out from my hiding place high in the rocks and grin as I take aim and land my spear with a satisfying *whoosh* directly in front of Buir's leather-bound feet.

She gasps and hops backward. "I wish you wouldn't do that," she shouts, her eyes roving in vain over the jagged outcroppings. She won't spot me; at best, I'll be a streak in her vision against the burning sun. I can leap as nimbly as any sham, and vanish like a vapor into the dark crevices in these formations. I come here to be alone—when the sense of not belonging anywhere becomes too overwhelming.

"That was payback," I say, splaying my fingers in greeting as I vault down from behind a large luminescent indigo boulder. "You scared off the herd of shams I've been tracking all afternoon, and I was in sore need of that kill." I gesture at the latest tear in my shamskin cloak—a fault line, even by my tolerant standards, and the third cloak I've ruined this month.

Buir raises a filigreed brow at me. As always, she is immaculately turned out—her gleaming hair woven tightly around her scalp, her shamskin accessorized with an enameled brooch fashioned by a revered Cweltan craftsman.

"Your father won't be pleased that you were hunting where the dead are mourned," she scolds. "Or that you greet the oremongers in such disheveled shape."

Buir takes her advisory role in how I present myself in affairs of state more seriously than I'd like. Her father died fifteen moons ago in service to my adoptive father, the chieftain, and she strives to honor his memory in every way she can. I link my arm in hers and tug her playfully to my side. "We'll strike my first misdemeanor from the record as we both know you're not going to rat me out." I throw a quick glance down at my ruined cloak, and shrug. "As for my shoddy appearance, my only defense is that I wasn't expecting visitors after this many moons of isolation."

Buir's the only person who knows I hunt in the sacred triangle, and despite her disapproval, she indulges me on this one issue. She understands that at times I need to rest my head against the coolness of one of its magnificent boulders when the pain inside me swells until my chest hurts. Something about the solitude here has a healing quality to it.

Cweltan legend claims warring galactic gods hurled the spectacular luminescent rocks at each other, and that they hold some mysterious power. Since our elders still haven't figured out what that power is, snagging the odd kill here doesn't seem unreasonable to me.

"Hurry!" I say, unlinking my arm from Buir's. "I don't want to miss the landing."

We tuck our cloaks into our leather belts and break into a run toward the settlement that houses our thirty-thousand-or-so strong population. Cwelt is a tiny, fringe planet in the Netherscape, outside the jurisdiction of the Syndicate, and also beyond their protection. Navigating the Netherscape is fraught with danger, not the least of which is the risk of encountering Maulers who regularly hijack trading vessels, seize slaves, and invade sovereign nations to extend their reach and resources. The Syndicate occasionally patrols the Netherscape, but only attempting to protect its own borders. The fate of other sovereign nations is only of interest to them if resources are at stake, and Cwelt has no tribute worthy enough to offer a protector.

My breath tingles the back of my throat as I run. My heart beats wildly, not from exertion—I can pound the dirt for hours like any long-legged Cweltan—but from exhilaration. I've dreamed of this day for many moons. Pictured it in my loneliest moments staked out on a hunt, my cloak wrapped tightly around me against a bracing solar wind. I'm hoping, of course, that there are people like me on board the ship. Fiery-haired and white-skinned. At the very least, they might know of others like me.

Apart from the lights of the odd Syndicate patrol with its distinctive insignia of a flaming planet, I've never seen a ship, other than the few wrecks half-buried in the desert beyond our farms. Ordinarily, the Syndicate patrols give planets like Cwelt a wide berth. Fringe planets are too remote and primitive for them to bother with. But no one has an explanation for why the traders don't come anymore. Astro fruit from our farms and our shamskins used to be highly prized commodities along the eastern arterial trade route. In return, my father purchased educational materials from the Syndicate EduPlex system, technical and medical DigiPads from societies advanced far beyond our own. He takes great pride in the fact that I have absorbed it all and deciphered things the elders could not understand. I fear it's the only area in which I truly please him.

I glance again at the unseemly tear in my tunic. Despite my nonchalant response to Buir, I'm secretly worried about my father's reaction to my less-than-regal appearance. As chieftain, he demands a certain level of decorum from his daughter. He's almost always sorely disappointed. I'm nothing like my graceful mother. I'm not like anyone on Cwelt. No fully grown adult here is under six feet tall, and the hair on their heads is waterfall-straight and shimmery white from birth, which is why they are endlessly fascinated by the way my red hair ripples uncontrollably over my freckled shoulders when I turn it loose.

The ground beneath us begins to vibrate and an unfamiliar rumbling fills our ears. "This way!" I say, grabbing Buir so that we don't get separated.

We elbow our way to the front of the seething crowd and stare in awe at the oremonger's ship powering down in a shroud of dust on the far side of the settlement. A crude patchwork of soldered metal, for the most part, totally unlike the intergalactic cruisers, battleships and trading vessels the elders describe from moons gone by. It's more like the wrecks buried in the desert, but to me it is the most beautiful sight I have ever seen. My nostrils twitch at the unfamiliar odor of fumes wafting our way. "Do you think they will let us on board?" I whisper to Buir.

Her ice-gray eyes widen. "I'm not going anywhere in it. They could be kidnappers."

I laugh. "I just meant to look around. Not to go anywhere."

Buir has little desire for adventure and none for risk. Like many other Cweltans, she's convinced she will die the moment she leaves Cwelt's atmosphere. Campfire folklore, of course. I've already been beyond it.

I glance around and spot my father a few feet to my left. He's robed in his finest shamskin and wearing his three-horned headpiece encrusted with augamond stones from our neighboring planet, Oxtian. In his gnarled right hand, he clutches his spear. From his waist dangles a ray gun salvaged from one of the ships that crash landed here many moons before I arrived. It doesn't work, but the oremongers won't know that.

At my father's side, as always, is his advisor, Parthelon. His long frame bends as he whispers in my father's ear. At almost eight feet tall, Parthelon is the tallest man on Cwelt. He dislikes me, although he hides it well around my father. My mother once told me that Parthelon tried to talk them out of buying me from the traders who brought me here, even though he knew how much they longed for a child in their old age. He was worried I would taint the Cweltan genes if I married among them. But there's no danger of that. Cweltan men view me as a curiosity, not an attraction.

My fingers instinctively reach for the tiny bracelet engraved with my name and birthdate that hangs from a chain around my neck. I suspect it may have contained a tracking device at one point, but the electronics inside are dead. I don't know if my birth parents are dead too, or if I was stolen from them by Maulers. Or perhaps they were sent to an interplanetary penal colony and forced to give me up, which is not uncommon on planets in the four quadrants under Syndicate jurisdiction.

My eyes settle hungrily on the visiting ship. If I bought passage with traders, I might be able to find out where my bracelet was forged. I sigh inwardly. As the chieftain's only heir, the elders would most certainly forbid it. I swallow down a familiar painful lump. My destiny is here now. Only Parthelon would be pleased if I disappeared with the oremongers.

A collective gasp ripples through the crowd as the ship's enormous cargo bay slowly hinges open revealing centrifugal mining gear and impact grinders. I recognize the equipment from the educational materials I have pored over. The oremongers will be sorely disappointed to learn that Cwelt has nothing to offer them after they risked passage through the Netherscape.

Buir elbows me excitedly when several figures emerge on the deck. "So … strange-looking," she gasps.

I scrutinize the group of four oremongers as they descend the metal ramp and begin making their way toward us, led by a stocky, flat-nosed woman. They're shorter than Cweltans, dressed in simple tunics of earthen shades, shod in leather boots. The most striking thing about them is that they're bald-headed. All but one. He walks at the back of the pack, the subservient position, yet his stride is assured—verging on a swagger. He's taller than the rest of the party and broader, but nowhere near as tall as Parthelon. My lips curve upward when I see his caramel-colored skin and long, glossy black hair, woven into skeins and bouncing off his back. He too is a stranger among his people.

I gesture discreetly at him and whisper to Buir, "Look at the dark one! He rides too close to the sun."

"Either that or he's ill. He's got some strange marking on his neck, too." She leans over and whispers in my ear. "Can you believe they expose their heads like that? They look naked!"

My father steps forward and splays his hand in greeting to the stocky woman. "Salutations!"

The oremonger returns the greeting with a quick nod of acknowledgment and introduces herself as Sarth. She grins patronizingly at the crowd of onlookers, displaying an assortment of dingy-looking teeth. Brows like angry dashes frame her dark, unsmiling eyes. The other three members of her party hang back, their expressions guarded. Directly behind Sarth is a tall, narrow-hipped man with sturdy shoulders, a beaked nose, and a knot in his neck that looks like a tumor. By his side is a much younger man with a squashed face, built like a boulder, and then the caramel-colored outsider. All three look as if they're poised to bolt if anything untoward happens. If they're armed, they're hiding it well.

"Cwelt welcomes you as the first traders in fourteen moons,"

Parthelon announces, with a flourish of his hand.

Sarth flicks a disinterested glance up at him and then addresses my father. "My ship, the Zebulux, has an ailing thruster. I request safe haven here until we can repair it."

"You come unarmed?" my father asks.

Sarth gives an unconvincing nod. "We left our weapons on board. We come in peace."

"Then your request is granted." My father motions behind him at the crowd pressing in. "You must forgive my people's curiosity. It's been many moons since we've seen a trading vessel of any sort. How did you find your way to us?"

A wary look comes over Sarth's face. "We stumbled on a tertiary route through the Netherscape. It brought us past several old fringe trading posts such as yours." She looks around with a sharp eye. "I had hoped to find parts, but I see you have no fleet."

"Our population is small," my father explains.

Sarth tents a hand over her eyes and surveys the craggy hills behind our settlement. "What *do* you have of interest to a speculative oremonger operation?"

"Our trade in the past consisted of shamskins and astro fruit," my father replies. "We harvest several different varieties that aren't grown anywhere else in our planetary system."

Sarth's brow ripples with displeasure. "Skins and foodstuffs trade for nothing. Don't you deal in minerals or metals at all?"

Parthelon straightens up to his full height. "There is nothing worth mining on Cwelt." He gestures at his spear. "Even the tips on our spears were bought from traders in moons past. Like the chieftain said, we trade in shamskins and rare fruit, both of which are highly prized on Syndicate planets."

Sarth curls her bottom lip. "*Were* highly prized. I'm not interested in schlepping a cargo of fruit along the trade route without a guaranteed buyer. The Syndicate has hortoreplication plants everywhere to create foodstuffs nowadays." She turns back to my father. "They'll still pay a handsome sum for the right minerals and metals, though. Perhaps we can run some core samples, now that we're here."

My father inclines his head. "You have my permission, although I must warn you that oremongers have tried in the past and found nothing. But first, allow my people to refresh you with some sustenance."

Sarth gestures behind her to the rest of her party and they step forward to follow my father and Parthelon. The crowd parts to let them through. Cweltan children point and whisper excitedly to one another as the oremongers pass in front of them.

I freeze when my father's gaze falls on me like a dark cloud harboring rain. When he waves me over, I stand rooted to the spot until Buir pokes me into action. "Go!" she hisses in my ear.

Smoothing down my cloak as best I can, I pick my way over to my father, one elbow pressed against the gaping tear in my shamskin.

Masking the disapproval in his eyes, he turns to Sarth. "Allow me to introduce my daughter, Trattora."

Sarth's eyes rove over me with the calculating gaze of a trader for whom everything is for sale. "A fine specimen, Chieftain. Evidently not from your loins or these parts. Impressive, what your prized fruit can be traded for."

My father's knuckles tighten around his spear. A faint smile appears on Parthelon's lips.

I flush and toss my head, inadvertently catching the dark-skinned stranger's eye. He winks brazenly at me. My cheeks burn even more and I turn away, hurrying after my father as he leads the oremongers to the Great Hall.

I don't escape the stranger's attention for long. Parthelon seats me next to him at the main table. It's a subtle insult; placing the chieftain's daughter beside the lowest person of honor in the oremongers' party. Parthelon knows exactly what he's doing, but it will pass as an oversight in the midst of the excitement of welcoming our first guests in fourteen moons. My father has every intention of sending the oremongers on their way with a good report of our hospitality. Our finest musicians stroll through the Great Hall with their lyres, while shamskin horn candelabras flicker in the center of the sumptuous spread of fruit, nuts, vegetables, and cold cuts of meat that the women have pulled together from their homes.

I reach for the wooden bowl of astro fruit being handed to me and offer it to the dark-haired stranger. His fingers briefly brush mine as he takes it. I flinch, startled by the tingling feeling that runs up my arm. Maybe Buir is right, and he is indeed sick.

"I'm Velkan." He leans toward me conspiratorially. "You're not *really* the chieftain's daughter, are you?" He raises his brows. "I mean, they seated you next to me after all, and with your flaming hair … you don't look remotely Cweltan."

I peel the delicate yellow skin of the astro fruit in my hand and take a hearty bite from it. "Maybe I'm a genetic anomaly."

Velkan laughs. "That goes without saying. Compared to everyone else here, you're somewhat on the short side."

"More *your* height, you mean."

He grimaces. "I'm used to towering over the crew, but I'm on the short side here. So, are you going to tell me how you ended up here?"

"The traders who came through fourteen moons ago brought me here." I grin across at him. "Did you bring anything more interesting?"

His lips twitch. "I doubt it. I've never met anyone with hair the color of an angry sun before. Where did the traders find you?"

I wipe the juice from my chin and shrug. "They didn't give too many details, but they were in an awful hurry to get rid of me." I twirl my finger around a lock of red hair that has tumbled out from the coil on my head. "They were afraid of this."

Velkan lets out a snort. "Some of the primitive planets in the Netherscape live in mortal dread of encountering a half-breed species. They probably thought you had some kind of power in your hair." He leans closer until I can feel his breath on my cheek. "Do you, *Girl of Fire*?"

I laugh. "My hair holds no secret power. What about you?" I ask, reaching out to touch his hair. I twist a piece between my fingers. It's a strange, wiry texture, nothing like Buir's silky mane or my own soft waves. "You don't look anything like the other oremongers. I've never seen anyone so dark."

He glances furtively across the table at Sarth. "I'm not one of them," he says, the mirth gone from his voice. "Sarth's my owner. I've been a trade serf since I was a child." He twists his head and points discreetly to a holographic tattoo projecting two inches out from the side of his neck. "My owner's brand. She calls me her first helmsman when she's in a good mood, but I'm still just a serf."

I pull my lips down in an apologetic gesture. I'm shocked, but I don't want to show my naiveté. I guessed he was in Sarth's employment, but not as a slave. Whatever my origins were, at least I was fortunate enough not to be indentured as a child. "Where did she pick you up?" I ask.

Velkan leans back in his chair. "Near the outer rim of the Netherscape. She was on a remote mining operation. She wouldn't tell me the name of the planet."

I steal a glance across at Sarth. "She seems a sly trader. What did she trade for you?"

"Nothing. She got lucky."

My eyes widen. "You mean she acquired you … in a bet?"

Velkan shakes his head. "Even crazier than that. You wouldn't believe me if I told you."

"Try me."

He flicks a skein of black hair over his shoulder and leans in to whisper in my ear. "She dug me up in a casket."

Chapter 3

I pull away and roll my eyes at Velkan. "The oremongers must keep you around for entertainment. For a moment there, I really thought you were going to tell me how Sarth acquired you. But you actually don't know, do you?"

"I knew you wouldn't believe me." Velkan reaches for a red-skinned astro fruit. I wait for him to burst out laughing, but instead, a wistful expression comes over his face.

I frown at him. "You don't *really* buy that story Sarth told you, do you?"

Velkan shrugs. "She made it sound pretty convincing. *Someone* buried me alive, a kidnapping for ransom gone wrong, she reckons. I was in a high-tech oxygen pod. Sarth said she got a small fortune for it. My birth parents might be from Aristozonex."

I run a hand distractedly over my half-coiled hair. The Syndicate is headquartered on Aristozonex, one of the largest and wealthiest planets, and home to the Syndicate's formidable fleet of warships. I don't want to crush Velkan's spirits, but I have a strong suspicion Sarth enjoys taunting him with hints of a wealthy background. Just like she taunted me with a stab at my worth in astro fruit.

I place my hands beneath my chin and eye Velkan playfully. "So, how can I be sure you're not really a ghost?"

A flash of irritation goes through his eyes. Almost as if he realizes I don't believe him, and that I'm trying to soften the blow with humor.

"I was—" He clamps his lips together when the room suddenly falls silent. At the center of the table, my father rises to his impressive height.

He raises a wooden mug of fermented astro fruit juice in a salute of respect to our guests. My mother gazes up at him adoringly, her hair shimmering silver down her back. Sensing my eyes on her, she glances over and splays her long fingers at me. I smile back. She's beautiful, inside and out. Despite all my shortcomings as a daughter, she never shows me anything other than unconditional love and acceptance. Even though I've never quite fit in here, I've been lucky. I shudder at the thought that it could have been me Sarth acquired all those moons ago. I can only imagine what she would have used me for.

"My fellow Cweltans," my father begins, "this is a day of great rejoicing as we enjoy the privilege of hosting the first traders to our humble planet in fourteen moons. Let us drink a hearty toast to their health, prosperity, and safe passage through the trade routes."

The room fills with the clink of mugs, laughter, and goodwill cheers. Glancing around at the rapt, glistening faces of my father's subjects, I catch a fleeting look of contempt on Parthelon's face before his studied mask slips back into place. I frown, troubled by the thought that perhaps it's not only me whom Parthelon secretly despises.

"Regrettably," my father continues, "today is also an occasion of great sorrow. Sarth informed me over dinner that Maulers have seized control of the eastern arterial trade route. They are building up vast interstellar armies through illegal serf trafficking and imposing tariffs on vessels passing through these territories, even seizing the occasional Syndicate ship. This, of course, explains the absence of traders to Cwelt in recent times. But my heart is heavy with a worse woe." He reaches down for my mother's hand and squeezes it before continuing. A somber expression settles in the folds of his ninety-year-old face. "Despite their aged warships, the Maulers succeeded in extending their reach to the fringe planets. They have invaded Oxtian and indentured its people."

A collective gasp ripples around the Great Hall, blood draining from faces that moments earlier were flushed from merrymaking and drink. Oxtian, our nearest neighbor in the fringe, is a rudimentary planet like ours, also without its own fleet of spaceships. What we know of Oxtian is all hearsay from traders. But we've always felt a kinship to its people who are reputed to be skilled hunters and farmers like ourselves.

"I will assign guards to man the tower day and night to watch for approaching ships," my father adds.

As though sensing the futility of such a gesture, the room remains respectfully silent.

Parthelon gets to his feet and flings his shamskin cloak over one shoulder, commanding the crowd's attention. "Sarth also informed us that the Syndicate refuses to deploy forces to resolve the situation. They have abandoned the fringe planets to their fate. We have been forewarned. Manning the tower is only a first step. We must move to the underground caves at once and begin preparations to defend ourselves."

Sarth cocks her head and looks up at him, the palm of her hand resting on one knee. "What preparations are you proposing, wise one?" She curls her lip into a scathing grin. "There's nothing you can do to defend yourselves against Maulers. They have ships, weapons, armor. You have—" She stops abruptly and makes an elaborate gesture of scratching her bald head. "Shamskins and spears."

One of the oremongers seated at the table next to her snickers. I suppress a grin when Buir shoots me a scolding look that says I shouldn't be enjoying the spectacle of Parthelon, writhing beneath the scorn of a woman half his height, when the fate of Cwelt is at stake.

Parthelon glowers down at Sarth, his silver-white goatee twitching side to side as he sizes her up. "How dare you mock the chieftain in his presence."

My father lays a hand on Parthelon's arm. "Enough. Sarth has greatly aided us. We will discuss our options further in private. The oremongers are eager to draw their core samples. Let us escort them."

Parthelon inclines his head, but I can tell he's seething inside. My father reproved him in front of a stranger and he won't readily forget such an insult.

Sarth beckons Velkan to join her.

He pushes his chair out and stands. "Thank you for the meal," he says to me in a tone that lacks some of the warmth it held earlier. "The astro fruit was excellent."

A smile plays on my lips. "You're offended because I didn't believe your story. I'm not calling you a liar, but I think you've been deceived."

"That's because you're too hot-headed to listen to the whole story!"

I toss the core of my astro fruit onto my platter. "Then I'll come with you so you can tell me the rest of your tale of woe while you draw your samples."

Velkan raises amused brows. "Better yet, you can ask Sarth herself about it."

I roll my eyes and get to my feet. "Should be fun. She seems like an excellent conversationalist when she's not putting a price on my head."

We make our way to the center of the long banqueting table. Parthelon gives me a dark look when I ask my father's permission to accompany the oremongers to observe the sampling process. After his earlier confrontation with Sarth, Parthelon won't be invited to tag along.

My father beams proudly at me. "Excellent idea, Trattora. You can report the oremongers' findings back to the elders."

My mother splays her hand good-bye. "Your father is pleased to see the future chieftain of Cwelt taking an interest in such affairs," she says in her voice that washes over me like a gurgling spring. Somehow, she always finds things to praise in me and subtle ways to connect me with my father.

I give her an awkward smile. I hate deceiving her. Truth is, I'm a lot more curious about the oremongers' serf than the oremongering process itself. I tell myself it's just because he's different too.

"Take Buir along," my mother adds. "I will rest easy knowing she is with you."

I chuckle as I exit the hall. I wouldn't dream of leaving Buir behind. We've been best friends for as far back as I can remember, and I don't have any memories of my life before Cwelt. Buir is my guiding star; she spends half her time reining in my crazy ideas and the other half soothing my mother's fears about my wellbeing, which is why she's beloved by us both. Mother says she has an elder's head on her shoulders. Which is why I plan to make her my closest advisor when I become chieftain. Although that didn't impress her much when I told her. She says I don't listen to her now.

I spot her chatting with friends on the main boulevard behind the bustling food stalls laden with fresh produce from the farms. "Buir!" I yell, waving across to her.

She looks up and splays her fingers in acknowledgment before taking leave of the group.

"Father gave us permission to accompany the oremongers to observe the sampling process." I squeeze her elbow in excitement.

Buir angles an elongated silver eyebrow. "You mean he gave *you* permission, and your mother wants *me* to tag along."

I give my chin a vigorous rubbing. "Something like that. They went to the Zebulux to pick up their mobile testing equipment. They'll be back in a few minutes."

Buir sighs. "Does this have anything to do with the sunburned serf?"

"His name's Velkan." I give a cocky grin. "And it isn't sunburn—"

"Tratt!"

"Yes! Okay. Sort of. It might have something to do with him. He intrigues me."

"He's a serf, not a trader," Buir says. "How intriguing can he be to a chieftain's daughter?"

"He's a good storyteller." I link my arm with Buir's. "Did you know Sarth found him buried alive in a casket?"

Buir's eyes widen. "She actually told him that? The woman is despicable."

"She hinted that it was a kidnapping gone wrong," I say. "I feel sorry for him. He believes it." I trace my fingers absentmindedly over the tear in my cloak. "Maybe *I* can get the truth out of Sarth."

Buir's face softens. "You understand better than most what it's like to live with questions about your origin. That's why you're drawn to him. But you should guard against coming between a serf and his owner."

I throw her an irritated look. "Someone needs to get in there and advocate on his behalf. Sarth knows more than she's letting on. She wouldn't even tell him the name of the planet she found him on—some place near the rim."

Buir gives me a skeptical look. "She's not going to tell you either."

"She's on my planet, eating my food and drinking my astro juice. That might give me some sway."

Buir opens her mouth to respond and then glances up at an unfamiliar throbbing sound.

My jaw drops when I spot a tan-colored vehicle rolling over the ground toward us.

"What on Cwelt is that thing?" Buir says.

"Some kind of surface vehicle," I say, mesmerized by its speed as it powers over the ground faster than the venomous sand snipers that emerge on Cwelt at night.

We jump back when the vehicle brakes hard alongside us, sending a volley of sand and rocks skyward. My pulse quickens. I throw an admiring glance over the riveted body panels, making note of every detail: the mesh tires coated with some type of metal strips for traction, and the T-shaped controller for steering. My mind is already racing with possibilities of everything I could do if I owned a machine like this on Cwelt.

Sarth pulls her goggles up to her forehead and jerks her head toward us. "Hop in. Throw your spears in behind, although why you drag those things around with you is beyond me."

Buir takes my spear from me and lays it alongside hers in the cargo bed at the back of the vehicle.

Velkan holds out a hand to me. I stare at it uncertainly, then tentatively reach out and grip his forearm. I'm sort of leery of touching his fingers again in case he really is sick. Rumors of disease-ridden planets and slave ships run rampant. But something tells me the tingling sensation I felt when his fingers brushed against mine in the Great Hall was not that kind of fever. He pulls me into the open seat behind him and then helps Buir in after me.

She scoots nervously into the corner, her expression a mixture of dread and guilt. "We don't have the chieftain's permission to ride in the oremongers' vehicle," she says to me, her voice higher than usual.

Velkan laughs. "Relax! It's perfectly safe."

"Where are the other oremongers?" I ask. "I didn't catch their names."

"Ghil and Nipper," Velkan replies. "They're working on the thruster. Cameras are down too. Always something. The wiring needs to be replaced."

"So, who's who?" I ask.

"Nipper's the one with the face that looks like it's been punched in," Velkan says. "Ghil's the tall, skinny one."

I'm relieved they didn't come along. Neither one of them gives me a warm and fuzzy feeling, but there's something especially unnerving about the younger, heavyset one with the flattened face and roving eyes.

Sarth revs the engine and takes off without warning. My insides light up like a falling star. I never in a thousand moons thought anything could feel this exhilarating. I throw my head back and close my eyes, savoring the wind hitting my face as we pick up speed. My hair whips around me in a mad frenzy. Maybe Velkan doesn't have it so bad after all. In many ways, he's more free than I am. At least he goes on adventures.

"What do you call this thing?" I yell at the back of Sarth's shaved head.

"A LunaTrekker," she calls over her shoulder. "Nifty little design. I picked it up in Aristozonex. Traded a quarter ton of helickel for it. Like I said, rare minerals are a hot commodity these days."

I run my hand over the unfamiliar material of the seat. My brain races to compute the possibilities. If we had a helickel mine, whatever that is, we could purchase a LunaTrekker, and maybe a spaceship or two. I turn to Buir, unable to suppress the smile breaking across my face. Hunting three-horned shams is highly addictive, but I'd trade my shamskin and spear for a fleet of spaceships in a heartbeat.

Buir eyes me suspiciously. "What are you grinning at?" she squeaks out, clinging to the side of the LunaTrekker with white-knuckled fingers.

I curtail my fervor and opt for a less dramatic version of what's unfolding inside my head. "I was just imagining you and I driving around Cwelt in a LunaTrekker."

She gives a disgruntled shrug. "That's not a great visual. I'm barely holding down my food."

"This looks like a good place to start," Sarth calls over her shoulder. She slows to a halt that jolts us sideways and points to some craggy domes on our right. "What's your take?" she asks, frowning at Velkan.

He tents his hand over his eyes and peers in the direction she's pointing. "Interesting-looking extrusive rock topography. I say we check it out."

Sarth rams the controller into gear, backs the LunaTrekker over to the domes, and jumps out. Buir clambers out after her, swaying dangerously back and forth on her feet before she gets her bearings. I lean forward in the seat and study the LunaTrekker's controls. I paid close attention to what Sarth did, and I know I could drive this thing myself. Persuading Sarth to let me try will be the hard part. Maybe if I find her some helickel, she'll be more agreeable. Reluctantly, I climb out and join Buir.

"Are you all right?" I ask.

She presses her lips together tightly. "I will be once we get back to the settlement."

Velkan strides around to the back of the LunaTrekker and activates a machine of some kind that's protruding from the rear of the bed. "This is our mobile Pneumacorer," he explains. "I built it myself. Raw beam technology. The laser can cut through rock and go down a couple hundred feet. If it picks up anything interesting, we'll bring in the heavy equipment."

I give a distracted nod. My heart is drumming in my chest, but it's not because of Velkan, curious as I am about him. I'm in love with the world of technology he brought with him and terrified of being left in my all-too-familiar environment when the oremongers leave.

I frown at the craggy mounds I played on throughout my childhood. They don't look like anything much to me, but then I've no idea what helickel looks like. I should know better than to get my hopes up, but I can't help dreaming.

In less than a minute, the Pneumacorer brings up the first sample. Sarth and Velkan lean over it and study the readings.

"Anything?" I ask.

"Igneous crystals." Sarth gives a dissatisfied grunt. "Parabasalt scrap for the most part."

Buir raises bewildered brows at me, and I give a disappointed shrug.

"We'll take another sample before we pull out," Sarth says. "Just to be sure." She backs up the LunaTrekker several more feet, and Velkan starts the Pneumacorer up again.

I take a quick breath when they bring the second sample up. Even a trace of a valuable mineral would be enough to persuade the oremongers to bring out the heavy equipment. Sarth leans over the display panel and studies the readings. After a moment, she throws up her arms in disgust and turns to me with a scowl on her face. "Don't you have anything but sand on this wretched planet?"

I open my mouth to echo Parthelon's words—that there's nothing on Cwelt worth mining, and then I hesitate.

What about the luminescent indigo boulders in the sacred triangle?

Chapter 4

Sarth pins a distrustful gaze on me, her brows fusing in a forbidding "V." "Speak up, girl. We don't have all day to waste cruising around sand dunes. We've a thruster that needs repair and a ship that needs rewiring at the next port. If there's nothing here worth mining, we'll be on our way."

"I know where there are some unusual rock formations," I say, repressing my desire to rebuke her for her insolent tone. "Luminescent rock, crystalline mineral of some kind."

Her face lights up in a lustful grin. "Well, why didn't you say so?"

I give a nonchalant shrug. "I just did."

Velkan busies himself with the Pneumacorer, trying to contain a grin. Sarth slides her jaw back and forth as if trying to decide whether I intentionally insulted her, or am merely a plainspoken primitive.

I smile serenely back at her, adding to her perplexity. I'm obligated to maintain a certain level of civility, but it doesn't mean I can't toy with her in return.

Buir shoots me one of her famous disapproving looks. A

warning, no doubt, to show more respect to our visitors. Or maybe she thinks I shouldn't have mentioned the boulders in the sacred triangle.

"What are we waiting for?" Sarth barks.

Velkan starts up the LunaTrekker and waits for everyone to climb back in.

Buir hesitates, then pulls back her shoulders as if steeling herself for something painful.

"You don't have to come," I say. "You can walk back to the settlement if you want."

"*Someone* has to make sure a bunch of strangers don't trample all over our ancestors' gravesites," she mutters, plonking down beside me on the seat.

"Where to?" Sarth calls back to us.

"East." I point over her shoulder. "I'll direct you when we get a little closer."

I sink back down and turn to Buir. "Relax. My father didn't say there were any areas that were off limits."

"Because you already *know* there are," she hisses back. "The elders would never grant the oremongers rights to mine in the sacred triangle, even for their precious helickel. If nothing else, you're wasting Sarth's time."

I shrug. "No harm in them looking around. Besides, my father wants us to be hospitable, and where else are we going to take them? They're not interested in the astro fruit farms." I lean a little closer, a smile tugging at the corners of my lips. "And personally, I can't picture Sarth in a shamskin."

Buir angles a brow, trying not to laugh as she reaches for the side of the LunaTrekker. She lets out a long sigh. "Parthelon better be right that there's nothing on Cwelt worth mining, or this is going to turn into a nightmare."

We give up on conversation as we rattle our way over the rough terrain and up the mountain pass toward the sacred triangle, shielding our eyes from the dust. Buir's right that my father wouldn't approve of me taking the oremongers here. I'm not even supposed to hunt here. But I want to impress them with something, and besides, what harm can it do to look at a few boulders? The likelihood that they'll turn out to be helickel is slim to none.

"This is a good spot," I call up to Velkan.

He brakes hard and pulls over a few feet from a cluster of luminescent rock. Sarth jumps out, eying the formations curiously. She runs a calloused hand over the smooth surface of the nearest boulder and circles it slowly like a predator admiring its mesmerized prey.

"Do you know what it is?" I prompt.

She rubs her fingertips together and sniffs them tentatively. "It's not igneous, so that's a good start."

"Let's hope it's what you're looking for." I shiver with excitement. "I wouldn't mind a LunaTrekker of my own. A ship would be better."

Sarth snorts. "If that's what you're after, you're talking a bigger vein of helickel than I've ever found."

I give her an understanding smile. "Figures, your ship is a bit of a wreck."

Her eyes narrow, but she masks her displeasure and turns her attention back to the rocks. She's not about to get into it with me before she has a chance to check out the boulders. Buir, on the other hand, glowers at me.

Velkan tosses a skein of dark hair over his shoulder and grins as he fires up the Pneumacorer. I suspect he's enjoying watching Sarth get back what she doles out for once. He angles the Pneumacorer over a knee-high boulder and flicks a switch to activate the raw beam laser. I hover impatiently until it retracts with a core sample. Sarth and Velkan lean over it and study the readout briefly before exchanging guarded looks.

"Well?" I demand, looking from one to the other. "What is it?"

"It's not helickel," Sarth says abruptly.

I can't help but feel a flicker of disappointment. I didn't really think it would turn out to be anything valuable, but a part of me secretly hoped Parthelon had got it wrong and that Cwelt had something worth mining after all.

"Do you know *what* it is?" Buir asks.

Velkan's brow wrinkles, but he clamps his lips tight. I study him, puzzled by his reaction. I have a hunch he knows exactly what it is, but for some reason, he's waiting to see if Sarth will tell us first.

Sarth smooths a stubby hand over her glistening head. "Hard to say without bringing in the rest of the equipment for an exploratory dig. I can take a couple of rocks back to the ship and try to verify the readings."

I give an exasperated sigh. "Are all oremongers this cryptic? If you want Cwelt's permission to bring in your heavy equipment, you'll need to do better than that. Tell me what you *think* it is?"

Sarth runs the back of her hand across her mouth and studies me through narrowed slits.

I cross my arms and stare back at her.

"Remember those rare minerals I said were a hot commodity?" she says after a few minutes.

"What about them?"

She sniffs into her sleeve. "It might be one of them. Dargonite."

My heart begins to race again, the LunaTrekker suddenly back within my grasp, but I don't want to get ahead of myself again. I compose my features to mildly curious. "How hot are we talking exactly?"

The corners of Sarth's lips curl upward. "Hot enough to buy you that fancy ship you're after."

I gulp down a gasp of excitement and glance across at Buir. Disbelief is written all over her face. She presses her lips into a disapproving line. I frown and glance back at Sarth. Maybe I should be more skeptical too. "So how come oremongers didn't discover it moons ago?"

"Dargonite had no value back then." Sarth takes a step closer to me, her eyes glittering. "Not until the Syndicate discovered its use in cloaking technology for warships. The minerals in it can be combined with any metal to render it invisible to the naked eye."

My mouth drops open. I clench my fists to keep my hands from shaking. *So much for keeping my composure.*

"If I'm right about this," Sarth says, looking around with a smug expression, "Cwelt's about to become a very wealthy planet, and the Zebulux is about to get a much-needed facelift."

Buir turns to me, her silver brows slanted inward. "*Tell* her, Trattora."

Sarth pins a steely gaze on me. "Is there a problem?"

"More of a technicality," I dart a warning look at Buir. "I'll

41

need to clear things with the elders before you begin."

Sarth gives a curt nod. "There's protocol to follow. I get it. Let's load up the bed with what we've got for now."

On the bumpy ride back to the settlement, I go over in my mind how exactly I'm going to persuade my father to allow the oremongers to mine in the sacred triangle. Even if I can persuade him, he won't overrule the elders for any reason other than our survival. But if Oxtian has fallen to the Maulers, we're in danger. Maybe I can convince him that granting the oremongers mining rights would give us the means to purchase the weapons and ships we'll need to defend ourselves.

When we arrive back at the settlement, Buir pulls me aside. "You're not really going to try and sway the elders, are you?"

"You heard Sarth," I whisper. "We could procure our own ships and weapons in exchange for a few rocks."

"It's sacred ground. What you're proposing is treason. You could lose your claim to the High Seat of Chieftain."

"Do you really think Father is going to let that happen when I'm his only heir?" I shoot a quick glance across at Velkan, who is watching our conversation with interest.

Buir grabs my arm to draw my attention back. "Parthelon will enforce a sentence of treason. He seeks to disgrace you at every opportunity. Can't you see how he craves the position of chieftain?"

I shake my arm free of her grip. "Are you seriously suggesting my father would disown me and appoint Parthelon to reign after him?"

"I'm not suggesting it, I'm *telling* you it's going to happen. The elders will see you as weak and easily manipulated by foreign traders for even proposing such a thing. And Parthelon will waste no time seizing the opportunity to showcase your growing list of infractions." Her gaze travels pointedly over the tears in my tunic. "The least of which is destroying three cloaks in one month."

I frown. "If you're alluding to me accidentally setting the Great Hall on fire, that was—"

"I'm alluding to how people perceive their future chieftain," she says.

I toss my head. "The only people who will see me as weak and easily manipulated are those who lack the vision to see the advantages this will bring to Cwelt. I will not be intimidated by Parthelon or his personal agenda. It's time to show him I'm my father's daughter."

Buir looks at me with a mixture of sadness and resignation in her eyes. "If you divide the elders, your father will divide his household."

I swallow down the lump in my throat. "I will not let the fate of Oxtian become ours. I won't give up without trying."

I turn to Sarth and Velkan. "Let me talk to my father alone first. Buir will take you into the Great Hall and provide nourishment for you while I am gone."

"I'm going to make a quick detour to the Zebulux to check on the rest of my crew," Sarth says. "Buir can take Velkan inside."

I grab my spear from the cargo bed and make my way down the main boulevard to my dwelling. It's the largest in the settlement, a dome-shaped structure fashioned from the chestnut-colored sand that covers much of our planet. Like all the dwellings on Cwelt, it's on a raised platform of brick columns to deter the venomous sand snipers that come out at night to feed. They writhe across the ground at high speeds on lizard-like appendages, but thankfully they can't climb.

I mount the front steps with a fluttery feeling in my stomach. Maybe the rocks in the sacred triangle have a form of power after all. What I'm about to propose could change the course of Cwelt's history, for better or for worse.

To my disappointment, Parthelon is seated at my father's side in the communal greeting room. I should have expected as much. The oremongers' visit and dire news about the Maulers necessitates a plan of action.

I incline my head, avoiding Parthelon's inquisitive gaze.

"Greetings, Trattora," my father says. "Have you satisfied our guests' request?"

I draw myself up to my full height, which always feels inadequate, even when my father is seated. "I need to speak with you about the oremongers, *alone.*"

He raises his bushy silver brows a fraction of an inch. "Parthelon is my most trusted advisor. If there is something that concerns you, he should hear it too."

I frown in Parthelon's direction. He gives me an acid-eyed stare in return.

I turn away and beam at my father. "Nothing of concern to report. The chieftain's daughter would simply like a word with her father alone."

My father gestures apologetically to Parthelon. "Make sure the tower is manned. I will meet you in the Great Hall with the other elders in a few minutes."

Parthelon rises, his lips pinched and bloodless. He flings his shamskin cape over his shoulder and departs the room. In my heart, I know Buir is right about his lust for power. It's not me or my father he despises as much as our claim to the High Seat of Cwelt. A position he desires for himself.

I sink down in the chair Parthelon vacated.

My father leans back against a large cushion. "What is it you wish to discuss with me?"

Despite my heartbeat clattering in my chest, I hold his gaze. "Parthelon said there was nothing on Cwelt worth mining. He was wrong."

My father furrows his well-lined brow and waits for me to continue.

"The oremongers believe they have discovered a rare mineral."

He straightens up, his eyes alert. "This mineral … is it of use?"

I hesitate. It may not be wise to lead with the information that the mineral will be used by the Syndicate to enhance their military supremacy. My father's feelings about the Syndicate and how they operate are conflicted.

"Sarth tells me its value on Aristozonex is astronomical," I say. "Enough to trade for ships and weapons."

He rubs his forehead with his long fingers. "You are suggesting we trade it to arm ourselves."

I lean toward him, barely able to contain myself. "Father, we don't have to fall to the Maulers like Oxtian did."

He nods thoughtfully. "This is indeed welcome news. The elders have been discussing our options for surviving an invasion.

They see no alternative but to retreat to the underground caves."

"Perhaps we won't have to after all. The oremongers await your permission to begin exploratory mining."

My father gets to his feet and reaches for his headpiece. "I will direct the elders to ratify their request. The sooner we confirm the findings, the greater chance we have of being prepared when the Maulers come. Follow me."

I swallow back my misgivings as he sweeps from the room. I wanted to break the news to him about the location Sarth seeks to mine before he addresses the elders, but maybe it's better this way. He won't want to lose face in front of the elders, so he may defend my request. I hurry out the door and join him, pushing down my apprehension.

When we enter the meeting room in the Great Hall, my father comes to an abrupt halt in front of me. The Council of Elders and Parthelon are gathered together in the room. Before them stand the three oremongers and Velkan, gagged and bound.

Chapter 5

My heart squeezes in on itself when I see the Cweltan guards standing to attention behind Parthelon, their spears aligned perfectly with their rigid posture. Why did they arrest the oremongers? I stare at the back of Velkan's head, willing him to turn around and see me, but he keeps his gaze forward. I glance around looking for Buir, but I can't see her anywhere.

My father's eyes rove over the elders' faces, missing nothing. When he speaks, his voice is low and strained. "What is the meaning of this?"

Parthelon draws himself up to his full height and gestures at Sarth with a dismissive wave. "We've been deceived by this reprobate captain."

"Explain yourself!" I burst out, my pulse pounding. "You insult our guests!"

Parthelon swivels in my direction and fastens metallic eyes on me. "They are our guests no longer. They came here under false pretenses, likely hiding from a Syndicate patrol ship. Sarth and her crew are no ordinary oremongers and their cargo is not comprised only of minerals. While *you* were off conducting your sightseeing tour, *I* sent a scouting party to the Zebulux." He pauses and addresses my father. "We discovered several large torpor vats concealed behind a false wall draped with netting at the back of the cargo bay."

My father's face blanches. "Are you sure?"

Parthelon gives a smug nod.

"What is he talking about?" I ask.

My father clenches a gnarled fist to his chest. "Illegal transport of cryogenically frozen heads. The elderly from wealthy planets who choose to undergo the procedure are taken to an undisclosed location in the outer ring and reattached to donor bodies."

"The practice is outlawed," Parthelon adds, his voice booming throughout the Great Hall. "The Syndicate has denounced it for decades. All ships engaging in the cryogenic trade are to be seized, and their crews executed, by order of the Syndicate."

Blood drains from my head. *Executed.* I've heard stories of the only execution ever carried out on Cwelt. A trader who attempted to kidnap a Cweltan woman. The elders buried him up to his head in the sand and left him for the snipers. A slow and excruciating death by all accounts. His head had swollen to twice its normal size by the time they found him the next morning. I open my mouth to say something, but my throat closes over.

Parthelon arches a brow at me. "Be abhorred by the crime, not the punishment. *Donors* are snatched from impoverished planets by body poachers. As you might imagine, there are no volunteers for such a procedure."

"Enough, Parthelon!" my father snaps, assuming his authority. "Is this the entire crew?"

Parthelon throws a scathing glance Sarth's way. "According to the captain, although she's hardly a reliable source." His gaze bores down on Velkan. "Maybe the serf has been disciplined enough times to keep him honest," he says, yanking the gag from Velkan's mouth.

"We are the entire crew," Velkan says, his face taut.

"What do you have to say in your defense?" my father asks Sarth, gesturing at a guard to remove her gag.

She scowls and curls her lip. "There's a fine line between trade and crime when it comes to making a living. We don't all get to choose which side we walk on."

Parthelon throws his arms out, appealing to the elders. "She condemns herself. She doesn't deny the charges."

My insides are knotting up so tight I can barely breathe. How could Sarth even think of participating in something so horrific? I sneak a glance at Velkan. Surely he didn't know about the illegal transport. "This is Sarth's crime," I blurt out. "She's responsible for the cargo she was paid to haul."

Parthelon stares me down with a satisfied air of superiority. "The exterior thermostats on the vats are set to -196C, the temperature liquid nitrogen is kept at to preserve human tissue. The crew knew exactly what they were transporting."

"Aren't you at least going to let them defend themselves?" I cast another desperate glance at Velkan, but he lowers his head.

"The face of guilt," Parthelon sneers. He turns and scours the elders before addressing my father. "We must act swiftly. If the Zebulux is being tracked by a Syndicate patrol, we will be called to give an account of our handling of the situation."

My father throws his shamskin robe over his shoulder and faces the Council of Elders. "All in favor of convicting the crew of the Zebulux, make your ruling known!"

One by one the elders cross their forearms in a giant "X" over their chests signaling a binding Cweltan ruling.

My legs shake as an icy fear creeps through me. The entire Council just ratified a Cweltan-style execution for Velkan and the rest of the crew. My mind churns in a sea of confusion. I can't process that this is happening. A few short hours ago, we were toasting these people in the Great Hall. I can still feel Velkan's warm breath as he whispered in my ear.

"Take them to the retribution hut," my father orders, his features grim. "They will be buried tomorrow night. The Cweltan elders have spoken."

I watch, helplessly, as the guards line up the oremongers and shackle them together. I cannot defy the chieftain's decree in front of the Council, but they can't stop me talking to my father alone. I can't let this happen.

Velkan stumbles as he passes me, and I reach out a hand to steady him before I realize his misstep was intentional.

His breath brushes my cheek. "There's a laser gun in—"

A guard pulls him away from me before he can finish what he was saying.

His eyes lock on mine with a plea so strong that my heart is crushed beneath it. I can't give him a weapon he could use to kill the guards with, but I won't let him die without trying to help him. I give a subtle nod before the guard yanks him forward and escorts him out of the Great Hall.

"Father," I say, grabbing his sleeve. "You must intervene! The crew can't be held responsible. They were merely following Sarth's—"

"Enough, Trattora! You are ignorant of such matters," he replies as Parthelon comes walking over. "The Syndicate's edict is clear if we fail to comply. Any planet that knowingly or unwittingly supports the practice of body poaching can be annexed as a conscription colony under Syndicate Domain Law."

I shake my head in disbelief. "But ... they don't even know the Zebulux is here."

"If Syndicate patrols were tracking the Zebulux and its cargo, they could arrive here at any minute," Parthelon says.

"We can't take a chance," my father says. "We must adhere to Syndicate law."

"What about the cargo?" Parthelon asks.

"Remove the vats and bury them in the sand pits," my father replies. He rubs a hand wearily over his brow. "About time those souls were laid to rest." He throws a sorrowful look at me, as if he regrets that I had to witness this, and then strides in the direction of the door.

"This is wrong," I say, appealing to the elders as they file silently after him. My insubordination will do little to win me support among them, but I'm past the point of caring. I'll find that laser gun on the Zebulux and hold the guards up myself if I have to.

Parthelon turns to me, a slow grin spreading across his angular face. "Your father is correct in his assessment. You are ignorant of affairs of state, which makes you ill-equipped to lead in his place."

"And you're qualified?" I reply with a snort.

He sidles closer. "I haven't spent all this time groveling under your father for nothing. He listens to me."

I glare up at him. "You won't have my ear when I'm chieftain."

A cord of anger ripples across his face. "*If* you're chieftain." He turns on his heel and stomps from the hall.

For several minutes, I stand rooted to the spot. Buir was right all along.

He seeks every chance to disgrace you. Can't you see how he craves the position of chieftain?

Parthelon has an agenda, and he's probably gained some more followers after I advocated risking the wrath of the Syndicate to save a murderous bunch of oremongers.

I breathe slowly in and out as I mull over Buir's words. Parthelon made sure to remind all the elders that he was the one who went to the trouble of investigating the oremongers' story while I blithely showed them around. The elders already view me as gullible. They completely ignored my plea for clemency and voted unanimously to execute the entire crew. Parthelon has more supporters among them than I realized.

I hurry out of the room intent on finding Buir. If I'm going to save the oremongers, I'll need her help. When I reach the main boulevard, I cinch up my robe and break into a run. Whatever despicable trade Sarth is tangled up with, her crew members don't deserve the excruciating death that awaits them. And I don't have much time to figure out a way to stop it from happening.

Once I arrive at Buir's house, I lean my spear up against the outer wall and jog up the familiar steps. The murmur of voices drifts toward me from the kitchen. Buir is seated at the table, her knees drawn up to her chest, in conversation with her mother. She looks up startled, then jumps to her feet. "Did you hear?" she asks, grasping me by the arms. "They arrested the oremongers."

I give a grim nod. "I just came from the Great Hall."

"The elders should never have let the two of you go off with them alone." Buir's mother says, her face rutted with worry. "Why did they arrest them?"

"They were transporting torpor vats," I reply.

She takes a sharp breath and claps both hands over her mouth.

Buir throws her a frightened look. "Mother! What is it?"

"Cryogenically frozen heads," her mother replies in a hushed whisper. "A dark market trade, punishable by execution."

I clench my fist into a tight ball. "The elders sentenced the entire crew to execution tomorrow night. They're being held in the retribution hut."

"Does the captain deny the charges?" Buir's mother asks. "I've heard of vats being planted on trade ships, disguised as other cargo."

I shake my head. "She knew what it was."

"Then nothing can be done to save the crew." Buir's mother lets out a heavy sigh. "The Syndicate has a zero-tolerance policy on the cryogenic trade."

"They don't all deserve to die," I say. "Velkan's an indentured serf. He had no say in the cargo Sarth contracted to transport."

Buir's mother shakes her head sadly but says nothing.

"I'm going to the retribution hut to talk to the crew," I say.

"Maybe they can tell me something that will make the elders relent." I turn to Buir. "Coming?"

She throws me a dubious look as she gets to her feet. "I don't think it'll do any good."

Buir's mother splays her hand good-bye. "Stay close to the guards. Be careful."

"Always," I call over my shoulder as Buir and I race down the front steps into the main boulevard. She sets out in the direction of the retribution hut but I grab the tail of her shamskin. "Wait! I need to swing by the Zebulux first."

Buir spins to face me, an uneasy look in her eyes. "What for?"

"I might be able to find something to help the oremongers."

"Like what?"

I reach for my spear and run my fingers over the tip. "Something … that might make the elders pay attention."

Buir's lips part. "You mean … weapons? Trattora! No!"

I drop my jaw and stare at her. "Now, that's *not* a bad idea. Good thing it was yours."

Up close, the Zebulux looks even uglier than when we first saw it coming in to dock. Its scarred hull is a scabbed assortment of riveted panels and salvaged parts, and its rear stabilizers give it the appearance of a crouching insect of war. It doesn't bode well for the condition on the inside. A Cweltan guard stands on either side of the rugged metal ramp leading into the cargo bay.

I give a nod of acknowledgment as I stride up to the guards with all the swagger of a chieftain's daughter who has every right to board a seized ship. "Did Parthelon remove the torpor vats yet?" I ask curtly.

The guard closest to me bows. "Not yet, High Daughter, but—"

"Good. My father wishes me to view the workings of the ship."

The guard bows again as I sweep past him, steering a reluctant Buir by the elbow.

Inside, the cargo hold reeks of oil and fumes. I wrinkle my nose at the foreign scent of toxic chemicals and glance around curiously. Thick netting holds a large quantity of gear in place; tool chests, oil drums, coiled cables, crates piled on top of crates, even a second LunaTrekker. I raise my brows and look pointedly at Buir. "Sarth didn't mention that they had more than one of these nifty little vehicles."

Buir grimaces. "Hardly surprising, after everything else she hid from us." She points toward the back of the cargo hold. "Those must be the vats."

We step around the half torn-down false wall and stare in awe at the giant thermostat-controlled drums, partly concealed by heavy netting.

Buir shivers. "I can't believe they're full of human heads," she says. "I wouldn't be able to sleep at night on this ship."

I gesture to an iron stairway. "Let's see where this leads. We need to find Sarth's room."

Buir looks at me suspiciously. "Why Sarth's room?"

"Because ... all the important stuff will be in there, like weapons," I say, grinning at her.

Buir presses her fingertips to her lips and throws a nervous glance over her shoulder at the guards standing outside the ship. "This is a really bad idea."

"Do you have a better one? Besides, the cameras are out on the ship, remember? They won't have a clue what we're doing."

She gives a resigned sigh and follows me up the stairway to the upper deck. A hexagonal utility hallway leads back into the bowels of the ship.

"This must be where the crew eats," I say peering through a porthole at a sparse-looking galley, dining room, and communal area. Most everything inside is fashioned out of metal and bolted to the floor; seating, tables, chests and cabinets.

"The Zebulux is no luxury liner," Buir remarks.

"She may not be pretty, but she's seen a lot more of our planetary system than we have," I say wistfully.

"Or want to!" Buir retorts. She wanders off down the hallway and peers into the next room. "Looks like supplies," she says, when I join her.

"Let's keep going," I say. "We don't have much time and we need to find Sarth's quarters before the guards grow suspicious and come looking for us." More than anything, I wish we had time to explore the control room, but that will have to wait.

Halfway down the corridor, we come to a small room with two recessed bunks. "The sleeping quarters aren't very impressive," Buir says, wrinkling her nose up and sniffing at the air delicately as we step inside. "This must be crew quarters. I can't imagine Sarth sharing a room with anyone."

The bunks are neatly made up but there's barely enough room to turn around.

"Definitely crew quarters," Buir says, squeezing past me to get back out.

"We can't be sure of that," I say, pulling open a steel drawer in a locker beside the bottom bunk. It's filled with personal items; a small knife with a carved handle, a collection of rocks of various hues, an assortment of prints from ports around the galaxy. *A comb.* I frown, suddenly feeling uncomfortable. Only one person on the Zebulux could possibly need a comb. I'm looking through Velkan's things. I take a quick breath to remind myself why I'm doing this and dig a little deeper. Maybe the gun is stashed in here. My eyes widen when I spot something familiar-looking in the bottom corner of the drawer.

Instinctively my hand flies to my neck. My throat feels like it's closing over.

"What's wrong?" Buir asks.

With shaking fingers, I pull the chain out from beneath my shamskin and point to the tiny metal bracelet on the end. "Look in the drawer," I say, in a scratchy voice.

Buir steps back into the room and peers into the drawer.

I don't dare breathe again until she confirms it.

"They match," she says in an awed whisper.

Chapter 6

I close my fist protectively over the bracelet in the drawer. All those lonely times when I cried in the crevices high above the sacred triangle flash before my eyes. Somewhere deep inside I never felt like I belonged anywhere, until now. A fluttering feeling creeps up my throat. "You know what this means?" I say to Buir, barely able to quell the tremor in my voice as I take a closer look at the bracelet. "Velkan and I are from the same planet."

Buir contemplates this for a moment. "How do you know it's his?"

"Because his name's on it!"

"It doesn't mean anything," she says, frowning at the bracelet. "He could have stolen it and had it engraved."

I shake my head. "It was lying right there with the rest of his things. He wasn't trying to hide it."

Buir looks unconvinced. "Why would he? Sarth's a crook. I doubt she cares if her crew help themselves to a few things when they're docked at trading ports."

I stare down at the tiny bracelet in the palm of my hand. Buir does have a point. The bracelet could have come from any port along the trading routes. But I don't want to entertain that possibility, not now when I might have stumbled on an opportunity to learn something about my origin. "I need to talk to Velkan," I say, slipping the bracelet into my pocket, "before anything happens. Let's hurry. Sarth's quarters must be close by."

Buir frowns and peers into the hallway. "I think I hear the guards coming."

I step back out into the corridor just as Parthelon strides around the corner. A furrow forms on his elongated forehead. "The guards said we would find you here," he growls. "A little late to be investigating the oremongers now."

I open my mouth to remind him who he's talking to just as my father comes into view.

"Trattora!" he exclaims. "What are you doing on board?"

I walk up to him and link my arm through his. "Buir and I were educating ourselves on the inner workings of an oremongers' vessel. You know how I love to learn. This is the first functional ship I've had a chance to explore."

His face softens. "It's not safe for you to be here. We're working on a way to remove the torpor vats, and the chemicals inside are hazardous. You and Buir need to leave the ship until we're finished."

"How long will it take?" I ask.

My father rubs his brow. "I'm not sure. Between the hazardous materials involved and the sand snipers, we can't bury the vats in the dark. We may wait to move them until morning."

I unlink my arm. "As you wish." I incline my head to

Parthelon, reveling in the thunderous look in his eyes, and then follow Buir back down the hallway to the front of the ship. Inside, my heart is racing. I run through our options as I go. It's too risky to try sneaking back on board after my father explicitly commanded us to leave. We'll have to wait until they're done with their assessment and then come back later tonight.

Once we exit the ship and are out of earshot of the guards, I turn to Buir. "My father and Parthelon will be occupied here for the next couple of hours. We might as well make use of the time and find out from Velkan where exactly their weapons are stashed on board, and where he got that bracelet."

Buir looks pensive. "Don't get your hopes up. I know you always believed your bracelet was significant. But if a lowly serf owns one, the truth is it could have come from some cheap market stall that charges a few extra credits for engraving a name."

"Not if Velkan was wearing it when Sarth dug up his pod."

"Right, *that* story." Buir gives a dramatic sigh. "I can see where this is going. Come on, let's settle this once and for all."

I beam her a grateful smile and she rolls her eyes in response. "Your mother's going to kill me if she finds out I let you go out to the retribution hut."

I sidle over to Buir and squeeze her arm. "She has too big a heart to kill anyone, and anyway, there's no law against visiting the condemned."

The retribution hut is located about three miles out on the far side of our settlement. We're almost at the Great Hall when I have the brilliant idea that we could take the LunaTrekker parked outside and get there much quicker.

"Are you out of your mind?" Buir chides when I suggest it. "You don't even know how to drive that thing."

I shrug. "I got the gist of it this morning. Come on, it'll be fun."

I stash my spear in the bed, slide in behind the controller and beckon to Buir to join me. She lingers for a minute, her forehead puckered, then throws a quick glance across the street at a group of Cweltan women eying us curiously, before climbing into the passenger seat beside me.

"Don't worry about what they're thinking," I say.

"They're probably thinking what I'm thinking," she retorts. "We've no business being in this vehicle. You do realize if you run someone over we'll probably end up in the retribution hut ourselves."

I place my right hand on the dash. "I solemnly swear to avoid all obstacles, living *and* inanimate."

"That's no comfort," Buir responds with a groan.

I lean forward and depress the igniter switch. The engine roars to life and despite my excitement, I can't help flinching at the sound.

Buir clings to the side of the LunaTrekker in a death clutch that eclipses her white-knuckled grip from this morning. "Are you sure about—"

Her voice mounts to a scream as we lurch forward. "Slow down!" she shrieks.

I barely register what she's saying. Adrenalin rushes through me, taking over every neural pathway. While it was exhilarating riding in the LunaTrekker this morning with the oremongers, being in control of the vehicle, and feeling the power of an engine in my hands, takes the experience to a whole new level.

It's all I can do to keep from hollering out with glee as I steer the LunaTrekker down the middle of the main boulevard and out of town. Cweltans dart to either side of the street, shocked expressions on their faces as I drive by. I ignore them and focus instead on keeping the LunaTrekker moving in the direction we need to go.

Once we're past the outskirts of town, and there's no danger of running anyone over, I accelerate, grinning at Buir's predictable yelps each time our tires bump over rocks in our path. The wind whips my hair up around me and I shiver with delight, invigorated by the sensation. As crazy as it seems, I can't help thinking this is what I was born to do. And more. I want to fly next. I've studied every ship's manual I got my hands on, and spent many an hour in the wrecks in the desert familiarizing myself with the flight decks. Driving the LunaTrekker only makes me hungrier to experience what it's like to pilot a ship.

All too soon, the retribution hut comes into view. I wish I could keep driving, but Buir's so pale I don't think she'll make it any farther without passing out. After locating the brake pedal, I manage to slow the vehicle down in a series of jerks. We come to an abrupt stop thirty feet from a small guard station to the left of the hut. Buir tumbles out first, strands of shimmering silver-white hair plastered across her sweaty face.

I raise my brows at the sight. I can't remember ever seeing her look quite this disheveled before. Maybe I shouldn't mention it, considering her precarious emotional state.

"Just so we're clear," she gasps, smoothing out her shamskin.

"I'm walking back to town."

"Hey, harsh! It was my first time!" I say. "I promise the ride back will be better. You can even take a turn driving if you want."

She lets out a low groan. "I prefer my own two legs beneath me, thanks."

We greet the guards, and Buir goes inside the station to find some water. I make my way over to the retribution hut. Unlike the other dwellings on Cwelt, it is constructed of heavy wooden posts driven into the ground an inch apart and covered over by a thatched roof. It offers no safety from sand snipers, and no privacy to its inhabitants, which fits its purpose—to serve as a spectacle to Cweltans, reminding them of the consequences of crime. It's rarely needed. And never for something of this magnitude.

The crew of the Zebulux is huddled together on the floor on the far side of the hut. Velkan jumps to his feet when he sees me, dark skeins of hair flipping over his shoulder. "Did you find the gun?"

Sarth, Ghil and Nipper eye us warily from the floor, but don't attempt to get up.

I shake my head. "We didn't have time before my father and Parthelon came on board."

Velkan looks gutted. The disappointment in his face stirs up the guilt I'm already feeling. I should have worked faster to search the ship. And I shouldn't have wasted time on the bracelet.

"They'll confiscate the weapons." Velkan leans his forehead against the post between us, his holographed tattoo glowing in the fading light. "You've got to help us. Can you talk to your father?"

I dart a glance in Sarth's direction. I can tell she's listening, but pretending not to.

"There's nothing we can do for *her*," I murmur to Velkan. "She's guilty as charged. Did you know what you were transporting?"

Velkan lets out a snort. "Of course I knew what it was. Doesn't mean I had any say in it."

"What about the other crew members?" I ask.

"They knew all right," Sarth interjects, getting to her feet. "Can't hide vats twice the size of LunaTrekkers when you're loading up."

I narrow my eyes at her. "You set up the transport. You put your crew's lives in danger."

Sarth flashes a hideous grin. "And now we get to die together on your dreary little planet on the fringe." She spits on the ground and walks back to the others.

A shiver goes through me. How can she treat this as some kind of joke? It's a very real possibility that the crew will perish with her unless I can figure out a way to free them. Why isn't she trying to negotiate with me? It makes me wonder what she's planning. Surely she couldn't break out of here without help.

"As soon as the vats have been removed from the ship, I'll go back and look for the gun," I whisper to Velkan. "I'll force the guards to turn you loose. I won't let them execute you."

He nods but looks unconvinced. "Sarth keeps a laser gun under her bed, strapped to the frame. The other weapons are locked in the safe. I don't know the combination."

"I found something else on the ship," I say, pulling out the chain around my neck. "Recognize this?"

His eyes widen. "You scavenged my things." He gives a hollow laugh. "I'm not even dead yet."

"It's not yours," I say, reaching into my pocket. I pull out his matching bracelet and hand it to him. "But, yes, I did go through your things looking for the gun."

Velkan reaches for the bracelet and rubs his thumb gently across it in a familiar gesture that tells me he too has spent many a night clutching it close.

"Were you wearing it when Sarth found you?" I ask quietly.

He gives a wry grin. "That's *all* I was wearing, as she likes to remind me."

Sarth wanders over, her beady eyes glued to the bracelet hanging around my neck. A flash of recognition goes through her eyes. She glances down at Velkan's bracelet and then stares at me for a long moment.

I stare brazenly back at her. "What planet did you find Velkan on?"

She scratches her bald head for a moment, then tugs the corners of her lips downward. "Can't say I remember."

"Try harder!" I snap back.

Quicker than a sand sniper, she whips her fist through the slats and grabs me by my shamskin, rattling me against the slats. The stench of her yellowed teeth washes over me. "Listen, *Princess*," she hisses. "No one tells me what to do, especially not some sassy-tongued import from a poverty-stricken planet who prances around like she's the Syndicate's gift to Cwelt." She shakes me loose with a disgruntled snort when Buir and the guards come rushing over from the station, spears poised.

"I'm fine." I hold out my palms to keep the guards at bay. "Go back to your positions."

"Are you sure you're okay?" Buir asks, breathlessly.

I glare at Sarth. "I'm fine. It was just a misunderstanding of who's in charge here."

She watches the guards retreat and then fixes calculating eyes on me. "Let's try this again. I don't take orders, but I'll deal. You want information, and you got something I could use in return."

I frown at her. "I thought you said you didn't remember …" I break off when I see the amused smile that plays on her lips.

"Might come back to me, given the right … *motivation*." She rubs her jaw, eying me with a bored look.

"What kind of motivation?" I ask.

She edges closer and I take a step backward, not wanting to be yanked into range of her foul breath a second time. She presses her face between the posts. "Get us out of here tonight and I'll give you the name of the planet."

I open my mouth to respond, and then wince at a stinging pain in my arm. I glance down at Buir's fingers digging into me. "Don't do anything stupid, Trattora," she whispers from behind.

I take a deep breath as I weigh the wisdom of her words against everything that's at stake. The roar of the Lunatrekker's engine and the feel of the wind beneath my hair comes rushing back to me, and something inside me rises up and takes over. I study Sarth's face, a daring plan forming in my head. *Hazardous, but not stupid.* "I'm willing to deal," I say, "but first, let's get something straight. I'm the chieftain's High Daughter, not a princess, and not the Syndicate's gift to anyone."

Sarth splits a grin and claps a hand on Velkan's shoulder. "See how easy it is to wheel and deal with the friendly folk on the fringe planets?" The smile vanishes from her face as quickly as it formed. She jerks her head in the direction of the guards. "What's your plan to get us out of here?"

"First," I say, beckoning her closer, "we discuss my terms."

She shrugs, leans forward, and peers through the slats at me, her eyes glistening like orbs in the fading light of the day.

"Take me with you, and I'll get you out of here," I whisper.

Chapter 7

Sarth scrutinizes me through half-lidded eyes, calculating and suspicious.

"Take me to the planet where you found Velkan," I say, jutting my chin out.

She lets out a snort. "You would leave your privileged position on Cwelt to chase some fantasy of finding your family of origin?"

"My birth parents might still be alive."

"What makes you think they'd want to be found? What if *they're* the ones who sold you?" Sarth waves her hand dismissively. "Happens all the time on famine-ridden planets. Lowlife vultures. They'd eat their own children if they couldn't sell them."

Buir lets out a horrified gasp.

My insides recoil, but I glue my lips tight in a steely expression. Maybe I am being naive. What if my birth parents turn out to be from some arid terraform where famine turned the inhabitants into savages? It's no secret the Syndicate has abandoned terraform projects that turned out not to be lucrative, or too dangerous, leaving the settlers to fend for themselves against galactic pirates, Maulers, giant predator birds, face-eating monkeys, and a host of other monstrous species that may be more the stuff of solar myth than fact, for all I know.

"I'll deal with it," I say, curtly. "Take me to the planet, and I'll help you escape."

Sarth scratches her bald head with a ragged nail and casts a furtive glance through the wooden posts in the direction of the guards.

"I can be useful," I add. "I understand spaceship technology." *At least in theory.*

Sarth's eyes scan me skeptically one more time, and I'm afraid she'll see me for what I am: a misfit teenager from a primitive planet, full of grandiose dreams, and a headful of knowledge, but no experience beyond the dirt beneath my feet.

"All right, what's your plan?" she barks.

I blink, taken aback by her abrupt buy-in to my proposition. I was fully expecting to argue and wrangle until she saw no alternative. I don't have a plan, yet. But Sarth doesn't need to know that.

"I'll tell you when it's time." I harden my tone. "One more thing. You're going to teach me how to fly the Zebulux. I've studied all the ships the Syndicate put into production, but I need to practice. Once we reach Aristozonex I'm trading some of that dargonite for a ship of my own."

Sarth hefts her brows upward and stares at me like I'm a creature to be pitied. "Takes months to learn to pilot a ship like the Zebulux—and years to master it."

"I can guarantee you'll only have to show me once," I say. "If you'd rather stay here, I'll figure it out myself."

Her mouth falls open, but before she can counter, I turn around and stride away from the hut, my heart thumping a heightened rhythm that matches the icy solar gusts whipping up around us. I pull up a corner of my shamskin to shield my face from the dust.

Buir hurries after me, her leather boots crunching the gravel beneath. "You can't go with her."

I stop abruptly and spin to face her. "Why not?"

Buir's eyes widen in alarm. "You can't be serious."

I shrug. "We need weapons and ships to survive a raid by the Maulers; the chieftain agrees."

Buir puts a hand on her hip. "He didn't agree to you helping the prisoners escape."

"Would you rather see them die?"

"That is for the elders to decide. I can't be a part of this. You're going too far, Trattora." She storms past me and takes off in the direction of the settlement.

I jump into the LunaTrekker, pull on Sarth's goggles, and start it up. "Wait!" I yell after her as the vehicle surges forward with a deep rumble that drowns out my plea. I drive alongside Buir, trying to shout across to her at the same time. "Will you at least listen to me for just one minute?"

She keeps her eyes fixed in front of her and increases her pace, her arms pumping up and down, her breath like gossamer in the chill Cweltan air.

In desperation, I swing the LunaTrekker around in front of her and jump out. "Buir! This isn't just about me, or the bracelet," I plead. "If we trade the dargonite on Aristozonex, we can buy the ships we need to defend Cwelt from the Maulers. If we stay here and do nothing, we'll end up a slave colony, like Oxtian, or worse."

Buir grabs me by my shamskin and pulls me close, her eyes flashing an urgency I can't discount. "Sarth is engaging in illegal cryogenic trading," she says. "She might be wanted by the Syndicate, for all we know. If you go with her, you might be arrested too."

A faint whistle from behind distracts me. I spin around, scrunching my eyes up as I hone in on the figure. Someone is running toward us from the direction of the retribution hut. A flicker of apprehension goes through me. The scarlet scarf tied around the runner's upper arm is a clear indication that something is wrong.

"Jump in," I mutter to Buir.

This time she doesn't argue. She slides in next to me and grips the side of the LunaTrekker as I rev the engine and take off in a cloud of dust, thankful for the goggles that protect me from being blinded. Buir raises one arm protectively over her eyes. I plow over rocks and shrubs in our path, straining to keep the vehicle under control. Moments later, we pull up hard by the runner. "What's wrong?" I yell.

"Mauler warship," he pants, leaning against the LunaTrekker to catch his breath.

"Have they landed?" I ask, my thoughts somersaulting in a mad panic.

He shakes his head. "On approach. Chieftain's orders are to flee at once to the underground caves. He's sent out a search party for you."

My mind races, trying to piece it all together. "What about the prisoners?"

The runner heaves in another deep breath. "My orders were to leave them and dismiss the guards."

I grit my teeth and start the LunaTrekker back up. I promised Velkan I wouldn't let the elders execute him, but leaving him for the Maulers might be a worse fate. "Head for the caves," I order the runner. "Tell my father we're on our way."

He bows and sprints off as I twist the controller and turn the LunaTrekker around.

"What are you doing?" Buir asks, a tremor in her voice. "We need to go to the caves right away."

I accelerate toward the retribution hut. "We're not leaving them to die," I say. "We made a deal with them."

"That was before we knew the Maulers were coming," Buir protests.

"Going to the caves will only buy us time, and not much at that," I say. "If the Maulers land and set up a base on Cwelt, we won't survive underground more than a few months. What we need are ships to fight back."

"You can't do anything about that."

"I can try." I glance across at her. "Who else is going to save Cwelt?"

Buir remains silent for a few minutes as we bump our way over a rocky patch on the trail leading back to the hut. "If you go with Sarth, what's to stop her from killing you?" she asks in a resigned tone.

I grip the controller tighter. "I'll need allies on board. Velkan will help me. I can bribe Ghil and Nipper with a share of the dargonite."

Buir looks increasingly skeptical as the retribution hut comes into view.

"I can drop you at the mouth of the caves on my way to the Zebulux," I say, swallowing down the lump in my throat at the thought of parting ways with Buir.

She turns to me, a stricken look on her face. "I can't go down there without you. Your mother would—" She catches herself and gives a hollow laugh. "Not kill me, *exactly*." She frowns. "But the grief in her face might. And that would be worse than looking at Sarth's ugly mug for however long it takes to sell the dargonite and get back here."

I raise my brows questioningly. "Does that mean you're coming on a *real* adventure with me?"

She tilts her delicate chin up. "I want a custom LunaTrekker and my own driver."

"Done!" I grin across at her as I slam on the brakes and pull up in front of the retribution hut.

It's empty!

Buir turns rigid beside me, and then glances nervously around. "Do you think the guards took them to the caves?"

"The guards would never go against my father's orders," I say. "They must have escaped." I grit my teeth and make a sharp turn, steering the LunaTrekker back in the direction we came. "We have to reach them before they make it back to the Zebulux."

Buir yells something to me, but it's lost as the engine roars and we lurch forward. I'm fairly certain she was urging me to forget the oremongers and disappear underground before it's too late. But I can't let that happen. As we rip faster over the trail, rocks spewing behind us, the tires fighting for traction, my thoughts grow darker. If Sarth leaves without me, Cwelt is doomed, and so is my only chance of finding out where I came from. The hope of my future and the clues to my past both lie with the Zebulux. I need to be on that ship when it takes off.

"There they are!" Buir points up ahead.

I squint at the figures in the distance. *Five* figures. My heart sinks. "They have a hostage. Probably one of the guards. This complicates things."

"Are you sure you want to intervene?" Buir mutters. "Maybe we should get help."

"They're not armed," I say, "but we are." I gesture over my shoulder at our spears lying in the bed of the LunaTrekker.

Moments later, we reach the fleeing oremongers. I veer past them and cut them off. "You forgot your passengers," I say, jumping out and grabbing my spear.

Sarth shoves the bound guard in front of her, holding a knife to his neck. It's Meldus. Only sixteen, he is one of my father's younger and more inexperienced guards. I grimace. No wonder Sarth wasn't too worried about her impending execution. Somehow, she managed to conceal the knife from the guards when they arrested her. She probably grabbed Meldus through the slats, like she grabbed me, and forced the other guards to unlock the door before they fled to the caves. A shiver runs across my shoulders. There was nothing to stop her putting a knife to my neck earlier.

An ugly grin spreads across Sarth's face. "I thought we'd seen the last of you two. Shouldn't you be running like rats to the caves like the rest of your clan?"

"We had a deal," I say. "I stand by my word."

Sarth sniffs. "Deal expired. I don't need you anymore."

"Release the guard," I say. "He has no part in this."

"Not until we're safely on board."

I tighten my grip on my spear.

In return, Sarth jabs the knife further into Meldus's neck. Ghil and Nipper step forward, fists clenched, the resolve of desperate men in their eyes. Velkan tilts his head questioningly at me as I wrestle with my decision. Putting Meldus's life at risk wasn't a part of my plan. And we're wasting valuable time with a Mauler ship headed our way. I'll have to back down and go along with Sarth for now.

"All right." I toss my spear into the bed of the LunaTrekker and slide back into the driver's seat. "We'll deliver you to your ship. But as soon as we're on board, the guard goes free."

Sarth yanks Meldus toward the vehicle and forces him into the back seat. Velkan and the other oremongers climb in beside him. Sarth walks around to the driver seat. "I'll take it from here."

Reluctantly, I slide over beside Buir and let Sarth take the wheel. I have to let her think she's in charge until Meldus is safe. Maybe it's for the best that her hands are on the controller. Less chance of her trying to pull a fast one if she's driving.

Buir and I trade sober glances when we pass the deserted settlement. The doors to the abandoned Great Hall swing back and forth in the wind. The stalls along the boulevard are replete with fresh wares; meat hanging from hooks, astro fruit piled high in crates. No one risked taking the time to pack anything up. Without ships and weapons, we have no chance of staving off the Maulers, and my father knows it.

Minutes later, the Zebulux looms in front of us. Sarth brakes hard and then changes gear abruptly. She drives slowly up the docking ramp and parks the LunaTrekker to one side of the dingy cargo bay. The oremongers jump out and secure the vehicle to the floor with cables. Sarth nods in my direction. "This is where we part ways." She throws a tarp over the dargonite in the bed of the LunaTrekker. "Take the guard with you."

Meldus throws me a relieved look, scrambles out from the back seat, and turns to exit the ship.

A horrendous clang echoes through the chamber of the ship, sending him flying. He falls awkwardly, hands still bound behind him, and his head slams into the metal floor knocking him unconscious. Velkan staggers over to a control pad on the wall and a moment later, the massive ramp retracts, closing out the light of Cwelt.

"Start her up!" Sarth yells. Ghil and Nipper race down a flight of stairs to the engine room.

"What's happening?" Buir asks, in a panicked voice.

"Maulers," Sarth announces grimly. "They're shooting long-range plasma rockets to clear the area before they make a landing."

Another round hits the hull of the ship throwing me back against the LunaTrekker. I scrabble to get a grip and pull myself upright. "Can't you fire back?" I yell to Sarth.

"Wouldn't do any good. We don't have that kind of firepower. Time we were out of here. The Zebulux is a tough old bird, but she's no combat ship." She turns and jogs up the stairway to the flight deck.

"We promised Meldus we'd let him go," I say to Velkan.

"Nothing we can do now." Velkan reaches for the metal

handrail on the stairway. "If we open that door we'll all die. I've got to help Sarth. Get him up to the control room as quickly as you can. All the way down the hallway."

I stagger over to Meldus and with Buir's assistance drag him onto a pile of tarps.

Strip lights flicker around the docking bay. A look of sheer terror passes over Buir's face as the ship begins to vibrate.

I swallow hard and give her hand a reassuring squeeze. Even though I'm grateful she's here with me, I wish she were someplace safe. If we take a direct hit, we won't even make it out of Cwelt's atmosphere.

Meldus groans as he slowly comes around. He blinks up at me, his body tensing as he pieces together where he is. His eyes dart left and right. "We need to get off the ship."

"It's too late for that," I say. "We're under attack by Maulers."

"No!" Meldus struggles to sit up. "We have to get to the caves … your father …" He looks at me, confusion flooding his face.

"We had no choice but to close up the ramp when the Maulers started firing," I say. "We have to get out of here before they come any closer."

Meldus stares at me with a frozen look of horror on his face, as if wrestling with the reality that he isn't getting off this ship, that he's leaving Cwelt with Sarth and her crew, and that he's the chieftain's daughter's sole protector now.

"We're coming back," I promise him.

"Unless we're intercepted by a Syndicate patrol." Buir points to the back of the cargo bay.

I twist my head and peer into the shadows.

The torpor vats are still here!

Chapter 8

The Zebulux lifts off with a G-force that sends my breath down to the pit of my stomach. I feel like all the blood is being sucked from my head. Buir's eyes bulge with fear as she hugs a nearby crate to steady herself. Meldus is huddled against one of the wheels of the secured LunaTrekker.

"We have to get up to the flight deck," I yell to them. "It's not safe here." *Especially not with those torpor vats so close to us.* I shiver when I think of what will happen if we take a hit and one of them explodes. The last thing we need is frozen eyeballs staring up at us from the loading dock floor. Buir's already on the edge of spiraling into a full-blown panic attack.

Meldus fixes a stricken gaze on the sealed cargo door. "We're dead."

"Not yet. Last I checked, you were still breathing!" I rest a firm hand on his shoulder. "Time to move!"

He blinks back into action, the authoritative tone in my voice registering somewhere deep inside the vacancy in his eyes.

The ship's thrusters strain as it banks hard to maneuver along a trajectory leading us out of range of the plasma rockets. I help

Meldus to his feet and we stagger across to the stairway. The ship dips again, presumably to evade another missile, and we wrap our arms around the handrail and cling to it tightly until we level out once more.

"Hurry!" I yell back to Buir who's still hugging the crate. She throws me a petrified look before letting go and dashing across the bay to the stairs.

When we finally make it to the upper deck, we sway like drunks down the utility corridor to the door marked control room. Relief washes over me at the pneumatic hiss of the doors sliding apart.

Inside, Velkan and Sarth are seated side by side in two large, well-worn bucket seats taped together at the seams. Screens flicker cryptically all around them, a low humming drones in the background. Neither one turns a head when we lurch toward the fold-up chairs behind them and strap ourselves in.

"Has the hull been breached?" Buir gasps.

Velkan twists around in his seat and grins. "No direct blasts, thanks to some skillful handling on our part. Seals are tight due to the heat-shielding tiles. The Zebulux may not be pretty, but she was built to last."

"Won't they come after us?" I ask.

Sarth grunts, her back to me. "Maulers have no interest in chasing down a worthless oremonger's vessel. They're focused on invasion. I'm more worried about salvage hunters. They'd sell this old beast for parts if they got their hands on it." She lets out an unflattering snort. "But that won't be a problem for much longer. Once we trade that dargonite on Aristozonex, I'll be outfitting this mining operation with a state-of-space new freighter with shields."

"So we're heading straight to Aristozonex?" I say.

"Not unless you want to run out of fuel halfway there," Sarth replies.

"We passed a fueling port on the old trade route we came along," Velkan explains. "We're taking a quick detour there first."

"How long before we reach Aristozonex?" I press.

Velkan shrugs. "A few days, if all goes according to plan. But it rarely does."

I frown. "You mean … Maulers?"

"Maulers, solar storms, mechanical problems. But yes, Maulers are our biggest threat. We'll have to avoid the eastern arterial trade route, and that will delay us a day or two."

I sink back in my seat and stare at the floor. Realistically, it could take weeks to secure a deal with a buyer, and after that, I still need to procure a ship. And someone to captain it. At least until I get up to speed. I study the back of Sarth's bald head. Maybe I could persuade her to sell Velkan to me. After all, she's about to become a very rich trader. She could afford to hire a captain and a full crew for her new ship. Why would she want to hold on to a serf?

"It could be a month or so before we make it back to Cwelt," I say to Buir and Meldus.

"Our people have enough supplies to survive underground for at least three months," Meldus says. "The caves are stocked and habitable."

"A month isn't too bad then, is it?" Buir's eyes sweep my face for reassurance. "We'll be back to rescue them long before they run out of food."

I give a distracted nod. *If all goes according to plan.*

We fall silent as the adrenalin slowly leaks from us, the steady thrum of the engine lulling us into a hypnotic state. I look around, taking note of the compact layout of the control room. I know what every piece of equipment on the console is used for, but I haven't seen any of it in operation before, and I'm fascinated by every blinking light and screen. I picture myself setting a course on the nav system, adjusting the flight controller, banking, dipping, steering the Zebulux through a sea of asteroids, racing through arid canyons, streaking away from Mauler projectiles at the speed of—

I jolt out of my trance when Sarth yawns loudly.

"Where are we?" I ask, jerking upright in my seat to peer through the viewport. A vast expanse of glittering stars and moons draped in gauzy film fills the screen. My breathing quiets in sync with the silence of the scene. I've never seen anything so beautiful, and never felt so small. I'm staring through a peephole into a universe with no beginning and no end. I reach for my bracelet and twist it between my fingers as a familiar ache rises inside me. How can I ever find my place in something this large?

"We're well out of Cwelt's atmosphere," Velkan says. "And out of range of the Maulers."

Sarth stretches in her seat and turns to Velkan. "Go down to the galley and tell Ghil to make me up a plate of food. I've programmed our trajectory for the next several hours on autopilot, but I'll keep watch up here a bit longer, just to be safe."

Velkan gestures at us. "What about them?"

Sarth blows out a disdainful breath. "Take them with you. I'm tired of them yakking in my ear. And show them where they can bunk in one of the extra crew rooms."

"Come on." Velkan tosses a skein of dark hair out of his face. "It's time you officially meet Ghil and get a taste of what you're in for. He's our chef extraordinaire, and Nipper's our engineer, although how either one of them ever qualified for their position is beyond me."

On our way, Velkan points out the extra crew room next door to his—an exact replica of his room, and equally bleak. "Ghil's in the room on the other side of you, so you'll probably hear him snoring half the night. Nipper bunks with me. And those are Sarth's quarters." Velkan gestures at a steel door on the opposite side of the hallway. "No one goes in or out other than Sarth. She keeps it locked, but don't let her catch you even hanging around outside the door."

I stare at the door for a moment. I wonder what other secrets Sarth is hiding.

We continue down the utility hallway until we come to the communal area and dining room outfitted with a couple of metal tables surrounded by benches, which are bolted into position on the floor. At the back of the room is a small seating area with a dilapidated couch. Faded paintings of various planetary systems cover the gray metal walls. Someone is whistling loudly inside the adjoining galley, and judging by the amount of clanging and clattering going on, lunch is underway.

"Ghil!" Velkan hollers.

The room falls silent. A moment later, the tall, narrow-hipped oremonger with the knot in his neck sticks his head out.

"Our passengers are hungry for lunch," Velkan says.

Ghil casts a resentful glance our way, clearly communicating that we're unexpected additions to the manifest, and that translates to extra mouths to feed. I need to make sure we get off to a good start, or we may not see our fair share of rations.

"You sound awfully busy in there." I tip my head in greeting. "What's on the menu?"

He flashes me a treacherous smile and steps out from behind the door, clutching a butcher knife in each hand.

Meldus moves silently to my side, his training kicking in.

Buir's nails dig deep into my arm, and I give a little yelp.

The grin on Ghil's face spreads like a river flooding its banks. Without warning, he lets out a whoop and tosses the knives upward with a vertical spin that rotates them several times. Buir screams in my ear as he catches them again by their handles. He pulls a third, smaller knife from his leather boot and adds it to the mix. I watch, mesmerized, as he juggles all three with increasing velocity, finishing up with an under-leg throw. My heart races in my chest, but he nails the final catch unscathed.

Velkan leans back against the wall, arms crossed, looking amused as he waits for our reaction.

"Impressive," I say, trying not to sound overly impressed.

"Sadly, not an indication of his skill in the kitchen," Velkan says.

Ghil glares at him. "But an indication of what I'll do to anyone who insults my cooking."

"Duly noted," Buir says, releasing my pinched arm. "I'm not too picky."

I let out a gasp and quickly cover it up with a cough. This from the girl who dissects everything on her plate and organizes it into reject piles by food type.

"Sarth wants me to take her a plate when we're done," Velkan says.

Ghil nods. "I'll give you one to take to Nipper too."

Velkan turns to us and gestures to one of the tables. "Sit down. We'll eat first, and then I'll take the others their food."

Ghil wasn't kidding about lunch being done. I stare down at the plate of earthen-colored food he sets in front of me. It looks and smells like it was "done" an indeterminate number of days ago. Buir's face pales several degrees in quick succession when Ghil slaps a plate in front of her.

"Uh, what—" she begins.

"Bean mush," Ghil snaps, wiping his hands on his filthy apron. I catch a glint of a sheathed knife dangling from his waist. My gut tells me our chef has little training in the culinary arts, but a whole lot of experience wielding knives. If I'm not mistaken, he's made a recent career change.

"Mondays, Wednesdays, and Fridays is bean mush," Ghil announces with a loud sniff.

Buir blinks at him, a scarcely-daring-to-hope look in her eyes. "And the other days?"

"Mash!"

I raise my brows, knowing better than to ask what the distinction is.

Confusion, mixed with despair, clouds Buir's face. "What's in the ... mash?"

Ghil throws her a look as sharp as his knives. "Leftovers." He swivels his narrow hips and stomps back into the galley, whistling loudly.

My mouth drops open. "Is he for real?" I ask Velkan.

Velkan jabs a fork into his heaped plate of food and cocks his head to one side as if considering the question. "Yeah, except he sometimes cheats and serves leftovers on Fridays too."

"Leftovers of *what*?" I ask. "Doesn't sound like he ever cooks."

"He pretty much gets a pot going at the start of the week and keeps adding to it," Velkan acknowledges.

"I can't eat this stuff." Buir pushes her plate to one side. "Maybe I can find something else in the kitchen." She gets to her feet, but, Velkan clamps a hand on her wrist. "No! You don't go into the galley. *Ever*. Just like no one goes near Sarth's quarters."

Buir looks affronted. "Why not? I won't bother Ghil. I'm perfectly capable of making myself something to eat."

"Ghil's overly protective of his territory." Velkan releases her, a wary look on his face. "The last person who went in there uninvited never came out. At least not in one piece."

Buir's eyes widen to planetary dimensions.

Velkan winks in my direction. "Rumor has it he was in the mash that week."

Buir lets loose with an anguished scream.

I fall to one side, laughing so hard that tears run down my face.

Buir turns to unleash her fury on Velkan just as the doors slide apart and Sarth walks in.

"Hate to break up the party," she says, the look on her face clearly indicating otherwise, "but I ordered lunch a half hour ago."

Velkan jumps to his feet. "Ghil's making your plate right now."

Sarth swings a leg over the bench I'm sitting on and slides in next to me. "Nipper's watching the flight deck for a few minutes. I'll eat here now."

Velkan walks over to the galley entry and reaches for the plate Ghil quickly loads up.

"Mush or mash?" Sarth asks, raising a quizzical brow at Velkan as he sets it in front of her.

He hesitates, pretending to ponder the question. "Definitely got more of a mush tang going on today," he announces.

Sarth grunts, then shovels down several mouthfuls in quick succession. She throws a glance across at our plates and narrows her eyes at Buir. "Something wrong with your food?"

Buir gives a one-shouldered shrug. "Not that hungry."

"My ship, my rules," Sarth says. "We don't waste food, *ever*. You waste a meal, I cut your rations for a week."

Buir pulls the plate gingerly toward her, looking like she might gag at any minute.

Sarth turns her attention to me, chewing noisily as her beady eyes scrutinize my hair up close. "We'll be at the fueling port in another hour. Ghil will pick up a few supplies to tide us over until we reach the Aristozonex, and I have some business to take care of. Shouldn't take but a couple of hours to fuel up and get what we need. You can look around the port if you want, but I won't wait if you're late. Meldus can stay with Nipper and keep an eye on the ship."

"What about IDs?"

"The Syndicate issues everyone with CipherSyncs. It's an ID and communication device all in one that can be worn on the wrist or around your neck. It connects you to the StellarNet and handles credit transfers too. I'll hustle you up some on the dark market. But you don't need them at a fueling port. You get an automatic twenty-four-hour pass. So long as you're not holographed as a serf, you're free to come and go as you please."

My heart leaps. Maybe I'll have a chance to find out something about my bracelet before I reach Aristozonex. "In that case, I'll visit the vendor stalls."

Sarth shrugs. "It's the same junk they sell at every solar shop chain in every port. The *real* shopping is on Aristozonex." Her lips curl into a satisfied smile. "And that's where I'll be going as soon as we strike a deal on that dargonite."

I twirl the chain around my neck between my fingers. If it turns out the bracelets are common merchandise sold everywhere in the galaxy, then I'll have no way to trace them. But if no one's seen anything like them before, it will be an indication that they're only made on the planet Velkan and I are from.

Sarth shoves her plate aside. "Time I checked up on Nipper. Last time I left him alone in the control room, we almost clipped an asteroid."

"I'll come with you," I say. "You promised to teach me how to operate the ship. Now's as good a time as any to start."

Her lips twitch in amusement. "That deal's null and void. You're only on board this ship because the dang Maulers didn't give me enough time to toss you off."

"I'll double your split of the dargonite," I say. "And you can have a share of the mining rights on Cwelt."

She wipes her mouth carefully on her sleeve, studying me for a minute and then slaps the table. "Double it is!" She turns to Velkan. "Go down to the engine room and start prepping for landing. Stay there until Nipper gets back, then cover those vats up with netting again." She gestures dismissively at Meldus. "And take that mute with you and show him how it's done. Maybe he'll do a better job in the engine room than Nipper."

She nods to me and I climb out over the bench.

Buir gets to her feet to follow us.

Sarth wags a fat finger at her, grinning. "*You* can stay here and help Ghil clean up."

Buir's lips part but no sound comes out.

I frown. "She doesn't have to—"

"Is there something about, *my* ship, *my* orders, that was unclear?" Sarth growls.

"It's fine." Buir splays her hand to placate me. "Don't worry, Ghil doesn't intimidate me half as much as his cooking."

Sarth cocks an amused brow at her and then exits the room.

I leave Buir stacking the dirty dishes and follow Sarth back up the corridor to the control room.

Inside, I slip into the co-pilot seat and secure my harness. With only an hour to go before we reach the fuel port, Sarth wastes no time getting into the mechanics of piloting the Zebulux. Everything about operating the ship fascinates me, and I ply her with questions. "So, firing the auxiliary thrusters is enough to course correct if we deviate from our trajectory?"

"For normal flight iterations, but not enough for the maneuvers I had to perform to evade the Maulers' rockets earlier." She throws me a curious look. "How do you know so much about spaceship technology and the geography of the intergalactic quadrants?"

"Education is highly prized on Cwelt," I say. "My father

acquired a vast collection of Syndicate EduPlex reference materials for our studies from traders. And we have several wrecked space vessels. I know what every part of the ship is called and what it's used for."

She grunts and fiddles with the controls. "Let's go over the landing sequence. We're only fifteen minutes out."

Despite the powerful rushing sound of the thrusters as we begin a steep descent, Sarth's approach into the fueling station is smooth and steady, and I'm forced to admire her ability to steer the unwieldy Zebulux into a graceful landing. I'm so focused on the bustling fuel station through the viewport that I don't spot the knife in Sarth's hand until it's too late.

Chapter 9

I jerk sideways in my seat, but I can't get far enough out of range before Sarth grabs me by my hair and swings the knife. When she releases me, I stare in bewilderment at the long red lock of my hair she clutches in her fist. My fingers fly instinctively to the hacked strands dangling awkwardly across my left cheek.

I scramble to release my harness. "What did you do that for?" I yell as I jump up and back away, shaking and confused, and immensely relieved that she didn't slit my throat.

"You know more than you should about my cargo," she says in a dark undertone, surveying the red lock of hair as she rubs it between her fingers. "If you turn me in and run, this will be evidence you were in on it with me."

My breathing is still ragged, but I try to act nonchalant. "Fine, if you're that paranoid. Next time, ask first."

A scathing smile plays on Sarth's lips. "You'd best remember I own everything on board this ship." She turns her attention back to the ship's controls. "You have exactly two hours to be back on board."

"You don't own my share of the dargonite, remember that!"

I shout at her and then stomp out of the control room without a backward glance. It was a clever move on her part. And a wake-up call for me. There is no understanding between us. We're partners on the dargonite by default, not by choice, and that means Sarth doesn't trust me and she can't be trusted either. I weave my hair into a thick braid as I make my way back to the galley to look for Buir. The short strands bob at the side of my face like a nagging reminder that the world beyond Cwelt is fraught with the art of treachery, and I have yet to learn its ways.

To my surprise, Buir is seated at the dining table, elbows propped up, engrossed in conversation with Ghil. Judging by the animated look on his face, and his chapped hands flailing in every direction, he's thoroughly enjoying regaling her with whatever tale he's telling. I splay my hand in greeting as I step inside. Ghil stops mid-sentence and hefts an unruly brow at me. "Kitchen's closed."

"That's a relief." I barely suppress an eye roll, before turning to Buir. "Sarth's given us a couple of hours to look around the port while they refuel and pick up supplies."

Ghil narrows his eyes. "Buir's busy."

I open my mouth to protest, but Buir gives a subtle shake of her head. "Ghil and I worked up some new menu ideas. I'll go with him to buy the supplies we need for the galley."

"All right," I say with some reluctance. "Guess I'll see you back on board." I was looking forward to sharing the adventure of our first outing on another planet together, but I don't want to dissuade her if she's managed to persuade Ghil to expand the menu—there's a good chance Buir would starve to death on his original meal plan.

I leave the two of them to take inventory of the galley supplies and make my way down to the cargo bay just as the loading ramp opens up to a view of the teeming port. My eyes dart left and right struggling to absorb the sensory overload in one panoramic sweep. Several merchant ships of varying sizes are docked around the fuel hub. A neon hologram overhead flashes constantly changing fuel prices and fleet discounts. Maintenance workers dressed in grease-stained overalls and clutching wrenches are busy at work on the hull of one of the ships. Attendants in blue tunics monitor the pumps, reporting available slots to the control tower via their earpieces. The throbbing of engines and the smell of fumes is overwhelming.

I startle when Velkan walks up behind me. "Come to watch the Zebulux refueling?"

"Actually, I was about to take a stroll around the vendors' stalls. Do you want to come with me?"

He gives a rueful smile. "The fuel hub's as far as a holographed serf can go. They won't let me past the security gate. Everything I know about the Syndicate planets is what Ghil tells me. He likes to talk plenty and I'm a good listener."

I frown. "I forgot about that. I was hoping I could find out something about our bracelets."

Velkan's face clouds over. "Be careful. There are a lot of shady dealers at these isolated ports. A nifty sleight of hand and your bracelet might disappear right before your eyes."

"I won't take it off the chain. If someone tries to steal it, they'll have to take me too."

Velkan laughs. "Then they'll get more than they bargained for. And so will you, once you step outside. Ever seen a cyborg before?"

I shrug. "I know what they are. I've read about them."

"You mean *who* they are. Nothing to be alarmed about. They're just people with mechanical parts, but it can be a bit disconcerting at first."

"How do they end up like that?"

"Some choose to become enhanced—the middle class on Aristozonex for example. It's cheaper than cell regeneration and the results last longer too. Others have been repaired with aftermarket organs and limbs, especially after industrial accidents. It's syndicate law. All companies are obligated to underwrite the cost of rebuilding injured workers."

A shiver crosses my shoulders. "Sounds creepy."

"Not as creepy as androids." Velkan grins. "You may not run into any this far from Aristozonex, but in the event you do, they're *not* technically people. Although the new humanoid simulation chips can make it difficult to tell the difference."

"Anything else I should be aware of before I venture out?"

"Empty your pockets of any trash. The fueling stations are forced to comply with strict Syndicate environmental regulations." Velkan tilts his head in contemplation. "And don't act interested if you want to buy anything. The vendors will jack the prices sky high as soon as they know you're in the market."

I laugh. "That won't be a problem, I don't have any credits to buy anything with."

Velkan eyes my shamskin. "Most vendors will barter. A cloak like that should fetch a few credits." His face softens. "Sure you're okay venturing out alone."

"Of course. I can defend myself. Where's Meldus?"

"He's helping Nipper in the auxiliary engine room. We need

to take care of a few things while we are in port." He reaches out and brushes his fingers over the chunk of loose hair dangling over my face. "What happened here?"

I suck in a breath at his unexpected touch. "Sarth decided she needed some fire insurance." I gesture at the covered vats. "She's afraid I'll turn her in for transporting illegal cargo."

Velkan's eyes flicker with anger. "The woman's a brute."

"Just don't let her take off without me," I say. "I don't trust her."

"She isn't planning on leaving you behind," Velkan says. "Not if she took a lock of your hair."

He watches with an air of sadness as I walk down the ramp and exit the ship. He's pretty much a prisoner on it, other than when the Zebulux is mining on the fringe planets. I can't imagine what it would be like to grow up without knowing a day of freedom. The thought lies heavy on me. I want to help him, but the only way I know how is to purchase him from Sarth, and that doesn't sit right with me either.

I stride toward the security gate at the far end of the platform, trying to pass myself off as someone who's fueled up at hundreds of ports. Despite my laid-back stride, several people turn in my direction and rake a gaze over me in passing. It's not hard to guess why they're staring. My red hair stands out like a neon hologram in a sea of black and brown and blond tones, and my shamskin confirms that I'm not a frequent traveler to these parts, or at all. Most of the people milling around me are dressed in neutral-colored tunics designed for practicality. Thankfully, I'm used to being the center of attention, so their curious glances don't phase me. I'm not the only oddity here. Several cyborgs mingle among the crowd and one or two questionable humans that might very well be androids. I imagine Buir is attracting a fair amount of attention too, wherever she is.

I keep weaving steadily through the crowd in the direction of the metal exit gates. Just beyond the barrier, I see vendor stalls, crowded one on top of the other, and a steady stream of people moving up and down the street. I join the back of the line at the nearest security gate and study the list of items prohibited from entering the port; weapons and ammunition, illegal substances, livestock, *holographed serfs*. My stomach knots. I know what it's like to be different, but not to be excluded like an animal or something dangerous to the public. If this is how the Syndicate planets outside Aristozonex operate, I dread to think what kind of society exists within its borders. I take my turn at walking through the scanner and dutifully hold out my hand for a holographic reentry stamp.

"You have twenty-four hours before it disappears," the guard says, zapping the back of my hand. "No reentry after that without a term permit."

I nod and proceed out the exit gate, merging into the throng of people on the main thoroughfare. I have no idea what a term permit is, but I won't be needing one anyway. Sarth has only given us a couple of hours.

The relentless clamor of vendors yelling out *one time only* special offers to passersby, and the hustle and bustle of bodies pressing in on me from every direction, are terrifying at first, but I move with the flow and my fascination soon overtakes my fear. I scan the stalls as I go by, my pulse quickening in anticipation. It's a long shot, but I can't help hoping that someone here will recognize my bracelet.

The first stall I approach sports a strange mishmash of metal jewelry and decorative items built from recycled parts, many of which I don't recognize, but it's the elderly vendor himself who catches my attention. He's wearing a metal cast over his nose, and I immediately think *cyborg*. My suspicions are confirmed when his left eye whirs and focuses in on me with the unerring accuracy of a camera lens. I flinch beneath his penetrating gaze.

"What can I do the traveling lady for?" he wheedles, beaming at me from behind the table.

"Depends on what you're selling," I say, casting a bored glance over his wares.

His eye whirs again and I'm almost certain he's zooming in on my hair. A puzzled look flits across his forehead. He scans my cloak more closely, and a flicker of comprehension registers in his one real eye. "First trip out of the fringe, yes?" he says, getting to his feet.

I nod, mesmerized at the claw that reaches out and swoops up a metal box from the table.

"Then you need souvenir to mark occasion." He holds the box out for my inspection.

I frown down at it. "What is it?"

"This," he says in a hushed tone, as he leans toward me, "is genuine antique float chamber from Syndicate's first generation of ships."

I reach out my hand to touch it and he whips it back protectively.

"*Very* valuable antique," he adds, giving me a knowing look. "A rare find these days." He traces a curved finger over the cylinder with his left hand. "But for you, I make a bargain."

I pull a face. "What would I do with it? It's too rusted up to be of any use."

He works his wrinkled lips in and out as if assessing the situation. "You don't know what antique is, yes? This float chamber has been—"

"Don't listen to a word he says!" the obese vendor sitting at the neighboring stall wheezes. "Lies, lies, and more lies!" He waddles over, huffing between steps. "All he sells is junk!" He pulls something out of his jacket and sucks on it for a moment before continuing in a stronger voice. "Let me offer a woman of your impeccable taste something more appealing." He slings a sweaty arm across my shoulder and escorts me with a firm grip over to his stall. "Asteroid scrubs, magnetic perfumes—atomic body oils are the latest craze. I carry every scent in the solar system at discounted prices."

I wriggle out from under his grasp, trying not to look repulsed.

He studies my hair for a moment. "You have such an exotic look. Here, try this one. It's called *Crater* and believe me, it will turn heads. They're going crazy for it on Aristozonex." He winks at me, his eye so heavily lidded it looks like an overhanging lip. "Word on the street is even androids go weak at the knees for it, if that's your thing."

Before I can protest he squirts something foul-smelling on my neck. I wrinkle my nose in disgust at the pungent odor.

"Not your taste, eh? Yes? No? I have something lighter, electron-charged perhaps. Those oils run a little more, but I could cut you a good deal on two."

"No!" I hold out an arm to bar him from spraying me with

anything else. "I'm not interested in smells. I'm looking for jewelry." I pull the chain out from around my neck and hold up the bracelet to him. "Something like this."

He taps his chubby fingers on his table of wares and throws a quick glance down the street. "I have a friend who deals in spectacular jewelry. I'm sure she can help you find what you're looking for." He whistles to a boy assisting a customer at the other end of the vendor's table and points two fingers down the street. The boy gives a quick nod.

The disgruntled antique parts dealer scowls and folds his arms in front of him when we pass by. "He crook, that one!" he calls after us. "Scam you out of last credit that one will!"

The obese vendor gives a dismissive wave and hurries me on down the street. We walk past a dozen or so stalls before we come to a stop in front of a bustling brightly-colored stall with a shimmery purple awning. The vendor squeezes behind the table and exchanges a few words with a tall, dark-haired woman holding up several strings of beads between her fingers for a customer to take a closer look at. The woman gives a curt nod, her sharp eyes appraising me, before turning her attention back to her customer.

"Roma will take good care of you," the obese vendor says, and then disappears back down the street in the direction of his stall.

I study the rest of the wares on display while I wait for Roma to finish up. Trinkets mostly, gaudy and cheap. Nothing that resembles my bracelet in material or quality or design.

I'm about to give up and move on when Roma jerks her chin in my direction. "Let me take a look at what you've got."

I wait until her customer has walked away and then pull out the chain around my neck.

Roma walks around to where I'm standing in front of the table and takes the bracelet from me. She weighs it in her hand and then pulls out a loupe and examines it carefully from all angles.

"Have you ever seen anything like this?" I ask.

She slips the loupe back into her pocket. "Are you buying or selling?"

"Buying," I say, after a moment's hesitation.

Roma grimaces. "Tough to come by something like this. On the other hand, if you were selling this caliber of wares, I'd be willing to come in on it."

I furrow my brow in confusion. "In on what?"

She tilts an already arched brow upward. "You bring me what you help yourself to, and I resell it and give you a cut."

"I'm not a thief," I say, indignantly.

Roma purses her lips and busies herself straightening out the necklaces the customer was looking at earlier. "I've been doing this long enough to know that a bracelet like that doesn't belong to a savage dressed in some animal skin from a fringe planet."

I square my shoulders. "How dare you! I'm—" I clamp my lips together. It wouldn't mean anything to her that I'm a chieftain's daughter.

"It was a gift," I say, holding her gaze.

She folds her arms across her chest and gives me a penetrating gaze. "And you want to know where it came from."

Chapter 10

"Can you help me?" I ask.

Roma ignores me and busies herself pulling out some trays of rings for another customer before responding.

"I have contacts," she says in a low voice. "But they don't come cheap. And hunting down something like that won't be easy. Two thousand credits up front. Another two thousand once I have the information." She taps something on the CipherSync on her wrist and gestures to me. "Let me see it again."

I dangle the bracelet in front of her. After Velkan's warning, I'm not taking it off the chain for her to take a closer look. She holds up her CipherSync to it and a dotted red line frames the bracelet and makes a 3D holographic scan of it with a single click. "I'll make some enquiries," Roma says. "Come back in an hour."

I open my mouth to respond and then shut it again. Where am I going to find two thousand credits?

She reads my expression and irritation ripples across her face. "Unless, of course, you can't afford the asking price."

I toss my head. "You'll get your money, but *only* after you deliver, not before. I'll be back in one hour, and I'll double your fee if you have the information for me."

Her expression remains skeptical. After a moment's hesitation, she gives a curt nod. "Don't be late. I close up here soon."

My feet keep pace with the heightened boom of my heartbeat as I hurry back to the Zebulux. I know what I have to do, but it's risky. If Sarth catches me dipping into the dargonite before we reach Aristozonex, she'll throw me off the ship, or worse.

"Back so soon?" Velkan calls to me from the fuel pump. He wipes the back of his hand over his glistening brow.

"Just checking if Buir's done helping Ghil yet," I call back to him. "I want her to see the stalls too." I do want her to come with me, but that's not the real reason I came back. I hate deceiving Velkan, but I can't risk involving him.

"You just missed her. She headed out with Ghil a few minutes ago," Velkan says. "Sarth's gone too. She had business to attend to."

I give a disappointed shrug. "I'll ask Meldus if he wants to come instead." I turn and run up the docking ramp before Velkan can dissuade me.

Inside, I take a quick calming breath and smooth my hair back with sweaty palms before making my way over to the LunaTrekkers secured with the rest of the cargo. I walk around to the back of the LunaTrekker closest to me, pull back the tarp, and peer into the bed. *Empty!* The sickening feeling in my gut creeps slowly up my throat. I glance dubiously over at the second LunaTrekker tucked behind a row of fuel drums. I'm almost certain it's not the one we stashed the dargonite in, but maybe

I'm mixing them up. My mind churns furiously as I pick my way through the cargo toward the other vehicle. Is it possible Sarth moved the rock without telling me? I peer into the empty bed of the second LunaTrekker, confirming my worst fears. A flash of rage goes through me. I should have known Sarth wouldn't be content with splitting the proceeds, even with a bigger cut. What if she's selling the dargonite out from under me right now?

I clench and unclench my fists, wrestling with what to do. I need that dargonite. I have no other way to pay Roma for the information about the bracelets. I press my fingers to my temples and try to calm down enough to sort out my thoughts. It's unlikely Sarth is trying to sell the dargonite at a fueling outpost near the fringe. Most likely she'll wait until she gets to Aristozonex where she'll get the best price, which means she's hidden it somewhere on board—someplace no one can get their hands on it. *Her quarters.*

I turn and race up the stairway to the upper level, my footsteps clanging in my ear with every step. Halfway down the utility hallway, I run right into a stocky, shirtless man. "Nipper!" I gasp, stumbling back from him.

"Whoa!" He grabs me by my arm to steady me. "Where do you think you're going?"

I shake myself loose and throw him a contemptuous look. "I could ask you the same thing, prancing down the hallway half-naked."

He runs a calloused hand over his bald head and gives a sheepish grin. "First chance I've had all week to take a shower."

He stares unabashedly at my hair. "Is that real?"

I give him a disgruntled look. "Ask your captain! She hacked off a chunk as collateral to make sure I don't turn her in for illegal cargo."

A dark shadow comes over Nipper's face. "She has no boundaries."

I let out an appeased sigh. At least we share something in common. "I'm sorry I almost bowled you over."

Nipper leers at me. "It's my lucky day when a pretty girl runs smack into me."

I swallow down my revulsion. "I'll watch where I'm going next time," I say, and continue down the hallway at a casual pace. His eyes burn a hole in my back, so instead of heading to Sarth's quarters, I slip into my own room. As soon as I step through the door, I realize my mistake—I'm in Velkan's room.

My heart races. I need to wait a few minutes to make sure Nipper has cleared out before I go back out. I sit down on the bottom bunk and draw my cloak around me. I pick at my lip, picturing Velkan here, asleep, his dark skeins of hair spread like the paths of shooting stars around him. That shiver that went through me when his dark fingers brushed up against mine in the Great Hall goes through me again. I've never been attracted to anyone on Cwelt. I've always felt like a stranger in my own skin there, but with Velkan it's different, yet somehow familiar. I twist my chain distractedly between my fingers. Maybe our matching bracelets mean there's some connection between us.

I look up, startled when he appears in the doorway.

"What are you doing?" he asks, a puzzled look on his face.

My throat closes over when I try to speak. I didn't want to involve him, but I don't want to lie to him either. After all, this is about him too. "The dargonite's gone," I say. "I need to get

103

into Sarth's quarters and find out where she's hidden it. Nipper was wandering around in the hallways so I slipped in here to wait until it was clear. I ... mistook it for my room."

Velkan's jaw tightens. "Sarth's quarters are off limits to everyone. She'll throw you off the ship if she finds you in there."

"I need the dargonite to pay for information about our bracelets. I have a lead, a vendor who has contacts on Aristozonex."

Velkan leans the palm of his hand against the upper bunk and bows his head as he weighs my words. "She keeps her room locked at all times. If you break in, she'll turn you over to port security."

"Not if it looks like an outside job." I grin as I get to my feet. "And she won't be able to report it to the authorities because she won't want the ship searched."

Velkan studies me for a moment. "There's just one hitch. You said Nipper saw you come in."

I frown. "Yeah, I'll make sure he sees me leave again. I'll go down to the engine room, check up on Meldus, and tell them both I'm heading back into town."

Velkan gives me a lingering look of uncertainty. He's got to be as curious about our bracelets as I am, but there's a lot at stake for him. As an indentured serf with no way of making a living away from his master, he'd almost certainly be rounded up and sent to a penal colony if Sarth threw him off the ship for helping me.

"I need to get back to the fuel depot," he says. "I'll alert you if I see Sarth coming back to the ship."

I follow him down to the cargo bay and watch him walk down

the loading ramp before making my way to the engine room.

I step gingerly over the threshold into the smelly, cramped space. Half the bulbs in the overhead fixtures are burned out, and the room is filled with the sound of thrumming machines running ragged. I glance over the row of propellant tanks, but Nipper and Meldus are nowhere in sight. My eye falls on a crowbar lying among a pile of dirty tools beneath one of the turbines. I pick it up and tuck it into my belt below my shamskin. It's perfect for what I have in mind.

"Meldus!" I yell his name several times to no avail. I squeeze my way through the labyrinth of greasy pipes running the length of the room to the steel door at the far end of the engine room. I hammer on it with my fist and then yank it open. "Meldus, are you in—"

My mouth drops open. Meldus stares groggily back at me, face flushed, a glass filled with an amber liquid halfway to his mouth. A cigarette dangles from his fingers. Nipper lounges in a nearby chair, legs stretched out, a smirk on his flat face. "Come on in and join the party," he drawls, slapping a spot on the seat next to him.

Meldus sets down his glass unsteadily and makes a half-hearted attempt to stand.

"Don't bother," I say coldly. I turn my attention back to Nipper. "He's had enough of whatever you gave him. Make sure he's sobered up before Sarth returns. If he gets thrown off this ship, you're going with him. I have to go into town, but I'll be back to check on him."

An amused grin dances across Nipper's lips. "You're pretty good at giving orders, for a savage."

I jerk my gaze away from his laughing eyes and slip back out into the engine room. I can't risk Meldus getting kicked off the ship. I have enough to worry about already, but I need to make sure Sarth doesn't find him in a drunken state.

I make my way back up to the cargo bay and then continue quietly up the stairs to the upper level. My heart thunders in my chest as I creep down the utility hallway. Time to stage a robbery, and quickly. I begin by going into the crew rooms and tossing the contents of the bunks and drawers over the floor to make the place look like it was ransacked. When I'm done, I peer out into the hallway and make sure it's clear before darting across to Sarth's quarters. I take a deep breath and wedge the crowbar into the doorframe above the lock. It takes a few tries but eventually the door snaps open. I suck in a breath and step inside.

I'm sweating profusely—partly from exertion, mostly from fear. I sweep my gaze over the room, on the off chance the dargonite is somewhere in view, before proceeding to rip the covers from Sarth's bed. I peer underneath it and search the mattress, and then move on to the drawers, tossing everything out as I go. Doubt nags at me. What if I'm wrong and all this is for nothing? What if I can't find the dargonite and have nothing to pay Roma with?

I move on to the closet and begin rummaging beneath the haphazard heap of clothes and boots on the closet floor. To my relief, I find what I'm looking for—several medium-sized buckets filled with dargonite are stashed beneath a pile of dirty blankets at the back. I hesitate, my chest rising and falling as I try to calm my breathing. If I take it all, she'll know I had something to do with the break-in.

I stare at the buckets, my mind scrambling to make the right decision. A thief from the fueling port would be looking for jewelry or other valuables, not a bucket of rocks. I need to make this convincing. I reach for a fistful of pebble-sized dargonite and fill my pocket. Sarth will never notice that much is missing.

I replace the blankets and turn my attention back to the rest of the room. I see a gun safe in the corner, but I won't be able to break into that without the code. My eyes settle on Sarth's desk. First place a thief would look. I scatter the contents and knock over the chair, then reach for the drawer below the desk. *Locked.* Without hesitation, I raise the crowbar and smash it open. I rummage through the items and pull out some gold coins and an old compass that looks like it might be valuable. I must make sure there's enough missing to convince Sarth it was a robbery. I tuck the crowbar back beneath my cloak and slip quietly out of the room. Every nerve in my body is taut as I make my way back down to the loading dock. Everything depends on getting out of here without being seen by Nipper or Meldus. I slip the crowbar into the bed of the LunaTrekker in passing. I'll figure out how to return it to the engine room later. I tread quietly down the loading ramp, nod discreetly at Velkan leaning against the fuel pump, and then put my head down and make a beeline for the security gate. Once safely through, I let out a long breath and walk briskly down the thoroughfare, ignoring the shouts of the vendors vying for my attention.

Roma is already packing up her wares by the time I reach her table.

"You're late," she says, without lifting her head.

"Do you have the information?" I ask.

She flicks me a steely glance. "Money up front."

"Information first, *if* you want to double your earnings."

She sticks her palm out in front of me. "Pay up now or *leave*!"

I bite down on my lip. I have no choice but to trust her. I rummage around in my pocket for the smallest nugget of dargonite I can find. "This should be more than enough," I say, dropping it into her palm.

She peers down at it for a second, quickly closes her fist over it, and then glances furtively behind her. When she turns back to me, her face is bloodless, her eyes bulging.

"You stupid little fool!" she hisses.

Chapter 11

"What's your problem?" I ask, narrowing my eyes at Roma. "You want to get paid, don't you?"

"I know what that is," Roma mutters under her breath.

"So then you're aware of how valuable it is," I retort.

"Keep your voice down," Roma says curtly. "Do you want to get us both arrested?"

I blink in confusion. "What are you talking about? This is a market, isn't it? We're free to buy and sell."

A look of comprehension flits across Roma's face. She beckons me closer, her sharp eyes boring into me. "You don't know, do you?"

"Know what?"

"All dargonite mines in the four quadrants have been seized under Syndicate Domain Law. It's illegal to trade in dargonite, even be in possession of it, under pain of death."

I take a step backward, reeling from the impact of her words. "When did this happen?"

"Last week. The ruling was broadcast to every planet in the Syndicate. Any newly discovered dargonite mines must be declared to the Syndicate within forty-eight hours."

I run shaking hands over my shamskin. Images of Cweltans huddled together in the cold, damp underground caves flash through my mind. If I can't unload the dargonite, I can't save Cwelt from the Maulers.

Something in my face triggers a vein of empathy in Roma. "I have an address for you," she says. "Tango, thirty-nine, alpha, victor, zero. It's an upscale Pawn Emporium on Aristozonex."

"Do they sell the bracelets there?" I ask.

"The owner thinks he sold one, a few months back. That's all I can tell you." She casts a worried look around, then reaches over and slips the nugget of dargonite back into my pocket. "You need to go. I don't want to be anywhere near you when they find that stuff on you."

"Thank you," I say, splaying my hand in gratitude.

"You owe me," Roma says with a curt nod. "If that bracelet turns out to be worth anything, you might think of stopping back by and paying off your debt."

I give her a grateful smile. "I intend to."

I turn and hurry back down the street, blood looping madly through my veins as I repeat the address excitedly over to myself. *An upscale pawn emporium on Aristozonex.* I've already abandoned the idea of my parents being savages. If the bracelets are being sold on Aristozonex, I might have been kidnapped from a wealthy Syndicate official, or the owner of a glittering shopping emporium—at the very least a middle-class family. *Velkan too!*

Halfway back to the ship, I spot a stall selling navigational tools and equipment. My fingers tighten around Sarth's compass. I still have some time before I need to be back on board the Zebulux. I could at least get a few credits for the compass. Between that and the coins I took from Sarth's desk, Buir, Meldus and I should have enough to survive on if she throws us off the ship for any reason. *Like when she realizes we can't sell the dargonite.*

I stroll nonchalantly over to the stall and make a show of examining the items on display. The vendor is a bushy-haired, heavyset youth, but no sluggard. He's smoothly closing deals with the people browsing his wares while his eyes rove the crowd for his next customer.

"Looking for a gift or shopping for yourself?" he calls to me, sizing me up with one quick sweep.

I pull out Sarth's compass. "Actually, I was hoping to sell something."

He nods while wrapping up a sale. "Be right with you."

"What do you have?" he asks when he wanders over a moment later.

I reach into my pocket and pull out the compass. "Antique. Worth a lot, I imagine." I smile brightly at him.

He scans me slowly up and down and purses his fat lips. "Don't do much in the way of antiques, but I'll have a look."

He spends less time examining the compass than he did checking me out, so when he tells me it's a decent piece, I'm pretty sure he's embellishing the truth. "How much?" I ask.

"I could go three hundred credits on it."

"Three-fifty!"

"You drive a hard bargain!" He forks his thick fingers through his hair and sighs. "All right, you got a deal," he says, looking down at his CipherSync.

That's when I realize I have no way of accepting payment. I rack my brains for a solution. I could possibly trade the compass for something useful, but I really want the credits.

"How long are you here for?" the youth asks, his gaze fixed on his CipherSync as he taps methodically on it.

"I'm … leaving in a few minutes, actually."

"Shame. I could have shown you around this evening. It's not half bad here once you move away from the fueling port." He looks up expectantly. "Okay, credits are set to transfer."

I give an embarrassed shrug. "I … don't have a CipherSync." A puzzled look flits across his brow.

I need to think fast. I spread my palms in a gesture of apology. "I left home in a hurry—unexpectedly. Long story."

He raises a brow. "Ah, I get it." He leans over the table, his belly resting on a pile of old navigational charts, and grins at me like we've just become best friends. "I did the same thing myself. Blazed a trail off my planet when I was fourteen. Built this stall up from nothing and been loving every minute of it since."

I widen my eyes admiringly. "That's impressive! I hope to do that too." *At least the part about blazing a trail.* And I'm envisioning spending my days on a ship, not behind a stall.

"Tell you what," he says, with a wink. "I'll throw in a used CipherSync if you let me buy you dinner next time you're in port."

I make an attempt at a flattered gasp. "You'd do that?"

"Sure! It's a dated model, but functional. Fully refurbished."

"Thank you." I smile gratefully at him. "Dinner it is!"

He hesitates for a moment, blinks, and then swings into action with the air of someone who's accustomed to more success closing deals than landing dates.

After he loads the credits, I record the address Roma gave me and stuff the CipherSync inside my shamskin. I'll have to keep it hidden. It's best if Sarth doesn't know I have some credits to my name; she might decide she owns those too.

By the time I get back to the Zebulux, Sarth has already returned.

"Cutting it close," she says, eying me with a disgruntled air that seems to suggest she was hoping I wouldn't make it. "You're the last one."

I shrug in response. "There were a lot of stalls."

She motions to Velkan to close the cargo door. When it's sealed shut, she pulls out three CipherSyncs, lays them out on a nearby crate, and turns to me. "I got these for you, Buir, and Meldus on the dark market. You'll need them to enter Aristozonex." She raises a brow. "And to purchase a ship, of course, once we unload that dargonite."

My stomach muscles tighten. She still doesn't know about the recent ruling. I need to tell her before we arrive at Aristozonex, or we'll all be arrested.

"We're going to have to change our plans," I say.

Sarth eyes me suspiciously. "What are you talking about?"

"I heard something when I was browsing at the market stalls. The Syndicate has laid claim to all dargonite mines in the four quadrants under its jurisdiction."

"I know." Sarth rubs her hands together briskly and grins, her teeth a sickly shade of scum in the dimly lit cargo bay. "It's good news for us."

I wrinkle my brow. "How is it good news? It's illegal to trade in dargonite now, even to be in possession of it."

"And that," Sarth says, staring at me with a strange light in her eyes, "is exactly why its value just tripled."

"But they'll arrest—"

Sarth waves a dismissive hand at me. "We're not going to sell it to the Syndicate."

My mind races. "Who are you planning to sell it to?"

Sarth's eyes gleam. "There are always buyers on the dark market. We'll find a broker on Aristozonex and cut him in."

My eyes wander to the Lunatrekker in the shadows. "We, or you?" I say, fixing an accusatory gaze on her.

A muscle in her cheek twitches. "Don't miss a beat, do you?" she says. "I stashed the dargonite in my room. Can't take the risk of someone from one of the other ships wandering into the cargo bay while we're docked, can we?"

I grimace but say nothing. Sarth's paranoia about strangers coming on board will make the break-in seem even more authentic, but her rage will know no limits when she discovers what's happened.

"Doors are sealed," Velkan calls to Sarth.

She nods and heads for the stairs to the upper deck. My heart surges up my throat. "How long until we reach Aristozonex?" I blurt out, knowing I'm only delaying the inevitable.

She scratches the back of her bald head. "We have a detour to take first."

I stare at her. "What are you talking about?"

She thumbs at the cryogenic vats beneath the cargo netting. "We need to unload our contraband."

"Where?" I demand.

A grin seeps across Sarth's face. "There's only one buyer for cryogenic cargo." Her chilling eyes run up and down the length of me like the edge of a blade. "Body poachers."

Chapter 12

The clang of Sarth's boots ascending the metal stairs echoes in my head like a siren warning. Something about the look she gave me when she mentioned the body poachers was deeply unsettling. I know we can't trust her, but we can't divert her course. *Her ship, her rules*, as she's fond of reminding us. And anyway, she's right about the vats—we need to get rid of them before we go anywhere near Aristozonex.

"Brace yourself," Velkan says, walking up to me. "She's going to be hotter than the flaming core of a planet once she sees her quarters."

"I only took a few coins and an old compass. And several nuggets of dargonite, not enough to be noticed. I hid it in my shamskin."

"She'll go ballistic just knowing someone was in there."

I nod glumly. "So how do we get the vats to these body poachers she talked about."

"There's a penal colony on a planet called Diretus two days from here," Velkan says. "They produce weaponry for the Syndicate. The penal commissioner uses some of the prisoners to help run a dark market on the uninhabited side of the planet, unbeknownst to the Syndicate."

"Sounds risky. What if one of the prisoners says something?"

Velkan hesitates for a moment. "It's a maximum sanction colony. They've had their tongues cut out."

My eyes widen in horror.

"The commissioner on Diretus has a reputation for being the most brutal in the entire Syndicate."

A shiver run down my spine. "How do we know he won't kill us?" I ask.

A look of sadness comes over Velkan's face. He reaches out and gently traces the back of his finger down my cheek. His touch chases the breath from my lungs. "Nothing's going to happen to you. We have connections there. The commissioner is Ghil's brother, Crankilius—that's his real name, but everyone calls him Crank. Ghil worked for him years ago."

"I had a sneaking suspicion Ghil didn't learn to handle knives like that in a kitchen," I say. "So why's he working in a galley?"

Velkan raises his brows. "He knifed a visiting Syndicate official who criticized the way he was running things. He's had to keep a low profile ever since. Officially, he's a fugitive on the Syndicate's most wanted list. That's why he wears a beanie pulled down over his head whenever he leaves the ship at a fueling port."

"Sounds like he's as much a prisoner of the Zebulux as you are."

Velkan smiles. "Doesn't feel so bad since you came on board."

My cheeks grow warm and I drop my gaze.

A roar startles us. Our eyes lock in instant recognition. Sarth has discovered the break-in. Right on cue her voice booms over the intercom. "All hands to the galley, *now!*"

My stomach knots as I follow Velkan up the stairway. Beneath my shamskin, the dargonite grows heavy in my pocket. Maybe keeping it on my person wasn't such a good idea after all.

Nipper races up the stairs behind me, trailed by Meldus.

"What's going on?" Nipper yells.

"No idea!" I call back, painting on a bewildered expression.

We pile into the galley under Sarth's menacing glare and take a seat at the table beside Ghil and Buir. Buir splays her hand nervously and I give her a reassuring grin.

Sarth fingers the laser gun holstered at her waist. "Someone broke into my quarters while I was on shore," she begins, her voice barely repressing her rage. "The crew's bunks have been ransacked too. Anyone see anything, know anything?"

With great deliberation, she scans our faces. Is it my imagination or does she hesitate a little longer on mine? Heat rises up the back of my neck. When her gaze passes to Velkan, I breathe out a silent sigh of relief.

"The port security was lax again." Velkan frowns. "Half the time they weren't checking reentry stamps. Anyone could have come through."

Sarth slams her fist hard on the table. "Why do I pay a security fee to dock at these deadbeat stations when they can't even keep them secure?"

She paces and smooths a hand over her head before turning back to Velkan. "You were by the fuel pump the entire time. Did you see any strangers loitering around the ship?"

He shakes his head.

Sarth frowns. "Ghil, Buir, and Trattora all returned after me." She lifts her gaze and glances at Nipper. "That leaves you and Meldus. You two never left the ship, right?"

Nipper shifts uneasily in his seat. "Never left the engine room. Too busy doing all the maintenance checks."

Sarth takes a step toward him. "Are you sure about that?" she growls. "I'll bet the only thing you lubricated was your insides, you worthless piece of galactic garbage." Without warning, she whacks him across the face with the back of her hand. He cowers in front of her as if waiting on more blows to rain down on him.

I'm baffled by his submissive posturing. Why doesn't he defend himself? With his strength, he could squeeze the air out of Sarth's windpipe in minutes.

Sarth swivels abruptly and fixes an ugly gaze on Meldus next. "*You* stayed on the ship too. *You're* a stranger, and you had ample opportunity while Nipper here was passed out drunk."

Meldus shakes his head fervently. "No, it wasn't that bad. He … I mean …"

Sarth turns on Nipper like a tornado, whipping out her gun and cracking him over the head with it. He groans and falls to one side clutching his head.

"You good for nothing solar slug! I knew you were drinking again on the job."

Sarth straightens up and turns back to Meldus, her features hard and calculating. "Did you notice anyone coming or going?"

He blinks, but to his credit, he doesn't glance in my direction.

My heart thumps so loudly I'm afraid the others can hear it in the deathly silence that has fallen.

"No one," he says, firmly.

Sarth moves her jaw side to side. "Then that leaves *you* as the only possible suspect."

"I don't know anything about it," Meldus protests.

"Was anything stolen?" I ask, trying to distract her.

"Yesss." Sarth draws the word out into a menacing hiss. She reaches for Meldus and drags him to his feet, then gestures to Ghil. "Why don't you go into the galley and sharpen your knife collection? Then we'll ask him if he has anything belonging to me."

I jump to my feet, but quick as lightning Sarth pulls out her gun and holds it to Meldus' head. "Sit down or I'll blow his brains out."

I raise my hands to pacify her and take a step backward. "Okay! Take it easy!"

Buir presses her knuckles to her pale face. "Meldus wouldn't steal anything. He's completely trustworthy."

Sarth cocks an eyebrow at her. "Never trust a servant. First rule of power. And I don't trust any of you either." She tilts her chin toward Velkan. "Except for the serf. No reason for him to steal—he can't go past the fuel port on any planet anyway, eh?"

Velkan gives a hesitant nod.

"Go up to the flight deck and prep for departure," she orders him. "The rest of you stay here. Anyone makes a move, Meldus dies. I'm gonna search each and every one of you before you leave this room, right after I explain to young Meldus here what will happen if he lies to Ghil." She turns on her heel and leads a sweating Meldus into the galley.

In a flash, Velkan is at my side. "Quick! Give it to me!" he whispers.

With trembling fingers, I reach into the pockets of my shamskin and pull out the antiquated CipherSync, dargonite, and coins, praying I don't drop anything. I thrust everything into Velkan's hands and watch him disappear out the door just as Sarth reappears, dragging Meldus by the collar. Ghil looms behind them, a butcher knife glinting in each fist.

My eyes lock briefly across the table with Nipper. He witnessed the entire exchange between Velkan and me. I can only hope his hatred of Sarth runs deep enough that he won't turn me in. After a moment's hesitation, he gives a subtle dip of his head. Relief surges through me. Whatever his reason, he's not about to rat me out. If it's blackmail, I'll deal with it later. First, I have to get Meldus out of the line of fire.

Sarth beckons to Buir. "You first."

Buir gets to her feet, regal as always and walks across the room. She stands head and shoulders above Sarth, stiff and unyielding as Sarth gropes around in her shamskin pockets and pats her down. After a few minutes, Sarth nods and dismisses her. "Go clean up the crew cabins."

Buir throws me a worried look as she slips out the door.

Sarth turns her attention to me. "You're up."

I get to my feet and walk over to her. "Did they take the dargonite?" I ask, looking straight at her.

She ignores me and pulls open my shamskin. I bite down on my lip as her rough hands search through my pockets. When she's done, she surveys me through narrowed slits for a moment. "That leaves your guard here as a suspect. He was the only one who stayed on board, except for that drunken lout, Nipper."

"Don't be ridiculous," I retort. "Meldus had nothing to do

with some random robbery. My father's guards are trustworthy men."

Sarth steps closer and sticks her face up to mine. "Maybe it wasn't so random. Some people are a little too curious for their own good, and there's a price to be paid for that kind of behavior."

My pulse races. I can't let Meldus pay the price for my actions.

"Get out!" Sarth says. "I'm done with you for now."

"I'm not leaving here without Meldus," I reply.

Quick as a flash she trains her gun on him. "You'll leave without him if you want to see him again."

I back away slowly. "He doesn't know anything. If you hurt him, our deal is off."

She lets out a scathing snort. "What deal?"

My blood ices over as the truth dawns on me. She has no intention of splitting the dargonite with me. Maybe she never did.

Sarth turns to Nipper and scowls. "Get back down to the engine room and finish those maintenance checks."

Nipper climbs out over the bench and throws me a knowing look as he exits the room—a look that says *I owe him.*

Sarth presses her gun to Meldus' head and raises her brows at me. "I'll count to five. One, two ..."

My stomach churns as I turn and exit the room. I've got to get Meldus out of here, and quickly. If Ghil's knife skills were honed cutting out tongues on Diretus, there's no telling what he'll do to make Meldus confess. And what can he possibly confess to other than that he knows I returned to the ship?

Chapter 13

I hurry down the hallway to the crew rooms. Buir peers out of Ghil's room, her arms piled high with bedding.

"Forget that!" I call to her. "We have to help Meldus."

Her eyes widen. "Did he do it?"

I shake my head. "It was me."

Buir gasps, her eyes pooling with fear.

"I needed the dargonite to pay for information about the bracelets," I explain. "Sarth suspects one of us was behind it. I have to get Meldus out of there before she hurts him."

"How?" Buir tosses the bedding inside the room. "Sarth has a gun. We can't go back in there unarmed."

"I have an idea. But we'll need Velkan's help." I grab her hand and together we race down the hallway to the control room. The doors slide apart with a pneumatic whoosh to reveal Velkan at the controls. He turns and scrambles to his feet when he sees us. "Are you okay?"

My heart warms at the concern in his voice. He glances at Buir, but his eyes linger on me. "Sarth didn't hurt you or anything?

"We're fine," I say. "Did you hide it?"

He nods. "It's safe for now—I stuffed it in a slit in my mattress."

"What about Nipper?" Buir asks. "He saw everything."

"Don't worry about him," Velkan says. "I'll handle him. Anyway, he's loving the fact that you pulled one over on Sarth."

"I don't know why he puts up with the way she treats him," Buir says. "Surely an engineer could get work on another ship."

Velkan grimaces. "Nipper is Sarth's nephew. She adopted him when his parents were killed in a mining accident."

My jaw drops. Sarth is a *mother!* How can she possibly share that title with my loving, gracious, and compassionate mother?

"Nipper has a problem holding down jobs because of his drinking." Velkan glances across at the door. "Where's Meldus?"

"Sarth's interrogating him now, with Ghil's help," I say. "We need to do something."

Velkan furrows his brow. "We have no weapons."

"Yes, we do." I walk over to the pilot seat, sit down and study the flickering screens around me. "We'll launch the ship." I close my fingers around the joystick. "That should get her attention."

"You can't be serious," Velkan says.

I turn to him and grin. "I am and I need your help. Guide me through what to do."

He hesitates, wrestling with the enormity of what I'm asking of him.

"Don't worry about Sarth," I add. "Tell her I told you she ordered us to launch."

Velkan remains quiet for a moment. "What if she turns on you?"

"She won't. She wants those mining rights on Cwelt too badly. That's the only reason she didn't kill me when she had her chance."

Velkan slips into the seat beside me and fastens his harness with a resigned sigh. "We're already prepped for takeoff. Hit the ignition and throttle up the engines."

"Buckle up, Buir," I call back to her.

A familiar rumbling sound accompanies the hull's vibration as the Zebulux roars to life. Red lights turn to green across the array of monitors in front of me. Adrenalin courses through me as I'm thrust backward into the bucket seat by the sheer force of the thrusters accelerating. Seconds later we're airborne.

"I knew there was something beyond Cwelt for me," I say, smiling across at Velkan.

He opens his mouth to respond just as Sarth bursts through the door.

"What are you doing?" she screams, reaching for Velkan by his hair and yanking his head back hard, her eyes cold and feral.

"It wasn't his fault," I say, unbuckling my harness. "I told him you gave the order to launch."

Sarth hesitates, her chest heaving up and down as she weighs my words, spittle glistening on her bottom lip. She glances from me to Velkan and back to me again. Wordlessly, she releases Velkan with a shove and yanks me out of the pilot's seat. "Get out of my sight," she hisses. "If it weren't for those mining rights, I'd have gotten rid of you a long time ago."

She jerks her head in Buir's direction. "You go clean up those cabins like I told you to and then get back down to the galley and help Ghil."

"Where's Meldus?" I ask.

"In the engine room where he belongs." She lets out a snort. "Piece of scum admitted he was drunk too. They were both passed out. Useless—both of them. Anyone could have come on board."

A huge wave of relief washes over me. I wasn't sure how far Sarth would really take it with the interrogation tactics, but it was a clever play on Meldus's part to say he got drunk with Nipper. It might have saved him a world of pain, if not his life.

I exit the control room and walk with Buir back down to the galley. "See you at dinnertime," I say. "Is it mash again?"

She gives a half-hearted grin. "We have fresh supplies for a few days, so Ghil's given me permission to make something out of them."

"Phew! I can already feel my appetite returning."

Buir laughs. "What are you going to do until then?"

"First, I'm going to check on Meldus, make sure they didn't lob off an earlobe or something."

Buir shivers. "I'm sure Ghil's capable of it, but he's got a heart in there somewhere."

"You mean a soft spot for you," I say, with a wink.

She throws me a look of abject horror. "Don't even go there! He must be twice my age." She arches a brow at me. "Speaking of soft spots, I'm pretty sure our sunburned serf goes weak at the knees every time you walk into the room."

"Don't be ridiculous," I say, my cheeks growing warm. "He's just watching out for us."

"He's watching one of us, that's for sure." Buir sounds amused. She splays her hand good-bye and disappears into the galley.

I mull over her words as I make my way to the stairs leading down to the cargo bay. I can't deny I'm attracted to Velkan, but I wasn't sure if the feeling was mutual, or if he was just being friendly. Buir seems convinced it's more than that. I finger the chain at my neck. It feels so comfortable being around him—almost like I've known him all my life. Maybe that's how it's supposed to be when you're in love.

In the cargo bay, I grab the crowbar out of the back of the LunaTrekker and head for the stairs. This is as good an opportunity as any to return it before any questions are asked.

I open the door to the engine room and step over the threshold. I'm hit again by the oppressive heat, the incessant throbbing of the engines, and the foul stench of fuel. Silently, I slip the crowbar back among the tools lying under the turbine.

"Meldus!" I yell. "Are you down here?" I try to focus in the dim light and peer through the labyrinth of pipes and equipment to the far end of the room. There's no sign of him or Nipper. Surely they're not hitting the bottle again.

I pick my way through the disarray and random tools scattered across the floor of the engine room. The Zebulux could use a more conscientious engineer than Nipper. It's a miracle the ship stays airborne. A moment later, I catch my foot in a snake of wires and plunge headfirst to the floor. I spread my fingers wide to save myself, tracking my nails through a greasy puddle. "Ugh!" I pick myself up and look around for something to wipe my hands on. A rustling sound stops me in my tracks. "Meldus?" I call out. "Is that you?"

I wait for several minutes but hear nothing more. I make my way to the back of the room and push open the door to the small storage room Nipper and Meldus were drinking in earlier. A lone bottle sits atop the table in the middle of the space. I grab a towel from the counter, and wipe the grease from my fingers before turning to leave.

The blood drains from my head.

Nipper's muscular body fills the doorway—blocking my exit. He watches me with a peculiar grin, arms locked across his burly chest.

"Is Meldus here?" I ask, trying to sound nonchalant, even though my pulse is racing.

"Haven't seen him." Nipper's grin widens like a cavern about to swallow me up. "Just you and me." He takes a step toward me.

I take a couple of steps backward, bumping into the counter. I grope behind me, desperately trying to find something I can use to defend myself. Desperately wishing I still had the crowbar.

"Let me out, Nipper," I say. "You're in enough trouble. If you lay a finger on me, I'll see to it you don't get your share of the dargonite."

He laughs a deep-throated growl. "Sarth won't give it up. None of us will see one lousy credit from that rock."

Before I realize what's happening, his arms shoot out and wrap around me like pliers. "But you might give it up, if you know what I mean. After all, you owe me something for keeping your little secret."

I raise my arm to lash out at him. He grabs it and twists it behind my back. The pain is excruciating and I scream, "Let me go!"

He tightens his grip and moves his face toward mine, but I

wrench sideways and his slick lips plant on my cheek instead.

I knee him in the stomach as hard as I can—but not enough to force him to release me. He tilts my head back and leans over me again. I scrunch my eyes shut, nausea surging up my throat as I twist in vain to move my face away from his.

Suddenly, there's a cracking sound, like bone hitting bone, and my arm is released. My eyes pop open. Velkan stands behind Nipper, getting ready to take another swing. Nipper's face is flushed, his eyes narrowed. He charges head down at Velkan, and the two go flying across the floor, grappling at each other's throats. The empty bottle on the table teeters for a moment and then falls to the floor and smashes. Nipper pins Velkan beneath him and delivers a few powerful blows to the head before Velkan manages to throw him off. He punches Nipper in the stomach and the head, raining down blows incessantly, but Nipper flips him and kicks him hard in the lower back. Velkan grunts, then scrambles to his feet and retreats a few feet, fists at the ready.

"Is the lowly serf jealous?" Nipper taunts. He wipes the back of his hand across his bleeding nose and charges Velkan again. They exchange blow after blow until both their faces are bloodied, but it's obvious Velkan is struggling to keep up under Nipper's meaty fists.

I frantically scan the space for something I can use as a weapon before Nipper delivers a blow that kills Velkan. My gaze falls on the broken bottle. I wait for my chance, then dart across the floor and grab it. Heart pounding, I raise my arm to smash it across the back of Nipper's head just as a single gunshot rings out.

Chapter 14

I spin to find Sarth standing in the doorway. "What did you do?" I whisper.

She ignores me and calmly holsters her gun.

Frozen with fear, I stare at the tangle of bloodied bodies on the floor. For a moment neither one moves. Blood pounds in my temples as I wrestle with the unthinkable. Then I hear a groan.

I watch with bated breath as Velkan heaves Nipper off him and rolls to one side before struggling up from the floor. His eyes meet mine and a floodgate of emotion rushes through me.

Sarth brushes by me and kneels by Nipper to check for a pulse, before abruptly getting to her feet.

"You killed him!" I blurt out.

She looks at me sharply. "Saved you the trouble, didn't I?"

"I was trying to break up a fight, not kill him. How could you do that? He was your son."

Sarth grunts. "My brother's worthless spawn. Attempting to kill another member of my crew. I had to choose who was more valuable." She scowls at Velkan. "This was your lucky day."

"I had no choice but to fight him," Velkan says. "He attacked Trattora."

Sarth waves a dismissive hand, as if she already knows, or at least suspected. "Dispose of the body in the waste port. Then clean yourself up and show Meldus what needs to be done down here. He'll have to take over now."

She turns and beckons to me. "You can fill in for Velkan in the control room."

"Where is Meldus?" I ask, following her through the door. "I thought you sent him to the engine room."

"After he installs a new lock on my door," Sarth grumbles. "It's the least he can do for getting drunk and letting someone smash the place up."

It sounds like a reasonable explanation for why Meldus hasn't returned yet, but after what I just witnessed, I'll feel better when I see him with my own eyes.

"Don't you feel any remorse for what you did?" I ask.

Sarth pierces me with an accusatory gaze. "Should I? He was about to kill Velkan, and then he'd have had his way with you." She sniffs and runs the back of her hand across her nose. "Doesn't leave room for remorse in my book."

I follow her up the stairwell on shaking legs, wracked by a sense of guilt. Inadvertently, I had a hand in Nipper's death. Maybe it would have come to this anyway, but my deception hastened his demise no matter how I look at it. If I hadn't broken into Sarth's room, Meldus wouldn't have been forced to fix the lock, I wouldn't have ended up alone in the engine room with Nipper, and Velkan wouldn't have fought him.

I slide into the seat next to Sarth in the control room and

force myself to focus on her instructions as she reactivates manual navigation. Her tone is clipped and businesslike as she demonstrates how to design a reference trajectory and directs me how to use the plasma detection system for avoiding space debris. I struggle to collect my thoughts, disturbed by Sarth's callousness and lack of empathy, as I study the sensor displays.

When Ghil's voice comes over the intercom announcing dinner, it's a welcome respite.

Sarth stretches her arms out behind her. "Bring me back a plate, and make it snappy this time. I'm going to send a downlink to Diretus. We'll be there by tomorrow night at this cruising speed."

I tense at the mention of Diretus. "The penal colony, right?"

Sarth hikes a brow at me. "You know it?"

"Velkan said that's where you're planning to hand off the vats to the body poachers."

Sarth gives a curt nod. "It's a dark market for all sorts of goods."

"Velkan told me the commissioner was Ghil's brother—he sounds gruesome."

Sarth grunts. "Velkan talks too much. If he's not careful, Crank will make sure he never talks again."

A shiver runs across my shoulders. Whoever this Crank is, his name paints a disturbing picture in my mind. The sooner we unload the vats and set a course for Aristozonex, the better.

"How long will it take to remove the vats?" I ask.

Sarth scratches her pitted cheek. "Not long. Crank knows what he's doing. We'll overnight on Diretus and head off early the next morning."

I frown. "Why are we staying the night?"

"It would be impolite not to. Crank is touchy about things like that." Sarth throws me a sharp look. "Just remember, we're only there to deliver the vats. We keep the dargonite under wraps. If Crank gets wind of it, he'll want in on it. And what he wants, he gets." She peers at the view screen in front of her. "I'll send that downlink now and give Crank an ETA. Go get me some food."

I'm relieved to find Meldus seated at a table in the dining room tucking into a plate of food. "Thank you for not saying anything," I whisper to him.

He looks straight at me. "It's my job to protect you no matter the cost."

I give a grateful nod and head over to the galley to pick up Sarth's dinner. Meldus may be only sixteen, but he's as loyal as any of my father's guards. I'm thankful he's with me. On our return, I'll be sure and commend him to my father for promotion.

When I set a laden plate in front of Sarth a few minutes later, she stares at it for the longest time before reaching for her fork. "Never seen anything this good come out of Ghil's galley before. Let's see if it tastes as good as it looks."

She chomps noisily and steadily on the roasted vegetables and fried rabbit until her plate is empty. Then she leans back and belches loudly. "Bring me another one," she says, gesturing at the plate.

I smile to myself as I make my way back down to the galley. Despite her reluctance to embark on this adventure, Buir is quickly becoming the most popular addition to the crew.

We're almost at Diretus the following evening when Sarth spots a suspicious shape on the scanner. "Looks like a Syndicate patrol ship on our tail," she says through gritted teeth. "Headed for Diretus."

"Do you want to divert?" Velkan asks from the co-pilot seat.

"Stay the course, but go to blackout and prepare for a possible sweep and intercept."

"What does that mean?" I ask, leaning forward in my seat.

"The patrol could be heading to Diretus on Syndicate business, or they may be tracking us," Velkan says. "Some of the newer Syndicate ships have upgraded scanners that can pick up illegal cryogenic transports. If they detect our cargo, they'll try to intercept us. We'll dim all the lights on the Zebulux and hope they haven't picked us up on their radar yet."

"And if they have?" I ask.

Sarth cracks her knuckles. "We'll stall them and radio to Crank for backup."

"Doesn't he work for the Syndicate?" I say.

"He works for anyone who pays him," Sarth says. "He has an unregistered warship at his disposal as well as his official Syndicate frigate."

Suddenly, a low beeping fills the flight deck and a light on the dashboard flickers red. "They've locked in on us!" Sarth growls.

I stare at the screen in horror as the patrol ship accelerates toward us.

"Tighten your harness," Velkan calls over his shoulder to me. "We may have to do some evasive maneuvers."

"Get the shields up," Sarth orders. "It'll give us some initial protection if they fire."

A transmission from the approaching patrol ship crackles through the console. "Zebulux, you are ordered to reduce speed and prepare to be boarded."

I dig my fingers into the armrests of my seat. If I know Sarth, she won't go down without a fight, but the Zebulux is ill-equipped to take on a Syndicate ship. This could be the end for us.

Sarth grips the controller tightly. "Game on!" she mutters. She flicks the transmitter switch and responds. "Zebulux reports an ailing thruster, request permission to make haste to the nearest port on Diretus. Will prepare to be boarded there."

There's a few minutes of silence and then another crackling sound. "Permission granted. We will follow you in."

Sarth flicks off the communications system and narrows her eyes. "They don't have an upgraded scanner on board. They would never let us continue on to Diretus if they knew what we were transporting."

She fiddles with the auxiliary radio. "I'll radio Crank for backup."

"Won't the Syndicate pick up the signal?" I ask.

"Crank has a secure dark market channel," Velkan explains.

"Zebulux to Diretus, do you read me?" Sarth says.

A thick vibrato voice comes over the radio. "Go ahead."

"Coming in hot. Syndicate patrol on tail to intercept at port."

"Copy that." The radio clicks off.

Sarth grips the controller. "Prepare for port flyby and rapid course correction."

"On it," Velkan replies.

"What's the plan?" I ask.

Sarth turns to me and grins. "We'll lead the patrol into the mouth of the dragon and then swing around to the other side of Diretus to dock."

I furrow my brow. "That doesn't explain anything."

"Watch and learn, and quit yakking," Sarth snaps back.

I sink back in my chair, keeping my eyes glued to the view screen. "Thrusters to full power," Sarth says to Velkan. "I want us out of harm's way when Crank comes rolling in."

Minutes later, I spot the ominous shape of an approaching warship, a sleek row of missile launchers mounted on either side of the charcoal hull. I recognize it immediately as a Dreadnought XII, a ship built outside the jurisdiction of the Syndicate, and not subject to weaponry code which limits the size and number of weapons according to the class of ship. Alarm spikes through me. I hope Sarth is right—that Crank is coming to aid us and not destroy us.

Sarth swings the Zebulux around in a tight left turn, opening up a full view of the Syndicate patrol ship on our tail to the warship. The Dreadnought brings its laser guns to bear on the patrol and fires a volley of blasts that shakes the hull of the Zebulux. Another sizzling round follows. My eyes grow wide as I watch the impact on the screen. The patrol ship peels off to the left like crippled prey, desperately trying to evade a third round of fire. Seconds later, a massive explosion obliterates the ailing vessel. Chunks of its pulverized hull spiral out in all directions. I gasp at the billowing black smoke and field of debris that fills the screen where the patrol ship had been.

"Got the scum!" Sarth yells, shaking her fist.

Velkan wipes the back of his hand across his brow.

"Bring her in to dock!" Sarth says. "We're celebrating tonight!" She thumps Velkan in the arm. "Even you get to party, far from prying Syndicate eyes."

Not surprisingly, the dark market docking station where Crank conducts his business is a heavily guarded fortress. Buir, Meldus and I follow the oremongers' lead and disembark under the scrutiny of a small army of guards dressed in black fatigues. They usher Sarth and Velkan through a scanner, presumably checking for weapons. The scanner beeps and flashes red when Ghil passes through. The guard monitoring the scanner signals to him to remove his knives, but instead, he whips them out in a threatening display of force.

"I wouldn't mess with Crank's brother if I were you," Ghil growls.

The guard pales and looks around uncertainly at his colleagues.

"Ghil? Is that really you?" one of the other guards asks, stepping toward him.

Ghil sheathes both knives in one swift move and yanks off his beanie. "The one and only."

"He's new on the job," the second guard says apologetically. "Welcome back. Been a while."

Ghil gives him a curt nod and strides past him to join Sarth and Velkan.

The rest of us pass through the scanner without incident. The guard escorts us out of the docking station and over an iron drawbridge into the side of a craggy hill.

Roars and jeers mixed with the sound of raucous laughter

drift down a dark, damp tunnel carved into the rock and lit with burning torches. A lizard slithers into a crack a few feet in front of me. I wrinkle my nose at the oppressive odor of stagnant water that fills my nostrils as we go deeper into the mountain.

At the end of the tunnel, the guard leads us inside a cavernous room with a dirt floor, filled with an ugly array of scarred and tattooed faces, glistening with sweat in the flickering light. Most are turned toward a metal cage in the center of the room where two bloodied men with unidentifiable animal paws over their hands are locked in what can only be described as a dance of death.

Buir gasps and turns her face away.

Silently, Meldus steps to my side, his eyes scanning the room for possible threats.

"Cage fight," Sarth offers when I throw her a baffled look. She clicks her fingers at the guard and he quickly escorts us out of the fray and up a stairway that leads to a dark, paneled room outfitted with a rough-hewn wooden table and a miscellaneous assortment of seating. The room must be soundproofed, because as soon as the door closes behind us, the cacophony of sound from below cuts out.

"Now what?" I ask, looking around at the others.

"Now we wait on the commissioner," Ghil says.

Buir's perfectly arched silver brows raise a fraction of an inch, but she sets her face in a resolute expression. I'm proud of her for keeping it together in this frightening situation. This isn't the kind of adventure I had in mind for either of us, but we need to unload those wretched vats before we head for Aristozonex.

We don't wait for long. The heavy thump of multiple pairs

of steel-toed boots alerts us to Crank's arrival. Sarth gets to her feet and, after exchanging dubious glances, the rest of us do the same. A moment later, a tall, imposing figure in black enters the room flanked by two flint-faced guards.

I stare, fascinated and repulsed all at once, at the Syndicate's most feared commissioner. The whites of his eyes glisten as he surveys us, his pupils dark and dead. Purple veins pulse in his temple just below the horns attached to his forehead. A disconcerting, jagged scar runs like a trickle of blood from his top lip down the side of his mouth, under his chin, and halfway down his neck. His lips split in a grin of sorts when he spots Ghil. I cringe at his teeth—metal and meticulously shaped into points. "Brother!" Crank says, throwing his arms wide. Ghil embraces him and slaps him on the back.

"Please!" Crank gestures to the chairs and we hurriedly seat ourselves around the table. He fastens a steely gaze on Sarth. "You have a shipment."

She leans toward him in conspiratorial fashion. "Double the usual."

Crank grunts in satisfaction. "Glad to hear it was worth deploying the warship." He rubs calloused fingers over his stubble. His eyes pass briefly over Buir, then lock on me for a long moment before he turns and motions to one of his men. "Take them downstairs and feed them while I hash out terms with Sarth. Wait for us in the dining room."

A shiver crosses my shoulders as I get to my feet. If I'm not mistaken, it's not just cryogenic cargo he's interested in. Maybe we should have stayed on the ship.

Chapter 15

We follow the guard back downstairs and into the cavernous hall. The cage fight is over, and judging by the amount of blood on the dirt floor, it ended in death for one, if not both, of the opponents. The jostling crowd egging them on earlier has dispersed, but a few stragglers are gathered around a trestle table jeering and hollering at an arm wrestling match that is underway. Ghil, Meldus, and Velkan wander over. A man dressed in a sleeveless black shirt stands to one side, burly arms folded across his chest, gripping a leash in one fist. A hairy, wolf-like creature with feral eyes paws impatiently at the ground, growing more agitated as the hollering grows louder.

"I don't like the look of that thing," Buir whispers to me without taking her eyes off the wolf-like creature. "What if it gets off its leash?"

I throw a closer glance at its owner. He's wearing studded, leather shields on both wrists, confirmation to me that the creature is far from tame. If the look in its eyes is anything to go by, it could devour anyone unlucky enough to be in its path if it breaks free. Time for us to move on.

"We're hungry," I say to the guard. "Can we eat now?"

"Dining hall's this way," he says. "Call your friends."

I round the others up, and we follow the guard to the other side of the room and out into a dimly lit corridor, narrower and even darker than the main tunnel we came in by. We must be going deeper into the mountain.

We haven't gone more than twenty feet when an eerie howl fills our ears.

"What on Cwelt is that?" Buir gasps, digging her fingernails into my arm.

The guard smirks. "Want to see Crank's pets?"

Buir frowns. "That howl didn't sound too friendly. Are they safe?"

"They're caged up," the guard replies.

"Just don't stick your fingers in the cage," Ghil interjects. "Don't say I didn't warn you."

"Let's have a look," I say, curiosity getting the better of me.

Buir throws me an anguished glance.

Meldus frowns disapprovingly, but falls in behind me, along with Velkan.

The guard turns down a side corridor and we walk for several hundred feet before coming to a steel doorway. He keys something into the control panel on the wall and the riveted doors rumble apart. We step through to a high-ceilinged, windowless room with cages running the length of the walls. A foul stench of something unidentifiable fills my nostrils. I wrinkle up my nose, feeling like I could gag at any minute.

"The monkeys are the worst offenders," the guard says, when he sees the look on my face. He gestures at the nearest steel cage, at least twenty feet high and twice that across. Inside, five or six gray and white mottled monkeys with pointed ears fly across the cage at alarming speeds, screeching relentlessly.

Ghil sniffs. "Face eaters. They'll gnaw the nose and lips right off you if you get too close to the cage. In the wild, they fly right at their victim's faces, shred them in seconds."

A shiver runs across my shoulders. "I didn't really believe these creatures existed until now." I glance at Buir. Her eyes are wide as moons and she clutches nervously at her throat.

We observe the monkeys from a safe distance for several minutes before moving on to another cage twice the length of the first one. A canopy of trees stretches all the way to the ceiling, and at first, I can't spot anything other than vegetation inside the cage. "Is there anything in there?" I ask.

Velkan points to the far end of the cage. "Look up to the right."

I peer upward and catch a glimpse of a large mud-colored bird with a scrawny neck adjusting its wings at the top of one of the trees.

"Predator gulls," the guard offers when I pin him with a questioning look.

"They're not as picky as the monkeys— they'll eat almost any part of you, although they do seem to enjoy picking out the organs first."

Buir makes a soft bleating sound into the sleeve of her shamskin.

"Crank doesn't like his pets soft and cuddly." Ghil says in an apologetic tone.

"These are some nasty specimens," Meldus says. "Doesn't he keep anything less menacing?"

The guard gives a twisted smile. "Tank full of sand snipers."

"I've had my fill of those," I say.

"Why does Crank have a private zoo anyway?" Velkan asks. "Keeping all these animals fed must be a nightmare."

The smile vanishes from the guard's face. He throws a furtive glance at Ghil as though seeking permission before saying too much.

"It's not strictly a zoo," Ghil says, after a long moment. "Crank keeps it stocked for other reasons."

"What kind of reasons?" Meldus asks.

Ghil shrugs. "His enemies, anyone who crosses him in a deal."

My jaw drops. "You mean he feeds people to these creatures?"

The guard shuffles his feet, looking distinctly uncomfortable. "I shouldn't have brought you in here. Time I got you down to the dining hall."

We fall silent, mulling over what Ghil said as the guard leads us back down the tunnel to a low-ceilinged room with several rows of long wooden tables. We take a seat at the only occupied one and greet the group of men eating out of a shared pot. They eye us warily, chewing methodically all the while.

"How's the food?" I ask, with a disarming smile.

Wordlessly, one of the men pushes the pot down the table toward me. He gestures with his fingers that I should eat something. Buir throws me an imploring look as if to warn me away from the germ fest most certainly happening inside the pot, but I grin back at her and stick my fingers in it. I pull out an unidentifiable hunk of meat and pop it into my mouth. All eyes are riveted on me as I chew. The meat has a strange taste and strong odor, but the texture's not unpleasant. I swallow it and tilt my head to one side contemplatively. "Not bad."

The men at the table exchange approving looks. One of them pulls his chair closer. "I'm Furax." His eyes drift almost immediately to my hair. "Are you traders?"

I glance at Ghil and he gives a subtle nod.

"Uh, yes," I say. "Oremongers."

"I'm Crank's brother," Ghil explains. "I'm contracted on their ship."

Furax nods his head thoughtfully.

"What do you trade in?" I ask.

He runs the tip of his finger down the side of his nose. "Parts, mostly."

I raise my brows. "Really? Our ship could use a new thruster."

Furax's eyes darken a fraction.

An uneasy silence hangs between us. Something I said rubbed him the wrong way.

"Not those kinds of parts, Trattora," Ghil says in a low tone. "They're body poachers. Their cargo gets shipped along with the cryogenic heads to the cryosurgeons at an undisclosed location."

I stare at Furax, aghast, scarcely able to fathom that I'm looking into the eyes of a man who hunts human beings, knowing the bodies he sells will be reattached to another person's head.

I push the bowl back toward the body poacher. "Actually, I'm not that hungry." I stand and turn to the guard. "Can you show us around some more until Sarth and Crank are done?"

He eyes the pot and scowls. "Kitchen's closed after this. And Crank said you were to wait here for him."

"Go ahead and eat." Ghil nods to him. "I'll take it from here."

The guard wastes no time pulling out a chair, and Furax passes the pot down to him.

"You can stay here and eat too," I say to Meldus, who's eying the bowl with the air of a starving man.

He throws me a grateful look and pulls up a chair.

Velkan, Buir, and I follow Ghil out of the dining hall, our tone markedly subdued. The horrific reality of everything that takes place on Diretus is almost too much to comprehend. How can Furax even keep his food down when he thinks about what he does for a living?

"I'll show you around the rest of the place," Ghil says. "And where you can bunk down for the night."

We make our way farther along the tunnel until it opens into another large room with a raised stage at the front. To the side of the stage is a row of posts, each with an iron ring driven into it. Some posts have a piece of paper or torn swatch of material attached to them.

"What is this room used for?" Buir asks.

"This is where the live auctions take place," Ghil explains.

"*Live* auctions?" I wrinkle my brow, dreading asking the inevitable question. "Are you talking animals or people?"

"Serfs mostly, or prisoners who are of interest to the body poachers. It's getting tougher all the time to find bodies for their business, between the Maulers cutting off trade routes and the increased Syndicate patrols to clamp down on the cryogenic trade."

My heart races. I cast a quick glance at Velkan who has wandered over to the posts to examine the items attached to them. However bad his life as a serf is, at least the body poachers didn't get ahold of him.

"Looks like there's going to be an auction tonight," Ghil says. "Come on, I'll show you how it works."

He leads us to the front of the room and walks up to the first post. "These are tagged to identify the serf or prisoner up for bid." He jabs a finger at the description nailed to the top of the post we're standing in front of. "This one already has three bids, pretty popular." He looks around and points to a wooden board to the right of the stage. "That board up there is for specimens who will bring in the high bids—exceptionally strong prisoners and the like."

Buir shivers. "I can't believe humans are auctioned off in here."

Ghil raises a brow at her. "We'll see it in action in a bit."

"I don't want to see it," she retorts.

"Fair enough." Ghil smooths a hand over his head. "I'll show you the bunk room so you can find your way there later when you're ready to turn in."

The bunk room turns out to be nothing more than wooden cots, stacked two high in a long dormitory of sorts. Ghil gestures to the back of the room. "Empty bunks are down at that end for visiting traders. First come, first served."

"Why can't we just sleep on the Zebulux?" Buir looks around with distaste.

"I wouldn't snub Crank's hospitality if I were you. He places a lot of weight on his reputation as a host," Velkan says, quietly. "There's a reason they call him Crank."

Buir's eyes widen. "I guess I could suffer through one night in here."

"I hear some ruckus." Ghil gestures to the hallway. "Might be the auction getting underway. I'm going to check it out if anyone wants to come with me. We could use a new engineer."

Buir gives me an imploring look.

"We should go with him," I say. "It's not a good idea to stay here by ourselves."

She peers around the shadowy dormitory, pulls her shamskin tighter, and follows us out of the room.

The auction room is filling up rapidly by the time we get back. We jostle our way to the front of the crowd and watch as several serfs and prisoners are marched in, hands bound in front of them, and secured to the posts with a noose that passes around their necks and through the iron ring. Interested bidders circle like predators. One of them wrenches a serf's head back and inspects his teeth before letting go with a snort of disgust. "Piece of solar trash from a famine planet," he mutters to his companion. "Don't know why they bother picking them up."

"Look for anyone with mechanical experience," Ghil says to us. "I wasn't kidding about needing a new engineer."

I frown as I push my way forward. I don't like the idea of purchasing a serf, but at least we'd be saving them from a worse fate.

We split up when we reach the prisoners and mingle with the bidders wandering from post to post. Most of the serfs and prisoners keep their eyes downcast, but one young woman glances at me through matted hair when I go by. Her eyes pierce me with a plea so strong it makes me shiver. The description nailed to her post reads: *Tanner*. I look down at her bound hands. Her nails are thick and long and split like combs from many moons of tanning hides. She probably doesn't know the first thing about engines, but maybe I can talk Ghil into bidding on her anyway. The sadness in her eyes has burned a hole in my soul. I squeeze her shoulder gently in passing, reluctant to make any promises I can't keep, and then turn and push my way through the crowd, searching left and right for Ghil. There are more people here now than ever, and it's increasingly hard to make any progress through the sea of sweaty bodies. Eventually, I spot Velkan and force my way past a group of loud-mouthed traders to reach him. "Have you seen Ghil anywhere?" I gasp.

"He was by the stage a few minutes ago." Velkan grabs my hand. "Come on, we should stick together."

The warmth of his hand against mine sends a shiver through me, and despite the revulsion I feel at the impending auction, I'm comforted by his touch.

We force our way through the throng of traders until we make it all the way to the front of the room. Ghil stands off to the right, frowning at the wooden board.

"Ghil," I blurt out. "We need to bid on a girl. She's scared—"

"We've got bigger problems," he interrupts. Frowning, he pulls me around to the back of the board.

My skin prickles all over when I see what's nailed to the wood.

Chapter 16

My stomach churns like the eye of a storm. I stare at the lock of my hair, numb to the tips of my toes. I glance at Ghil's grave expression and confirm what I already know in my heart. *Sarth betrayed me.*

Velkan squeezes my hand until I think he's going to crush it. "I'm going to kill her for this."

"Never thought she would sink this low," Ghil growls.

"Maybe it's her way of avenging Nipper's death." My voice sounds strangely calm even though I'm unravelling inside.

"We need to go," Velkan says in an urgent tone. "Now!"

Ghil nods at me. "Put your hood up and follow me."

"What about Buir?" I ask.

"I'll go back and look for her," Ghil says. "Slip out the side door over there, and wait for me." He points to the other end of the auction room before plunging into the crowd.

Velkan and I push and shove our way through to the far side of the stage and make our way out the side door into a dimly lit corridor. I slump down in a dark alcove and draw my knees up to my chest. Velkan sinks down beside me. "I'm so sorry, Trattora."

"What for? It's not your fault."

"If I hadn't got into it with Nipper, this might never have happened."

I lift my head and stare at him. "If you hadn't got into it with Nipper, I might be dead by now." I reach out and brush my hand gently over his bruised jawbone. "Thank you for what you did."

He takes my hand in his and places his other hand on the small of my back, pulling me closer. Before I have time to process what's happening, his lips brush mine, and then he's kissing me gently. The horror of everything I've seen in Diretus, and the terror I felt at Sarth's betrayal, melts from my mind until all that's left is this moment between Velkan and me.

"Got her!" Ghil announces.

Velkan and I pull apart, startled out of an embrace that I wasn't ready to end. I scramble to my feet and step out of the alcove.

"We need to make a plan to get out of here," Ghil says, striding up to us.

"I already have one," I say. "We're taking the Zebulux and leaving Sarth behind."

Velkan frowns. "Crank will send the Dreadnought after us. We won't make it out of the atmosphere."

"Then we'll have to sabotage the warship before we leave," I say.

Ghil runs a hand along the sheath of his knife. "I can handle that if I can find a way on board."

"You're Crank's brother," I say. "How hard can it be?"

"No one boards the warship without clearance from Crank." Ghil rumples his brow and studies me for a minute. "But we might be able to pull it off if you're willing to play along with me."

He turns to Velkan and Buir. "Fetch Meldus and wait for us at the docking station."

Ten minutes later, Ghil and I stagger like two drunks up to the guard stationed at the boarding ramp to the warship. Ghil takes a swig out of the bottle in his hand and waves it in front of the sentry's face. "You luk like you could use a drink."

"Evening, Ghil," the guard says. He reaches for the bottle. "Don't mind if I do." He glugs back a few mouthfuls and then hands the bottle back to Ghil before turning his attention to me. I peer up at him from beneath my lashes and flash him a coy smile.

Ghil turns to me and jabs a crooked finger in the direction of the warship. "*This* here's the *beauty* that saved our hides from that maggot patrol."

I widen my eyes. "Can I see inside?"

The guard gives an apologetic shake of his head. "Not without clearance from Crank."

"Crank's brother don't need no clearance!" Ghil says with a dismissive wave of his hand.

The guard looks uncomfortable. "It's just that … you haven't been here in a long time, Ghil. I need to run it by Crank first."

I bat my eyelashes at the guard. "How about *you* show me around?"

Ghil yanks me hard against his body. "Hey! You're with me, remember?" He bends over and pretends to whisper something in my ear.

I laugh and nestle into him.

Ghil winks at the guard and offers him the bottle one more time. "How about you let us have some private time on board, and I'll let you take the pretty lady on a tour afterward."

The guard moves his jaw side to side as he weighs the offer. He runs his eyes over me, and I give him my best approximation of a drunken wink.

"All right." He casts an uneasy glance over his shoulder. "Fifteen minutes."

"That's my man!" Ghil thrusts the bottle to the guard's chest. "Drink up!"

Once on board, we head straight down to the engine room and Ghil moves into action. "I'll cut the fuel and coolant lines and damage a few of the gaskets. It should trigger enough warning lights to keep them busy until we're far enough away to lose them."

I keep watch by the engine room door. My heart trips in my chest at every sound wafting our way, but to my relief no one interrupts us. When he's done, Ghil gives me a curt nod. "Let's go."

A flicker of apprehension goes through me as we make our way back up to the cargo bay. "Give me one of your knives," I mutter. "Just in case the guard doesn't take kindly to me telling him I've changed my mind."

Ghil grins and pulls out a menacing-looking dagger. "How's this?"

I take it and slip it beneath my shamskin. "Adequate. I've speared plenty of shams with less." I don't tell him I've never hurt another human being before. I'm hoping I'll only need the dagger as a deterrent.

The guard straightens up when he sees us, a mixture of relief and anticipation flooding his face. I stride past him without a second glance.

"Hey!" he calls out, grabbing me by the arm. Quick as a flash I whip around and point the tip of the dagger at his throat. "Take your filthy hands off me."

He reaches down and fumbles for his laser gun in his holster, but Ghil snatches it first and stashes it inside his jacket.

"What are you doing?" the guard protests. "We had a deal."

Ghil leans into his face. "That was a test, you moron! Crank's not going to be happy about how lax you are on patrol duty."

The guard's face pales. His eyes flit from Ghil to my dagger and then back to Ghil. "Please don't tell him. He'll kill me. I was just trying to do you a favor."

Ghil shoves the guard against the hull of the ship. "This is the one and only break you get," he says striding off in the direction of the tunnel. "Next time I'll feed you to the face-eating monkeys myself."

"Wait!" the guard calls out. "My gun!"

"You'd better figure out how to explain that one," Ghil yells back to him. "Maybe you'll think twice before you override Crank's security protocol again."

"That was clever," I say, falling in beside Ghil.

"Let's hope he keeps his mouth shut long enough for us to move out of range of any land-based firepower," Ghil says.

We slip back into the tunnel and make our way to the far side of the docking station where Velkan, Buir, and Meldus are waiting for us. They jump to their feet when they see us.

"It's done," I say. "Time to go."

I throw a quick look around. The Zebulux is parked in a small bay alongside a smaller vessel. A couple of traders stroll by deep in conversation, scarcely giving us a second glance. A lone mechanic is bent over one of the access gates in front of the Zebulux, adjusting the locking mechanism. He looks up when he hears us coming. "You the crew?"

Ghil gives a curt nod.

The mechanic straightens up and wipes his hands on his overalls. "You're Crank's brother, right? I've heard some crazy stories about you."

Ghil scowls. "They're all true, and then some."

The mechanic scratches his ear as if digesting the implications. "Yeah, well, holler if you need anything."

Ghil dismisses him with a grunt and we continue up the loading ramp and into the cargo bay of the Zebulux.

"We can't take off with that mechanic hanging around," I say once we're inside.

"You stay here in the cargo bay and keep an eye on him," Ghil says to Velkan. "As soon as he leaves, pull up the loading ramp and radio up to the control room," He turns to Meldus. "Go down to the engine room. Do exactly what Nipper showed you. Velkan will be down there to help you as soon as he can."

"I'll prep for liftoff," I say.

Ghil nods distractedly as he peers around the cargo door at the mechanic. "Looks like he's wrapping up. I'll be right behind you."

"Are we really going to steal Sarth's ship?" Buir asks in a hushed tone as we climb the stairway to the flight deck.

I arch a brow at her. "If that's what it takes to save us from

Sarth's evil purposes, and me from the auction block."

Buir frowns. "I don't understand why Sarth would be willing to sell you all of a sudden. She'll never get mining rights on Cwelt without you. Maybe she doesn't believe we can oust the Maulers."

I grimace. "Or maybe Crank made it worth her while."

The doors to the control room slide apart with a familiar whoosh, and I quickly set about prepping for departure. Within minutes, Velkan's voice comes over the intercom. "All clear. Closing cargo bay."

I flick on the ignition just as Ghil walks in. He slides into the bucket seat behind me. "I can't promise you we'll make it out. We're rolling the dice on this one."

Buir lays a hand on his shoulder. "If we do make it out of here alive, it'll be because of you. I don't know why you're helping us escape from your brother, but we're all grateful."

After a long pause, Ghil responds. "There's nothing left in him but darkness. I don't want to join him in that place."

"You're nothing like him, Ghil," Buir says.

He looks at her with the eyes of a startled child. "I've done a lot of things I'm not proud of."

"But you still have a conscience," Buir replies. "It's not too late for you."

His face softens. "Well, that's something, seeing you think my cooking's a lost cause."

Buir laughs, and my heart warms at the sound. Everything that's happened since we left Cwelt has been so traumatic, and I've been worried she might crack under the strain.

The hull shudders as the Zebulux lifts off from the docking

station. One of the thrusters is still not operating up to par, but I blast it up to maximum power regardless. If we can make it out of here, we can worry about maintenance later.

I scan the viewer for any indication of rockets headed our way. Hopefully, everyone is preoccupied with the auction, and by the time they realize what's happening we'll be well out of range. My only regret is that I couldn't save the girl whose eyes pierced me with her pain.

We endure several minutes of strained silence, startling at every flash of the navigation lights. I'm half-expecting a laser blast to hit the ship and rip her apart at any minute, but the Zebulux ploughs steadily on, and the only hazards we encounter are the streams of debris I navigate around with ease—remnants of the Syndicate patrol ship perhaps? After a bit, I relax my shoulders and let out a long breath. "You did it, Ghil," I say, setting a course for Aristozonex. "We made it out alive."

"And ditched Sarth!" Buir adds. "I never want to set eyes on that evil woman again."

"She's not gonna give up the Zebulux that easily," Ghil says.

"It's not like she can report it stolen," I retort. "Not with the dargonite on board. They'd arrest her too."

"That's exactly why we need to watch our backs," Ghil says in an ominous tone. "When Sarth strikes, it will be swift and unexpected. Maybe at some lone port months from now. I'll have Velkan change the entry code on the cargo door, just to be safe."

"You may be right about Sarth, but we've had enough doom and gloom for now," I say. "Time to celebrate. And we're all starving, so let's start with a feast. Buir, you want to whip us up something to eat? That morsel I had on Diretus didn't do much to stave off the hunger pangs."

"Monkey brains," Ghil mutters.

I grip the controller tighter. "What did you say?"

"Monkey brains. That's what you ate. Made quite an impression on the body poachers. Apparently, it's an acquired taste. I never could bring myself to try it."

For a moment, my vision blurs and I think I'm going to throw up all over the console. I tighten my stomach muscles and set the controls to auto. "I'll see you all down in the dining room," I say weakly. I stagger out of my seat and totter down the utility hallway to the lav. Inside, I palm the wall panel to activate the toilet bowl and watch it rise from the floor, willing it to move faster. The room spins with alarming velocity. I'm not sure if I'm going to retch or pass out first, but I clutch the toilet bowl and hang my head over it anyway.

Ten minutes later, I stagger to my feet, still nauseous, but empty of the hideous contents of my stomach. I wash my mouth out at the basin and slowly make my way down to the dining room, vowing never to badmouth Ghil's mash again.

"Are you okay?" Buir asks when I step through the door.

Before I can respond, a loud beeping comes over the intercom and the ship pitches. A moment later, the lights flicker and die, plunging us into darkness.

Chapter 17

The ship shudders again and I'm thrown against the wall. Seconds later, the contents of the table crash to the floor.

"We need to get to the control room," Ghil yells. I hear him fumbling around for something, and then a beam of light searches out the door. "Crawl if you have to!"

"We're going to crash!" Buir wails.

"Not if we don't lose too much power." Ghil yanks the door open. "Let's go!"

We half-stagger, half-crawl along the hallway toward the control room.

"What about Velkan and Meldus?" I ask.

"Still down in engineering," Ghil calls back to me. "I'll try and touch base with them on the emergency comm."

To my relief, we make it all the way to the control room without losing any more altitude. The lights flicker once briefly, and my hope soars, but they don't come back on. Once inside, Ghil runs through some tests and then radios down to Meldus and Velkan on the emergency comm. It crackles briefly and then Velkan's voice comes over the line. "Mains are out, we can't get any power back."

"What about auxiliaries?" Ghil demands.

"We're working on it. Nipper didn't maintain anything properly down here. What's our vector?"

"Screens are all out," Ghil says. "I have nothing. Keep working on the auxiliaries. We need to stabilize our trajectory."

"I'll keep you posted—" Velkan's voice cuts out abruptly.

I take a deep breath, my mind racing to digest everything that's happened in the past few hours. It's a miracle we're still alive, but for how much longer?

"Are we still losing power?" Buir says, voicing my own worst fear.

Ghil's frown deepens. "We're stable for now, but unless Velkan figures out what's going on and gets us back up to speed, the power could fail completely."

Another dreadful silence falls over us as we contemplate our predicament. Minutes earlier we were celebrating our victory at ditching Sarth on Diretus. Now I wonder if I did the right thing by dragging the others with me.

Static comes over the emergency comm again and I jerk upright in my seat.

"I think I've figured out the problem," Velkan says. "A vent valve on the fuel line. I can do a temporary fix, but we'll need to head for the nearest planet to make more extensive repairs."

"Do what you can," Ghil says. "As soon as my screens are back, I'll calculate our closest possible landing."

We don't wait for long. The screens flicker back to life simultaneously and a low humming fills the control room, the reassuring sound of full power surging through the ship again.

Buir gives an audible sigh of relief.

Ghil wastes no time reorienting the Zebulux and adjusting our orbital vector to set us on the fastest course to the next habitable planet on the charts.

"What's it called?" I ask, staring at the planet looming larger on the viewer.

"Seinought," Ghil says through clenched teeth.

There's a note of resignation in his voice, and I'm almost afraid to ask why. But I'm more afraid of being surprised by what awaits us.

"You don't sound thrilled," I say. "Is it dangerous there?"

"No more so than any other trading planet." He scrubs a hand over the stubble on his chin. "It's just that I have some history there."

"What kind of history?" Buir asks.

"Not the good kind," he acknowledges with a wry grin. "I'm wanted for instigating a brawl with some traders that ended badly."

"You didn't kill anybody, did you?" I ask.

He hefts a brow. "Came close. He asked for it, though. He took a serf's eye out for dropping some cargo he hired him to unload."

I shudder. I can certainly see why Ghil was incensed enough to start a fight. "So, you think they'll remember you?"

"I reckon. It made Seinought news."

"You'll just have to stay hidden on board for as long as it takes to repair the ship," I say.

Ghil gives a tight nod. He leans over the controls and sets the A.I. system to guide the Zebulux in for a landing. "You got this from here. I'll be in engineering if you need me. Velkan could use my help with that vent valve."

He disappears through the door and I turn my attention to the looming planet. My breathing turns ragged as I watch our erratic descent.

"What's wrong?" Buir peers anxiously around at the flickering screens.

"The A.I. still isn't functioning properly after the power outage," I reply, adjusting a couple of switches. "I need to be prepared to take over if things go awry." Seconds later, the thrusters sputter and an alarm blares on the console. My stomach twists as the Zebulux lurches off course. I flick the systems back to manual and grab a hold of the controller.

"Hang on! We're doing this the hard way."

"Are we still on target to dock?" Buir asks, clutching her armrests.

"Not by a long shot." I grimace. "We'll be lucky if we land anywhere on Seinought unless I can get us maneuvered into a decent trajectory." I glance at the scanner and do some quick calculations. We're veering way off course, but it's too risky to take the extra time to recalibrate the coordinates for the docking station with the thruster as unstable as it is. I lock into our new course and steel myself for whatever lies ahead.

"Should I get Ghil back up here?" Buir says.

"Nothing he can do to help us now," I say through gritted teeth.

Buir frowns at the console. "We missed the docking station."

"I know, I'm locked in for a landing on the other side of the planet."

The intercom snaps back to life and Ghil's voice comes through. "What's going on?"

"The A.I. shut down," I respond. "We veered off course, but we're locked in for a landing."

"Hold the course," Ghil says. "I'll do what I can on my end."

We fall silent as the surface looms closer on the viewer. Holding my breath, I prepare for landing and wait to see what lies in store for us on the ground.

"It doesn't look inhabited." Buir's voice rises in panic. "We're heading for some kind of desert."

"It's the best I can do." I eye the flickering lights on the dash.

"Tighten your harness. It could be a rough landing." I wipe the sweat from my brow and focus on the screens in front of me, carefully going over all Sarth's instructions in my head.

Thankfully, the power doesn't cut out again and the Zebulux remains maneuverable for a relatively smooth landing on a powdery landscape of dust and rock. I kill the engine and sink back in my seat, panting with relief.

Buir unbuckles her harness and gets to her feet. "You're drenched with sweat," she says, running a practiced eye over me.

"I had no idea until just now how stressful that would be." I get to my feet and let out a long breath. "My first solo landing, and I averted a crash."

"You did great getting us down safely." Buir peers through the windscreen. "Now we just need to figure out how to get to civilization."

"We may not have to if Velkan can repair the valve causing all these problems." I wipe my forehead with the sleeve of my shamskin. "If he needs parts, we'll take the LunaTrekker and find the nearest settlement."

A moment later, Ghil appears at the door, his face taut. "Where are we?"

"I don't know, but it looks bleak." I gesture through the windscreen to the desolate landscape outside.

"What are our coordinates?" he asks.

"The celestial reference coordinates are putting us about three thousand miles due south of the docking station. We can take the LunaTrekker and look for a settlement if Velkan can't fix the ship."

Ghil frowns. "Fuel's going to be an issue if we have to travel any distance. We'll need to drain the fuel from the second LunaTrekker and take an extra can along."

"Let's see what Velkan has to say." I lean over and flick on the intercom. "Velkan, what's the report from engineering?"

"Looks like the main oxidizer valve is bad too," he says. "We're going to need a new one to make it all the way to Aristozonex."

Ghil cracks his knuckles. "I can take the LunaTrekker and try and find a settlement, but if I'm picked up, you'll all be arrested for harboring a fugitive."

"Buir and I will go," I say. "We might be able to get to a settlement and back in one day."

Ghil fingers the dagger at his waist. "The other unknown is what's out there." He gestures through the windscreen. "It's one thing refueling at a docking station, another thing entirely when you go beyond the station perimeter on any of these planets."

I hesitate for a moment as an unwelcome image of the face-eating monkeys comes to mind. "Doesn't look like there's much of anything out there," I say, peering through the windscreen.

"You'll have to wait until morning," Ghil says in a resigned tone. "You can't risk encountering whatever wildlife might be lurking around at night."

"All right," I say, reluctantly. "We'll leave as soon as it's light. Right now, we need food."

"Monkey bars coming right up!" Buir says in passing.

I shudder and swat at her as I follow her out of the control room.

Down in the galley, Buir doesn't take long to prepare a tray of hard scones filled with a delicious cheese.

"These are unbelievably good." I pop the last piece of my third scone in my mouth with a contented sigh.

Ghil rubs his belly, a hazy satisfaction in his eyes. "For these, I could share my galley."

Buir leans toward him with a mischievous look in her eye. "I'll divulge more of my recipe secrets if you teach me some knife handling skills."

Ghil raises a tentative brow. "That's a tall order. I didn't learn those skills overnight."

Buir smirks. "Trust me, it'll take you equally as long to turn that mush around!"

Ghil throws back his head and laughs. "You got yourself a deal."

The door to the dining room opens and a grease-stained and sweaty Velkan and Meldus traipse in. My heart pitter-patters a little faster when Velkan slides into the seat beside me. Even with the reek of fuel between us, I can still remember the sweetness of his lips.

"So we can't repair that valve?" Ghil asks, straightening up in his chair.

Velkan casts a hungry eye over the remaining scones on the platter Buir pushes his way before answering. "It's shot. We're not going anywhere until we replace it."

Ghil gives an exasperated sigh. "You and I can't go looking for a settlement. We're going to have to send the newbies."

Velkan gives a concerned nod. "We'll load the guns in the bed of the LunaTrekker, just in case."

"Of what?" Buir asks. "It's a civilized Syndicate planet, isn't it? We should be safe here."

Ghil gets to his feet. "If you call maiming your serf for dropping a package civilized."

Buir bites her lip.

"We'll get in and out as quickly and quietly as possible," I say, breaking the uncomfortable silence that follows Ghil's words. "For now, let's rest. It's been a long night."

Ghil nods. "You and Buir can take Sarth's quarters—more comfortable." He snatches up the last scone, winks at Buir and disappears out of the room.

Buir and I kick off our boots and curl up on Sarth's bed under our shamskins, too exhausted to be bothered undressing. Buir mumbles something to me, but one or the other of us drifts off mid-sentence because everything after that is lost in a black haze.

I wake the next morning and stretch my limbs out lazily. I haven't felt this refreshed in a long time. Buir stirs and sits up next to me, rubbing her eyes sleepily. "Is it morning?"

"It's light out. Time we got moving."

She yawns, flings her legs over the side of the bed and plods over to the viewport.

"You can check the view out all you want from the LunaTrekker," I say pulling on my boots. "We need to get going."

She turns around to face me, her eyes bulging. "Doesn't look like we're going anywhere."

Chapter 18

I race over the viewport and peer through it. A group of painted tribespeople, forty or fifty strong, riding on long-legged hairless creatures with large heads, flared nostrils and burning yellow eyes surround the ship. A rod of fear shoots up my spine and momentarily paralyzes me. Armed with crossbows, and daubed with ochre markings on their foreheads and upper arms, the tribespeople stare fixedly at the ship as if waiting on someone to emerge.

"Come on," I say, grabbing Buir by the hand. "We need to wake the others."

Huddled around the viewport in the dining room, we stare out at the intimidating tribe, their naked mounts snorting and pawing the dust.

"You were right about the wildlife, Ghil," Buir says glumly. "They look dangerous."

"Solarbald ponies," Ghil replies. "They roam wild on some of the more remote planets. Don't worry, they have a vicious kick, but they won't eat you."

"Can't vouch for the tribespeople," Velkan says, grimly.

Buir shrinks back from the viewport.

"We can't stay in here forever," I say. "We need to figure something out."

"We can't shoot our way out—there are too many of them," Ghil says.

"We may not have to shoot them," I say. "We don't know what they want … yet."

"They don't look too friendly," Buir says dubiously. "And neither do those ponies."

"But they're keeping their distance," Meldus says. "I think we should wait it out. They may be passing through on their way somewhere, and stopped out of curiosity—just to look."

"I'm with Meldus," Velkan says. "I say we give it a day and hope they disappear. But we should use the time to come up with some kind of plan in case they're still here tomorrow."

"I hate to be the one to point this out," Buir says. "But if they're a good representation of the inhabitants on Seinought, it's not likely we'll find the part we need unless we go all the way to the docking station."

Ghil scratches his jaw. "Buir's right. We need to figure out how to patch up that valve."

Velkan shakes his head. "I nursed it all I could to get us here, but there's nothing more I can do."

"There's always something more," Ghil says. "We'll build a part if we have to. First, let's take inventory on our weapons. I know the code to the gun safe."

To my relief, Sarth's gun safe turns out to be surprisingly well-stocked. We have plenty of options to arm ourselves with, and then some, but it still leaves us hopelessly outnumbered. If we try shooting our way out, the tribespeople will fill us with arrows from their crossbows in seconds.

"Let's go down to engineering and put our heads together," Ghil says. "Maybe between us we can figure out how to jury-rig that valve."

Velkan looks skeptical. "I'm open to suggestions," he says with a shrug. "But I already tried everything I could think of."

We spend the remainder of the day modifying several different spare parts and trying to fashion something that could tide us over and temporarily replace the main oxidizer valve. Instead of making any progress, Velkan makes another disheartening discovery—the valve that failed caused the heat exchanger to malfunction, which in turn damaged the turbo pump.

"We're screwed," Velkan says, tossing his wrench aside. "This ship's a disaster. We don't have any replacement parts, and a pump's not something we can build or modify."

"We'll just have to wait until the tribespeople disperse," Meldus says, wiping a greasy hand down his shirt.

"Our water supply's not going to last more than a few days. The longer we wait, the more likely it is we'll die of thirst before we find a settlement," Ghil says.

"Maybe our best option is to try and befriend them," I say.

"Too risky. Gives them all the control if we walk out there." Ghil frowns and folds his arms over his chest. "We could build a protective cover for the LunaTrekker and drive out through them."

"That's risky too," I say. "If those wild ponies panic, they could flip the vehicle and trample us to death."

"I like the idea of having an armored vehicle to flee in," Meldus says. "At least it gives us a fighting chance."

"And I like the idea of trying to reach out to them first," I say.

"All right," Ghil says. "If they're still here tomorrow, we'll initiate contact. In the meantime, let's start modifying the LunaTrekker in case we do need to make a run for it."

In the cargo bay, Velkan takes charge of welding the panels and roof for the LunaTrekker that will act as a shield against any arrows. Meldus and Ghil set about draining the second LunaTrekker of fuel while Buir and I practice drawing our guns and aiming. My hand itches to grip my familiar spear, but it would be inadequate for what we're facing. I just hope I can pull the trigger if the situation calls for it. Every time I take aim at something in the cargo bay, I hear the blast of Sarth's gun and see Nipper's lifeless body. As frightening an impression as the tribespeople make, I cringe at the thought of killing them. But I'm torn—I must do whatever it takes to get out of here and back to Cwelt before it's too late to save my own people.

Buir quickly tires of practicing with the guns and heads off to prepare some food rations to bring with us. If we do escape, it could be days before we reach a settlement.

I wander over to the LunaTrekker to inspect what Velkan has built so far.

"Jump in," he says, gesturing for me to climb through the open door. He clambers in after me and grins. "What do you think?"

"It's solid. Nothing's going to penetrate it."

"I left just enough of a slit at the front to see through, or shoot through," Velkan says. "Makes it dark in here … and private."

I turn to him and he leans toward me, his lips sealing with mine. For what feels like an eternity, I lose myself in his kiss, forgetting everything around us, and against us. When we break apart, he crushes me to his chest. "Trattora, if we don't make it out of here, I want you to know—" His voice cracks and he clears his throat. "I treasure every conversation we share." He twirls a lock of my hair in his finger. "You're a chieftain's daughter and I'm only a serf, but—"

I put a finger to his lips. "Don't talk like that." I pull out the chain around my neck, place the tiny bracelet in his hand and close his fingers over it. "Whatever other significance this bracelet has, it proves we were equally loved. I am no different from you, other than that my lot in life was easier. I have no royal blood in my veins, and you don't have the blood of a serf in yours. We are simply two people, Velkan. Two people with one destiny, I hope."

He smiles gently at me and slips the bracelet back into my hand. "You're a dreamer, *Girl of Fire*."

"Anything is possible." I reach up and kiss his forehead gently. "Now let's show the others our new armored escape vehicle."

At dusk, the tribespeople are still here, and they appear to be settling in for the night. Several campfires flicker malevolently against a backdrop of craggy rocks, and a perimeter guard circles the encampment.

"I wonder if they're guarding against us surprising them during the night, or guarding against whatever else is out there," I say.

"Maybe they'll move out at dawn," Buir says, sounding unconvinced.

I grimace. "They look like they're planning to stick around until we make an appearance."

No one seems inclined to try to sleep, so we hang out in the communal area, dozing and exchanging the occasional banter, but mostly monitoring the viewport in the hopes that our fearsome and unexpected guests will disappear as elusively as they came.

We take turns watching the flames from their fires burn steadily through the long watches of the night. When dawn comes, we are faced with the cold, hard reality that the tribespeople aren't going anywhere anytime soon.

We pick in strained silence at the breakfast Buir prepares for us with the last of our fresh food. We still have enough canned supplies left for a week's worth of mash, but after that, we'll be out.

Ghil sighs and tosses down his fork. "I say we load up the LunaTrekker and blast a trail out of here. I can't sit here and do nothing any longer. They won't be expecting a vehicle, so maybe we can make a getaway before they even realize what's happening."

"You're assuming a lot," I say. "We don't know how fast those solarbald ponies can run."

"What we need is a distraction," Velkan says, getting up and walking over to the viewport. "Maybe we can jam the accelerator on the second LunaTrekker and send it down the ramp first to scatter them."

"It might just end up blocking our escape route," Meldus points out.

"Hey! Check this out!" Velkan turns and gestures us over to the viewport.

We crowd around him, pressing in to get a better look. A lone tribeswoman is approaching the ship, arms outstretched. She appears to be unarmed, but after seeing how many knives Ghil can conceal under his clothes, it wouldn't surprise me if she had a weapon stashed somewhere on her person.

"What do you think she's doing?" Buir asks, when the woman sits down cross-legged in front of the ship and lays what appears to be a string of beads out in front of her.

My heart beats a little faster in my chest. "I think it might be a gift for us. They're initiating contact. Maybe they're trying to tell us they come in peace."

Ghil narrows his eyes at the woman. "Or trick us into coming out unarmed, more like it."

I scan the remainder of the tribespeople clustered in small groups behind the woman. Despite the intimidating symbols daubed on their foreheads, they don't look like they're preparing for war.

"I'll go out there and greet her," I say.

"No!" Velkan and Buir cry in unison.

Meldus gives me a stern look. "The chieftain would never allow such a reckless gesture."

I toss my shamskin over my shoulder. "I am your chieftain until you return to Cwelt," I reply sharply.

Meldus tightens his lips but gives a slight bow.

"It would be crazy to go out there alone," Ghil says.

"It's not crazy to reciprocate if they're trying to reach out to us," I argue. "If we send out an unmanned vehicle into their midst, we could end up killing some of them. No telling how they'll react then."

Ghil frowns. "You have a point."

Buir lays a hand on my arm. "I'll go with you."

I shake my head. "No, they only sent one messenger. It's best if we do the same. Woman to woman. The rest of you can take up positions behind the cargo in the docking bay. We'll open the door and see what happens. If they don't attack right away, I'll go out and greet the woman."

There's a long silence while everyone mulls over my proposal.

"If they do attack, we'll retaliate, you understand that?" Ghil says, frowning at me.

I nod, even though on the inside I'm shrinking from the thought of shooting one of them.

Ghil looks around at the rest of the group. "They've made the first move. We need to respond, one way or another. Either we make contact, or we blast our way out of here."

"I vote for leaving in the armored vehicle," Velkan says.

"I second that," Meldus echoes.

I fasten a disapproving gaze on him. "You don't have a vote; your job is to obey my orders."

"If we can avoid bloodshed, we should try that first," Buir says.

Ghil gives a curt nod. "I agree. Let's head on down to the cargo bay and begin strategizing."

Once we're gathered downstairs, Ghil wastes no time assigning everyone a hiding place with a good view of the entryway, and a decent angle to shoot from if it comes to that. My heart beats rapidly as I crouch behind several barrels to the left of the loading dock. I elected not to arm myself with a gun—I don't want to come across as a threat—although I keep Ghil's dagger concealed in my waistband.

"Opening the doors now," Velkan calls out. He keys the code into the control pad on the wall and then darts back behind a stack of crates.

Blood pounds like rushing water in my ears. The steel door of the cargo bay yawns upward at an agonizingly slow pace. I shield my face when the light spills through, my body tense as I watch from behind the barrels for any sign of sudden movement. A hush falls over the tribespeople. I wait, breath on pause, to see if any of them reach for their crossbows. But they leave them slung casually over their shoulders and make no attempt to approach the ship.

I wait for several harrowing minutes before stepping out into the cargo bay in full view of the tribespeople. The woman who was sitting cross-legged in front of the ship gets to her feet and holds out the beads like an offering. I walk slowly toward the loading ramp, smile, and lift my hand to splay it in greeting. The expression on the woman's face shifts to one of horror. Out of the corner of my eye, I spot an archer raise a crossbow, then someone slams into me from behind and sends me flying.

Chapter 19

"Don't shoot! It was my fault!" I scream. "They misunderstood!"

My mind races in circles as everything plays out again in slow motion. Splaying my hand in greeting, the five-pronged symbol on the tribespeople's foreheads—some kind of war cry perhaps? The archer drawing his bow, *someone slamming into me.* Fear prickles up my spine. I scramble to my feet and gasp when I see Meldus lying motionless a few feet away, an arrow protruding from his chest. I fall to my knees at his side and cradle his head, my breath icing over in my lungs. "Meldus! Can you hear me?" I scream his name repeatedly until I'm hoarse, but to no avail. His body lies limp in my arms. I rock him back and forth, tears welling up and streaming down my face. If ever I felt the burden of my legacy, it is now when I have witnessed one of my own lay down his life to protect his future chieftain.

The tribeswoman's shadow falls over me. Too grief-stricken to react, I bury my head in Meldus' chest and wait for her to do what she will to me. When nothing transpires, I lift my head in time to see her kneel reverently by Meldus' body. I watch through my tears as she takes her glittering beads and slips them over his head before running her finger down the center of his forehead.

I blink across at her, numb with shock, yet sensing empathy emanating from her expression; her caring gestures those of a mourner grieving for the dead.

"He's gone," I whisper.

She looks at me blankly and traces her finger down his forehead again. I crumple back over Meldus' body and sob quietly. The woman's hand slides over my shaking shoulders, rubbing tiny concentric circles of comfort into them. "Sah-pire," she whispers repeatedly.

The word has no meaning to me, but her comforting tone warms my broken heart and tells me everything I need to know. They meant no harm. My hand gesture indicated something else entirely to them that triggered their need to defend themselves, or perhaps their honor.

When my sobs finally subside, I lay Meldus gently back down and wipe my eyes with the palms of my hands. The tribespeople stand around us, still as shadows, heads hung low in a mark of respect for the dead—or shame perhaps? I glance around, but it's impossible for me to tell which one of them shot the arrow. Not that it matters. It wasn't their fault. I blame myself for my careless gesture. I should have been more cautious like Buir. I get to my feet and reach for the woman's hand. She studies my face for a long moment and then places her hand in mine. Murmuring ripples around the tribespeople, but they remain motionless.

I walk slowly toward the ramp, hand in hand with the woman, signaling to Buir and the others to stay put. I come to a halt at the top of the ramp and face the tribespeople. When I'm sure I have their attention, I shrug out of my shamskin and drape it around the woman's shoulders, before presenting her to them. Toothy smiles break out across their painted faces. A low warbling fills the air which I take as another sign of their approval. The woman tugs at my hand and pulls me toward her people. I walk down the ramp, my heart heavy with loss, but filled with a growing assurance that the tribe meant no ill-will. As I walk toward them, one-by-one they raise their fists in front of them and pump them up and down. The woman turns to me and smiles. She takes my hand and folds my fingers over in a fist. I nod to show her I understand, and then return the native greeting, the one I know now I should have given, the one that wasn't a call to war, or an insult to their deity, or whatever it was that it meant.

The woman ushers me along the line of tribespeople until we reach a man who I can tell is their leader by the command of respect in his gestures, and the wisdom in his eyes as he appraises me. The woman says something to him in their native tongue. He taps his knuckles to his chest. "Boshtee!"

"Bosh-tee," I repeat.

He nods and smiles.

"Trattora." I tap my fist to my chest in return.

He gestures questioningly at the ship.

I beckon to him to follow me and then wait for his response. He nods curtly to the men around him, and two of them move silently to his side. I turn and lead them back down the receiving line of people toward the Zebulux. The woman catches up with me and taps her chest. "Zindera!"

"Zindera! That's a pretty name," I reply.

She smiles as if she somehow understands that I've complimented her and grabs hold of my hand again.

I walk back up the ramp and into the cargo bay with my newly acquired entourage. Buir's eyes widen when she sees us. Ghil and Velkan freeze midstride, in the process of transporting Meldus' body over to the bed of the unmodified LunaTrekker. I signal to them to finish what they are doing, and hurriedly pull Buir aside.

"Do *not*, under any circumstances, splay your hand at them. That's what triggered their archer to shoot at me—something to do with the symbol on their forehead, I think. I either threatened them or insulted them."

Buir nods fervently, stricken with awe and terror at the sight of the tribespeople examining their new surroundings. Boshtee turns back to me and flaps his hands in the impression of a bird and cocks his head to one side questioningly.

I shake my head, then flap my hands downward and point at the floor in my best attempt to demonstrate that the ship is broken.

He seems to grasp what I'm saying and nods thoughtfully. He taps his chest insistently with his fingers and then points two fingers at his eyes.

"I think he wants to see what's damaged," I say to the others.

Ghil runs a skeptical eye over Boshtee and shrugs. "He doesn't look like the type to have a spare valve in his hip pocket."

"We're just being courteous." I give Ghil a dark look. "Keep your knives out of sight."

"I'll stay up here," Buir says. "It doesn't seem right to leave Meldus here, even though—" Her voice chokes and she turns and hurries over to the LunaTrekker.

"I'll stay with her," Ghil says. "It's not safe for her to be alone."

Velkan steps forward. He beckons to the tribespeople to follow him and then leads Boshtee and his men down the stairwell into the belly of the ship and through to the engine room. I follow behind with the woman.

"We have several problems," Velkan begins, gesturing at the equipment. "The oxidizer valve failed and messed up the—"

"Velkan, they don't understand you," I interrupt. "Just show them."

He tosses me an annoyed look but proceeds to demonstrate the problem using hand gestures and sounds.

Boshtee follows along with interest. When Velkan is done, he exchanges a look with the two men accompanying him before motioning to us to follow him.

Velkan turns and raises his brows at me. "Now what? Are we about to be kidnapped?"

I shrug. "Think positive. Maybe he's a parts dealer in disguise."

"And maybe I'm a Syndicate Commander," Velkan says.

"Just do what they want for now and don't insult them," I say.

We lead the party back up to the cargo bay where Ghil and Buir are waiting.

"They want us to go with them now," I say.

"What for?" Ghil asks suspiciously.

"I'm not sure," I admit. "But I think they want to help us."

Ghil scratches his jaw. "We'll follow them in the LunaTrekker. That way we can get away from them if we need to."

"That sounds marginally more appealing than riding those solarbald ponies out there," Buir says, frowning.

I tap Boshtee on the shoulder and point at the LunaTrekker and then at myself and the rest of the crew. He raises his brows and points at himself.

I smile at him. "You can come too if you want." I point at my ears and then the LunaTrekker, and make as loud an imitation of an engine sound as I can.

He turns and mutters something to Zindera. She bows and takes off down the ramp with the two men in tow. With any luck, he sent them out to explain to the other tribespeople what's happening and warn them how loud it's going to be when we drive out there.

"What do you want to do with Meldus's body," Velkan says when we reach the LunaTrekker.

The searing pain of his loss hits again. I won't dispose of him like Sarth did with Nipper's body. The least I can do is lay him to rest with all the dignity a Cweltan warrior deserves. "We'll take him with us and find a place to bury him."

Velkan gives a solemn nod. "I'll grab some shovels."

We pile into the LunaTrekker and Ghil starts the engine. Boshtee flinches at the sound but seems more excited than nervous when the vehicle rolls forward and down the ramp. The tribespeople stare at us wide-eyed, parting hesitantly to let us through. Boshtee points in the direction he wants us to go in. Once we are clear of the crowd, Ghil accelerates to a comfortable cruising speed. I'm half expecting Boshtee to panic and scramble to get out of the vehicle, but he's unperturbed by our increasing speed. I realize why a moment later when the solarbald ponies thunder past on either side of the LunaTrekker, kicking up a storm of white dust that severely impairs Ghil's vision. He brakes hard and waits until the cloud disperses before revving the engine up again. "And there I was thinking we'd be sitting around waiting for them to catch up with us," he grumbles.

"I'm glad we befriended them and didn't have to outrun them," Buir remarks.

"I wonder how far their settlement is?" Velkan asks.

I shrug. "We have extra gas containers. We should be good unless it's more than a day's journey from here."

As it turns out, we're underway less than an hour before Boshtee leans forward and jabs his finger excitedly at the sand up ahead. I frown and peer at the monochromatic dunes, unable to detect anything out of the ordinary. Ghil keeps on course, following Boshtee's instructions. We're rewarded minutes later when I spot a wrecked ship half buried in the sand.

"If I had to guess, I'd say it's been here for decades," Velkan says, leaning forward in his seat for a better look.

Boshtee nods emphatically, looking pleased with himself. He flaps his hands like a bird again and points at the ship.

I give him a frozen smile. I don't want to burst his bubble, but this ship isn't going anywhere ever again.

"We might be able to salvage some parts," Velkan says, sounding dubious.

Ghil pulls up alongside the ship where the rest of the tribespeople are waiting patiently. We climb out the LunaTrekker and make our way over to the downed vessel. My heart sinks. Up close, it's even more apparent that we won't be going anywhere in it. The hull is rusted up and corroded through in several places. Based on its condition, I can't imagine there's anything inside worth salvaging. Boshtee meant well, but it looks like we've wasted our time coming here.

"Might as well look inside now that we're here," Ghil says, sounding as frustrated as I feel.

I lead the way to a gaping hole in the rear of the ship and duck through it. The space is musty and my nose begins to itch almost immediately. The floor has accumulated a thick layer of sand, and every object and surface is buried in white dust.

"The engine room's probably filled with sand too," Velkan says.

"We brought shovels," I remind him. "We could dig it out."

"Waste of time. The equipment can't be saved now." He jerks his head at Boshtee, who's followed us inside the hull with several of his men. "We'd best tell him. No sense wasting his time either."

"I'll talk to him," I say.

I walk over to Boshtee and shake my head apologetically.

He frowns, a perplexed look on his face.

I bend over, lift a handful of sand and let it run through my fingers, before pointing to the equipment.

Boshtee snaps his fingers and signals to several of his men. They cross over to a pile of crates at the back of the bay and quickly clear off the sand, before prying off the lids.

Velkan walks back there and peers inside the first crate. "I can't believe it." He looks up with a glimmer of hope in his eye. "This must have been a transport vessel. These crates are full of parts. And they're in decent shape, thanks to the airtight containers they were shipped in." He casts a glance around the rest of the bay. "If we dig around, we might be able to find what we need, or at least something I can modify."

My gut tightens. A sliver of hope returns. If we can get the Zebulux airborne today, we might be able to reach Aristozonex tomorrow or the following day at the latest. There may still be a chance of saving Cwelt from the Maulers after all.

We spend the next hour sifting through the crates of parts and pulling out possible replacement valves and pumps. Boshtee and his men soon grow restless and wander back outside to wait with the rest of the tribe.

When Velkan is satisfied that he has salvaged everything that might be of use, we load the parts into the LunaTrekker and turn our attention to the question of what to do with Meldus' body.

"This is as good a place as any to bury him," I say. "I'll talk to Boshtee and make sure he's okay with it."

Velkan wrinkles his brow. "*Talk?*"

"In a manner of speaking," I say.

Velkan shrugs and pulls out a shovel.

I walk over to Boshtee and point to Meldus' body in the back of the LunaTrekker, and then to Velkan who's already hard at work digging a grave beside the wrecked ship.

A look of alarm comes over Boshtee's face. He yells something at Velkan and one of the other tribesmen rushes over and snatches the shovel from Velkan's hand.

"What's wrong?" I ask, raising my shoulders in a questioning shrug.

Boshtee gives a series of rapid orders to a couple of the tribespeople and they undo an oversized saddle bag on one of their mounts and pull out some wood and kindling.

Buir grips my arm. "I think they want to burn his body."

I grit my teeth. "If that's their custom, then that's what we'll do. We can't risk offending them again."

We watch in silence as the tribespeople build a pyre a short distance from the wreck and then ceremoniously pick up Meldus' body and hold it high above their heads as they march over to the stacked wood. They lay Meldus carefully in the center, Zindera's glittering beads still around his neck. Our mood is somber as Boshtee raises his hands over the body. I bite down on my lip when one of the tribesmen builds a tinder nest, rubs his hands briskly together to light it, and ignites the pyre. I close my eyes, shutting out the macabre sight. I promised Meldus we'd go back to Cwelt as soon as it was safe, but I can't keep that promise and it's tearing me up inside. Now, all I can do in his honor is liberate Cwelt from the Maulers.

Chapter 20

Once the pyre is burning steadily, Boshtee and his tribespeople begin quietly loading their packs onto their animals. One by one, they file past the flames and raise their hands to the sky invoking what I can only believe is a prayer before they mount their ponies. Zindera comes up to me, looking almost regal in her new shamskin. She presses a sack into my hands, then jabs her fingers to her mouth, pretending to eat.

"Thank you," I whisper, touched by her kindness and too choked up to say much else.

Not long after, we watch the tribespeople leave in a sedate procession, but the moment they disappear out of sight, the pounding of many hooves reaches our ears. Their strange hairless ponies have resumed their powerful stride across the shadowy desert, but where they are headed to remains a mystery, as does the cryptic symbol painted on their foreheads.

"I don't want to go back to the Zebulux yet," I say to the others. "It doesn't seem right to leave here Meldus alone." I slump down on a flat rock a short distance from the pyre, emotionally spent from hours of delicate negotiations with a tribe whose language I don't understand, and whose ways are not mine. Meldus' death seemed almost surreal as long as I was focused on dealing with Boshtee and his people, but now the raw pain of loss and guilt feels like a hot poker piercing my gut.

Buir sits down beside me and puts an arm around my shoulders. Ghil and Velkan busy themselves looking through the parts we collected.

I wait for several hours until Meldus' remains have been completely consumed. Then, with a heavy heart, I give the signal to start up the LunaTrekker.

I can tell Buir is relieved to be heading back to the ship before it gets dark. She smiles tentatively at me, and I squeeze her hand in return. I still don't have the heart for conversation. I'm struggling to come to terms with Meldus' heroic sacrifice; a moment of rude awakening for me. I've taken my role as the future chieftain of Cwelt far too lightly up until now. One of my own people died in my place today. I'm only just beginning to realize the weight that my position carries, and how important it is that someone as corrupt as Parthelon never gets the chance to lead.

"Maybe there's some astro fruit in here." Buir rummages around in the sack Zindera gave us and lets out a yelp. "Ugh! What is this?" She holds up a dried-out insect with shiny pincers and a dark red underbelly.

"Food!" Velkan reaches for it. "Let me try it." He bites the head off and chews tentatively for a moment. "Tangy, but protein packed no doubt."

Buir shudders. "Is there anything you won't eat?"

"He used to say nothing could taste as bad as my mash," Ghil says with a wink.

I smile, despite the ache in my heart. It's impossible for the others to understand the weight of the responsibility I feel for Meldus' death. I realize now how lonely my father must be at times with the burden he carries for the welfare of his people. When I return, I plan to do more to lighten his load and less to disappoint him.

It's almost nightfall by the time we arrive back at the Zebulux.

"I never thought I'd be glad to see this ship again," Buir remarks, as she climbs out of the LunaTrekker inside the cargo bay.

"Don't get too excited," Velkan says. "She's not flightworthy yet."

"We'll work on the engine in the morning," I say. "We could all use an early night. It's been a long and difficult day."

Buir accompanies me upstairs to Sarth's quarters and slips off her shamskin. "That was a generous peace-offering you made, and a wise move by a future leader of Cwelt." She runs her hand over her immaculate cloak as she drapes it over the bed. "I want to gift you mine in return."

"And subject a perfectly good shamskin to ruin." I smile at her. "Thank you, but no. Anyway, we won't be needing those on Aristozonex. We'll need to blend in a little better than that."

She sighs. "If we ever get there. Do you really think Velkan can make those parts work?"

"He seems to think so. Between us, we'll figure something out." I give an ungraceful yawn and flop down on the bed. "We'll work on it tomorrow. Right now, my brain's powering down."

I wake the next morning to the unmistakable sound of the Zebulux roaring to life. Buir and I bolt upright and exchange bug-eyed stares before jumping out of bed and racing down to the rumbling engine room. When we burst through the door, Velkan glances up and gives us a lopsided grin, sweat glistening on his face. His hair is knotted in a messy bundle on top of his head.

"Did you work on it all night?" I ask.

He shrugs. "Couldn't sleep. I kept jolting awake with ideas on how to make the repairs."

Before I can respond, Ghil barges in, an incredulous look on his face. "Son of a serf," he blurts out, rubbing the sleep from his eyes. "You got some kind of magic around machines."

Velkan runs a hand over the manifold in front of him. "Not magic. Just engineering."

Ghil scratches his bald head. "One and the same in my book."

"Does this mean we can leave?" Buir asks. "Breakfast at an upscale restaurant on Aristozonex sounds awfully good."

Ghil throws her a disapproving look. "Thought you said you weren't picky."

"I'm not!" She beams at him. "I'll eat at any establishment you take me to!"

He grunts. "Be dinner time before we get there."

"Then dinner it is!" Buir replies.

"First, we need to figure out what we're going to do with the dargonite," I say. "If Syndicate customs officials search our vessel at the docking station, their scanners will pick it up no matter where we hide it."

Velkan furrows his brow. "Not if we hide it in some kind of

a solution. It has unusual properties that render it virtually undetectable once it's immersed in liquid."

Ghil glances across at the pipes. "Are you thinking of putting it in the coolant or something?"

Velkan shakes his head. "That's an old trick—stashing dark market items in the equipment in the engine room. First place they'll search. It needs to be somewhere they would never even bother looking."

"I know how we can pull this off." I grin around at the others. "Ghil, how about you whip us up a little something in the kitchen with the rest of our canned goods?"

"Like what?" he asks, a confused look on his face.

Buir scrunches her brow. "You're not making any sense."

"We can hide the dargonite in a cauldron of Ghil's famous mash."

Velkan's lips tug up into one of his brilliant smiles. "Perfect! I'll grab the nuggets from my mattress and throw them in there too."

"Humph!" Ghil folds his arms across his chest. "Mash is leftovers. If I whip it up it's mush."

I roll my eyes at him. "So, you'll do it?"

He squeezes his brows together. "Waste of food if you ask me."

"Actually, it's a good use of our resources." Velkan winks at me. "That mush is practically inedible anyway. Besides, there are still plenty of those bugs left in the bag."

Ghil scowls. "I'll cook up a pot to hide the dargonite in, but it's the last one I'm making for an ungrateful lot like you." He turns and stomps over to the door.

We wait until he has stormed out before we all burst out laughing. I laugh until my gut hurts and tears trickle down my face, and then all of a sudden, I'm sobbing. Sobbing for Meldus, for my mother and father on Cwelt, for the family I once had, but may never know, for the burden I feel to protect Cwelt from the Maulers and Parthelon, for the sense of belonging I think will elude me all my life.

Buir wraps an arm around my shoulder. "Hey, it's all right."

"No, it's all wrong," I say with a loud sniff. "I promised Meldus we'd go back."

"You couldn't have done anything differently," Buir says. "He died a hero; his family can be proud of that. We will honor him on our return."

"If we make it back to tell them." I wipe the tears from my eyes with the back of my hands.

Buir gives me a long hug. "I believe we're going to make it back."

I let out a resigned sigh. "I'll go to the control room and prepare for departure. Send Ghil up to help me as soon as he's got his mush going—mash—whatever it is."

Six uneventful hours later we're on approach to Aristozonex. I'm convinced Velkan truly is a wizard with machines—the engine hasn't sputtered once throughout the flight, and even the A.I. system is operating properly again.

Ghil's mystical concoction is cooling in a cauldron in the galley. Buir assures me this latest batch smells worse than ever, so it's pretty much a given that the Syndicate customs officials won't go near it. Even so, we're all on edge as the Zebulux begins her descent into the large, brightly-lit Aristozonex docking station.

"There's a lot of security down there," Buir says, an apprehensive look on her face.

Ghil grimaces. "Here's how it works. We sit tight until the officials come on board and go over the manifest. We're short three crew so we all need to stick to the same story that we dropped them off in Seinought and we're picking them up on our way back."

I nod distractedly, glued to the view screen. The station is abuzz with a steady stream of ships moving in and out. Just when I'm wondering how Ghil will ever manage to avoid clipping the tail of another ship as he attempts to park, two steel cables shoot upward and lock onto our hull, guiding us into the narrow slip assigned to us.

When we finally touch down, my mind races in several different directions at once. As soon as we're cleared by customs, I need to find a buyer for the dargonite, and then somehow procure a ship. And I want to check out that address Roma gave me before we leave. Whatever the origin of our bracelets turns out to be, I can't help toying with the fantasy that Velkan and I will discover that we both belong on Aristozonex and that our parents are alive and well and never stopped searching for us.

We head downstairs and wait in the cargo bay until two Syndicate customs officials, dressed in dark brown skintight jumpsuits with the flaming planet Syndicate insignia on their collars, board the ship. The younger one gives a curt nod by way of greeting before proceeding to document the members of the crew and take inventory of our weapons.

"Any cargo to declare?" the other official asks in a bored tone.

"Nothing." Ghil hands over the ship's registration and manifest.

The younger official takes them and flicks a condescending glance over them. "We'll still need to search the ship." He looks around with a glimmer of satisfaction in his eye. I suspect he's new to the job and not nearly as jaded as his partner—which could work against us.

"This way," Ghil says. "We'll start down below." He nods to me and I join him. Maybe he needs a second set of eyes to keep an eye on them if they split up.

The two men follow us around the ship, inspecting every square inch of every room, scanner in hand. Despite what Velkan said about dargonite being undetectable in liquid, my heart pounds a death dirge in my throat as we near the galley. I push open the door and gesture Ghil and the officials inside while I wait in the hallway. I'm not sure I could disguise the guilt written all over my face if I set eyes on the cauldron. I lean back against the wall and close my eyes, my thoughts still with Meldus.

I startle upright when they reappear.

"Where are your sleeping accommodations?" the younger official says.

I signal politely down the hallway to the bunk rooms and Sarth's quarters. The older official falls in beside his partner, the look on his face a sure indication his interest in the Zebulux is waning rapidly. I exchange a fleeting look of relief with Ghil behind their backs.

When the officials have completed their inspection, they log our entry permit and abruptly take their leave. I let out a sweeping sigh of relief. We have a permit to move freely in Aristozonex for the next month. Except Velkan, of course. He's listed on the paperwork as cargo and instructed to remain on board at all times. The only exception for bringing serfs into Aristozonex is for auction. And that requires a special sales license.

"Let's go get something to eat." Ghil pulls on his dark beanie. "I know a low-key place off the beaten track that serves great food."

Buir's eyes light up. "Ooh! I've been dreaming about this all day."

"We'll bring you back some food," I promise Velkan. "We won't be gone long."

"Thanks." He stretches a smile across his face, but I know how he really feels inside—that ache of being a misfit in a world that doesn't see you as one of them, scarcely sees you as human. If there was anything I could do to change that for him, I would.

I drop several pieces of dargonite into my pocket and slip on my old CipherSync. Once I use up all the credits on it, I'll toss it for the newer model Sarth procured for me. I don't know if we'll have time tonight, but at some point, we'll need to buy new clothes. We can't hope to be considered legitimate traders dressed in Cweltan attire.

Outside the cargo bay, the bright lights and billboards of Aristozonex make for a blinding show. We look around, awestruck, as we wait in line at the security gate to leave the docking station. When we reach the front of the line, the guard stamps a holographic reentry permit on our hands and we step through to the opulent world of Aristozonex.

I stand at the curb in a daze, my head rotating side to side as I try to absorb all the sights and sounds assaulting me from every direction.

"Keep a low profile," Ghil says. "There are Minders everywhere. We don't want to attract attention to ourselves."

"Do you mean those creatures with the tentacles?" Buir points at a row of shiny black mechanized objects lined up on the opposite curb.

Ghil laughs. "No, Minders are Syndicate security forces, humans—for the most part. Those things are heliodrones. They deliver packages and other items throughout Aristozonex." He points at the sky above us. "Eases up traffic congestion."

I crane my neck to see. Overhead, the sky is thick with heliodrones silently following lighted laser paths. Some clutch packages to their bodies, moving like giant stealth spiders that could descend on us at any minute.

"LevCab service is over there." Ghil gestures to our right at a fleet of driverless shuttle vehicles displaying holographic images of hotels and shopping emporiums with constantly changing electronic deals and offers. "But we'll hoof it to the restaurant tonight. It's not far, and you'll see more that way."

Buir and I exchange flabbergasted looks as we follow Ghil along the sidewalk into the bustling metropolis up ahead. I can't help but stare at the people passing by dressed immaculately in iridescent jumpsuits. Their skin is eggshell flawless and the adults all appear to be a similar age. I haven't seen anyone who looks even close to my father's age.

A vast array of vendors line the sidewalks, but the businesses here are nothing like the makeshift stalls at the fueling port.

Elegant glass buildings rise to staggering heights in the sky, switching color and advertising flash sales and an ever-changing display of inventory at dizzying speeds. Tantalizing aromas of unidentifiable foods drift our way as we walk. My stomach rumbles in response and I quicken my pace.

I frown when we pass a sign for a dermal sculptor outside an elegant building, more understated than most. "What's a dermal sculptor?" I ask Ghil, as I scan the menu of services.

"Maintenance crew," he says with a grunt. "They keep you looking twenty-five for the rest of your life."

"So that's why everyone here looks so young." I read aloud to Buir and Ghil. "Facial reconfiguration, blemish removal: we'll rid you of your imperfections. Offering home visits for convenience. Discretion guaranteed." I laugh. "Anything you'd like to get rid of?"

Ghil throws me a pained look. "Yeah, hunger pangs."

"All right." I throw up my hands. "I'm coming."

Ghil takes us to a laid-back cafe on a side street that he assures us serves the best galactic tacos he's ever tasted. Neither Buir nor I have any idea what tacos are, but as soon as I bite into mine, I moan with pleasure. "Ghil, you've outdone yourself. I forgive you for the mush."

He stops chewing and stares at me for a minute as if he's trying to decide whether I'm serious or not.

"Come on, Ghil!" Buir pulls a humorous pout. "You've got to admit that your mush doesn't come close to this."

He shrugs and takes another bite of his taco. "Like I said, I ain't making any more for you lot anyway."

When we're done, we order an extra portion for Velkan, and

enough for breakfast for all of us, and then pay our bill using credits from my CipherSync. To my relief, it works flawlessly and we are free to leave without being arrested on our first night on Aristozonex. We exit the restaurant and make our way back toward the docking area, our stomachs bloated from our flavorful feast.

As we pass by the dermal sculptor, I glance at the sign again: *We'll rid you of your imperfections ... discretion guaranteed.*

And then a radical thought occurs to me.

Chapter 21

"You two go on ahead! See you back at the ship!" I call to Ghil and Buir before pushing open the door to the dermal sculptor.

Hypnotic music envelops me, luring me inside the foyer. My feet seem to bounce beneath me on some type of cushiony surface as I walk. Several cylindrical acrylic tubes filled with luminescent fish stretch all the way from the floor to the ceiling at various points throughout the space. Monochromatic lounge chairs in the seating area to my left float out from the white walls. A crisp, citrus fragrance wafts through the air as I make my way to the desk on the right side of the room, where a perfectly coiffed woman graces me with a flawless smile. "How may I be of assistance to you today?"

I open my mouth to respond, and quickly close it again. I study the woman for a moment, my heartbeat quickening. She's not just sculpted to look impossibly younger than her years; *she's an android.*

I narrow my eyes and stare at her from several angles to be sure. She gives a tight, condescending smile and casually brushes a strand of hair back from her face. "If you have any questions about our elite services, I would be happy to answer them for you."

I blink away my confusion and peer over her shoulder, hoping to spot another human being, but there's no one in sight. "Uh, yes. I'm interested in blemish removal."

"It would be my pleasure to assist you with that today."

"The home service," I add hastily.

"Of course." She smiles as she hands me a flat device. "Discretion is our specialty. Just fill out these details on the DigiPad to begin the process."

"It's not for me," I explain. "It's for a friend."

"I understand, just fill it out as best you can."

I sit down with the tablet and glance over the questions. I don't know the answers to most of them. I could guess at Velkan's height and weight, but as for where he was born, I don't have a clue. But then neither does he. I shrug and mark his birthplace down as Seinought, and fill in the rest of the blanks with whatever comes to mind, before handing it back to the receptionist.

She scans it and blinks up at me. "As your friend is interested in the home service you will need to fill out the address section," she says in a pleasantly chiding tone.

"I don't have a home address. We're docked at the port."

The android's left eyebrow shifts upward a fraction of an inch. "I'm afraid we don't offer home services on ships."

"The ship is our home."

The android assumes a neutral expression, the chip inside her head reciting from some pre-programmed script. "Syndicate law 5-07B8H2 states that dermal sculptors are not authorized to perform services on board foreign vessels."

"Why not?" I demand, barely able to contain my irritation.

She tilts her head at an annoying angle and smiles serenely at me. "I detect that you are frustrated and unnecessarily elevating your blood pressure. Please allow me to explain."

I briefly consider reaching for her head and pulling it off her neck, but I can't be sure it wouldn't trigger an alarm.

"It is a documented fact that unscrupulous renegades move among us," the android continues. "Some fugitives attempt to conceal their identity through dermal sculpting, and even serfs have been known to hire dermal sculptors to remove their holographic markings." She gives me a penetrating glare while carving her lips into an ambiguous smile.

My blood chills. Does she read minds too? Maybe I should have asked Velkan more about these androids. I dismiss the thought and steel myself for a fight. I need to escalate this beyond the standard script to accomplish what I came here for, and quickly. A human can always be bribed.

I lean my elbows on the counter and stick my face up close to hers. "Get me your boss, and make it snappy before I take that perfectly sculpted face of yours and melt it into something unrecognizable!"

"That won't be necessary," an icy voice calls from behind me.

I spin around and stare at the slender woman standing in an archway by the seating area, sleek hair pulled into a tight knot, a slash of red across her even tighter lips.

"I'm Doctor Azong. This is my practice."

"At last, a human," I say, walking up to her. "Your pre-programmed assistant is impossible to reason with. I need to procure your home services for a friend. We're docked here for the next few days."

"As my receptionist has already explained to you, it is a violation of Syndicate Law to perform dermal services on a foreign vessel," she says in a placating tone.

"I can't imagine you've never performed services on a ship before." I lower my voice. "*Discretion guaranteed.* Why else would a dermal sculptor set up shop on this end of town if not to service the ships?"

The doctor runs her eyes up and down me and twists her lips disapprovingly. "You don't look like you can afford my services."

"I like to be discrete too," I retort, holding her gaze.

"Come with me," she says, her tone all at once sharp and businesslike.

I glance at the android, imagining her eyes boring into me, but her head is bent.

Doctor Azong leads me through the archway, down a short hallway and into a small conference room. Instead of offering me a seat she presses something on the underside of the table. The wall behind it slides apart revealing a smaller office beyond. She ushers me inside and gestures to a chair before sitting down behind the desk.

"You're not my usual type of client." She leans back and lights up an herbal cigarette as the wall slides shut behind us. I frown and throw a nervous glance behind me. I don't like being trapped in this windowless space with a stranger.

"What's your usual type?" I ask.

She pulls down her scarlet mouth. "Older, male—for the most part. Fugitives seeking a new identity to reintegrate into

Syndicate life." She peers at me keenly. "Tell me about your *friend*."

A flush creeps over my cheeks. "He's a serf. He needs his holographic tattoo removed."

Doctor Azong takes a puff of her cigarette. "Why?"

My mind whirls as I make some snap decisions about what to share with her. Maybe we can pass Velkan off as Ghil's serf if she agrees to do the dermal sculpting. "He saved the crew's lives. The captain wants to give him his freedom as a reward."

Doctor Azong flashes me the kind of smile that's appropriate for a heartwarming story, but I can see by her eyes that she's busy calculating how much of what I said is true. "House visits are double my usual fees, ships are triple," she says after a long pause.

Relief cocoons me like a soft blanket. She doesn't believe my story, but she doesn't care. "Triple it is," I say, a tad breathlessly.

Doctor Azong stubs out her herbal cigarette. "You can pay my receptionist. She'll run half the credits up front, the balance to be paid once services are rendered."

"What's your fee?" I ask.

"Three-hundred thousand credits."

I shift uncomfortably in my seat. "I don't have that many credits—yet. I need to sell some cargo first."

Doctor Azong looks at me with a bored expression. "Come back when you have the money."

I run through my options in my head, reluctant to walk out of here without sealing the deal. There's no guarantee she'll even agree to it if I come back later. I can't take that risk. I fumble inside my tunic and pull out a small nugget of dargonite. I clutch it in my hand for a moment or two, weighing my decision. After seeing how Roma reacted, I'm not sure it's a wise move. But what choice do I have if I want to help Velkan? Slowly, I stretch out my hand and set the nugget of dargonite on the table between us. "I can give you your money—just in a different currency."

Her eyes widen and gleam like a predator going into stealth mode. She flicks a burning glance my way and then reaches for the nugget and turns it over in her hand. "Is this what I think it is?" she asks, arching an accusing brow.

My pulse drums against my temples. I lean toward her, hoping the gleam in her eye was greed. "Dargonite. That nugget alone is worth ten times three-hundred thousand credits."

She pulls out a laser loupe and studies the nugget intently. "How much do you have?"

"None of your business."

She drums her fingers impatiently on the desk between us. "You'll never be able to sell it on Aristozonex without contacts. I could help you."

I narrow my eyes at her. "All you need to concern yourself with is performing the services I'm hiring you for."

She stares at me for a long moment, as if weighing up how far she can push me, and then closes her fist over the dargonite. "All right. Here's how it will go down. Fill out a maintenance request slip for a new turbo pump and turn it in at the dock. I'll arrive in a maintenance van—my mobile sculpting unit—early tomorrow morning. I'll drive right into your cargo bay so clear a space for me. Your friend better be there. We only get one shot at this, so don't screw up."

I nod, dizzy with elation. "Thank you," I mutter, sinking back into the chair. I went with my gut on this one and it paid off. Not only is everything about to change for Velkan, but Sarth was right about the dargonite only increasing the interest of buyers now that it's a dark market item. We shouldn't have much trouble selling our supply.

"You love this serf, don't you?" Doctor Azong peers at me through half-slit eyes.

"Excuse me?" I say, flummoxed.

A smile tugs at her lips. "I could have been a Syndicate undercover officer for all you knew, and yet you came in here and risked your freedom—your life even—to help your *friend*."

I glower at her. "What's it to you?"

She laughs. "Prickly little thing, aren't you?"

I open my mouth to snap back but decide against it. I don't want to risk souring the deal. Anyway, what would I be defending? Maybe I am in love with Velkan. I push out my chair and stand. "I'll see you in the morning."

Doctor Azong gets to her feet and escorts me back out to the reception area before taking her leave. The android receptionist looks up and blinks in my direction. "I trust we answered all your questions to your satisfaction. Please don't hesitate—"

I hurry out the door before she finishes her spiel, disinclined to engage in any more small talk with an irritating android.

I walk back to the docking station with a spring in my step. We've only been on Aristozonex a few hours, and I've already found a way to help Velkan, and successfully negotiated a deal involving dargonite. We won't be needing Sarth after all.

Once I pass through the security gate, I check in with the port authority and fill out a maintenance request slip as directed. Then I head back across the dock to the Zebulux.

Buir's eyes widen with relief when I enter the cargo bay.

"Where were you?" Velkan demands.

I grab him by the shoulders and smile up at him. "Making my first deal on Aristozonex. I found a dermal sculptor to remove your holographic tattoo."

His brows flick upward. "They know I'm a serf?"

"A nugget of dargonite goes a long way."

Velkan shakes his head. "No wonder Buir and Ghil were so tight-lipped about what you were doing. Is he coming to the ship to perform the procedure?"

"*She*. Doctor Azong. She'll be here in the morning disguised as a maintenance worker—obviously, this isn't the first time she's performed illegal sculpting services on ships."

Ghil narrows his eyes at me. "Who did you tell her Velkan's owner was?"

I tell him the whole story, beginning with the android receptionist who freaked me out so much I considered terminating her. "Doctor Azong specializes in fugitive transformations," I add. "Maybe you should think about it, Ghil. We've got the credits now."

He folds his arms across his chest and frowns. "I'm used to my ugly mug."

"At least talk to her about it," I say. "You could ditch the black beanie."

I barely sleep through the long watches of the night, knowing that tomorrow Velkan will become a free man, free to love me on and off this ship. Free to move openly through the Syndicate. My heart pounds with excitement. I rise before anyone else and grab a cold taco from the galley before heading down to the cargo bay and opening the door. I sit down on a crate to wait for Doctor Azong and take a bite of my taco. Even cold, the flavors are equally as mouthwatering as I remember them from the previous night. I chomp down on another bite just as Velkan appears at the top of the stairwell clutching another cold taco. We burst out laughing. He jogs down the steps, sets his taco aside, and takes me in his arms. "Thank you," he whispers in my ear.

I reach up and wave my fingers through the holographic tattoo projecting from the side of his neck. "It could have been me," I say. "Do you ever wonder why some suffer a fate that others escape?"

A troubled look flits across Velkan's face. "Only those who escape a fate such as mine have the luxury of asking why."

I drop my gaze, struck by the truth of his words. My life of ease has bought me much education and many hours to contemplate it. My thoughts drift to Cwelt and my parents. I miss them. They'll be safe in the underground caves for now, but if I don't return in the next month or two, their fate at the hands of the Maulers is sealed.

The humming of a machine startles me out of my reverie. "That must be her!" I say to Velkan.

We jump up just as a large white beetle-like vehicle zips up the docking ramp and into the cargo bay. The lettering on the side reads *Azong Mechanics & Maintenance*. A moment later, Doctor Azong and two men climb out, all dressed in mechanic's jumpsuits.

"Close up the cargo door," Doctor Azong says, sharply.

Velkan raises his brows at me but walks quietly over to the control pad.

"You didn't mention bringing anyone with you." I gesture to the men standing by the vehicle, faces set like flint. "Who are they?"

"My assistants," she replies, watching the cargo door close. As soon as it's sealed, she inclines her head to the men. They reach inside the maintenance vehicle and turn to face us. I gasp when I see the red dots from their laser guns lined up across Velkan's forehead.

Chapter 22

"What do you want?" I cry out.

Doctor Azong smiles serenely at me. "I'm an expert at sniffing out weakness. As lovesick as you are, I've no doubt you'd rather die yourself than see anything happen to the serf."

I throw a desperate glance at Velkan.

"Where's the dargonite?" Doctor Azong's eyes pierce me like steel.

I glare back at her, determined not to show weakness again, even though I'm trembling inside with rage and frustration. I shouldn't have been so trusting. Her reaction when she saw the dargonite was warning enough that she had an unhealthy interest in it, but I was so caught up in the excitement of helping Velkan that I ignored it. "I already paid you ten times over," I retort. "Unless you came here to perform the service I purchased, you need to leave."

"Search the ship!" Doctor Azong orders her men. One of them breaks away and marches mechanically toward the stairwell. I shrink back in horror when he passes by me. *An android!*

"So that's how you keep your dirty dealings secret," I say, turning back to Doctor Azong. "You don't employ humans."

"Human's lips flap too much." She gives me a thin smile. "I prefer to write the scripts and androids like being told what to do—the perfect working relationship."

I sneak another glance across at Velkan. One lone laser dot glows in the center of his forehead. I've no doubt of the accuracy of the android's aim. I don't dare try anything rash.

"Move it!" Doctor Azong gestures to the stairwell.

Velkan and I exchange guarded looks before heading toward the stairs. Doctor Azong and the remaining android fall in behind us. I'm worried about Ghil and Buir. They have no idea what's going on down here. If Ghil encounters the android he might try to fight it—feisty as he is—and end up dead, which doesn't bode well for Buir.

When we reach the top of the stairs, I turn to Doctor Azong. "Where to?"

She arches a brow. "Take me to your captain. Maybe he'll be more cooperative."

I lead the way down the utility hallway to the communal area, my feet heavy as boulders. If Ghil is inside, I have to warn him not to charge the android accompanying us. When the door slides open, I tentatively peer around it. My eyes bulge and I repress a gasp. A decapitated android is slumped over on the floor by the dining tables. Ghil puts a finger to his lips and then beckons me inside. I give a subtle nod.

"He's here," I call to Doctor Azong.

"Step aside." She motions to the android to follow her. Seconds later, Buir's piercing shriek electrocutes my ears. I rush inside just as the second android crumples to the floor. Buir peers out from the galley, one hand clapped over her mouth. The android's head rolls listlessly to a halt under a table. Ghil holds a knife to Doctor Azong's throat. "This your dermal sculptor?" he growls.

I grimace. "Turns out she engages in more than illegal dermal sculpting services when the price is right."

"She came here for the rest of the dargonite," Velkan explains.

Ghil shoves her down on a bench. "Are you even a doctor?"

She flashes him a venomous look. "Of course, I'm a doctor. You can't operate a business on Aristozonex without legitimate qualifications."

Ghil eyes her skeptically. "If you're running a bogus ship maintenance business on the side, I'm willing to bet you're not making your money sculpting. You're moving dark market cargo through Aristozonex."

Doctor Azong tightens her lips.

"All the answer I need." Ghil scowls. "The question now is what are we going to do with you?"

"First," I say, glaring at Doctor Azong, "we're going to put her to work doing what we paid her to do. And as penance for this stunt she pulled she can throw in a complimentary facial reconfiguration for you, Ghil."

He shakes his head vehemently. "Don't trust her. I'm not letting her anywhere near me with a knife."

"I'm not a butcher," Doctor Azong says, sounding exasperated. "Dermal sculpting is a robotic laser procedure. The face is partially dissolved and remolded during the process."

Ghil grunts. "Don't matter."

"She has no choice but to cooperate now," I say. "Unless she wants to leave this ship in the back of her maintenance van, piled up with her androids' corpses, she'll perform whatever procedures we tell her to."

Ghil nods to Velkan. "You first."

"Does it hurt?" Velkan looks directly at Doctor Azong.

She gives a quick shake of her head. "Your pain receptors will be in a state of deep freeze during the procedure. You won't feel a thing."

"If anything happens to him, you won't leave here alive," I say.

Her cheek twitches once, but her glacial eyes betray no emotion. "My sculpting record is flawless."

"Good, let's begin then," I reply.

Ghil turns to Buir. "You go with them, I'll clean this place up."

Buir gives a grateful nod and steps gingerly around the headless androids.

Ghil picks up a laser gun and hands it to me. "Just in case."

I point it at Doctor Azong and gesture for her to exit the room first. Velkan follows, and I bring up the rear with Buir.

"Do you think androids feel pain?" Buir whispers to me.

"Of course not. They shut down the instant Ghil cut their wiring."

Buir sighs softly. "It was a horrible way to go."

"Ghil did what he had to do," I say. "If he hadn't, we'd all be dead by now."

Back downstairs in the cargo bay, Doctor Azong moves swiftly into professional mode. She opens the back of her van to reveal a gleaming gurney surrounded by a dazzling array of unfamiliar equipment. She reaches inside and dons an electronic full face mask with robotic eyes and then gestures to Velkan to lie down on the gurney. "On your right side," she instructs him.

Buir and I watch from outside the van. I squeeze her arm, a mixture of apprehension and excitement tingling through me. "I can't believe this is really happening."

Doctor Azong pulls an overhead light into position and settles down in front of a row of screens.

"What are you doing?" I ask.

"Capturing the 4D image of the holographic tattoo and then programming the laser to extract it at the right depth. After that, it will simply be a matter of touching up the wound with regenerated cells. In a couple of hours, you won't even see a mark."

"Doing okay, Velkan?" I call to him.

He lets out an exaggerated yawn. "Just trying to nap, if everyone would quit hollering."

I give a nervous laugh. He's way more relaxed about the procedure than I am.

Ghil appears at the top of the stairs dragging the decapitated bodies of the two androids. He yanks them unceremoniously down the steps and tosses them in a heap a short distance from the van. "I'll load them up inside once she's done. She can take her trash with her." He disappears back up the stairs and returns a few minutes later with the heads.

Buir shudders and backs away from the pile of android remains. "I know they're not human, but they seemed so real. That's what makes it disturbing."

Ghil shoots her a sympathetic look. "You can wait up in the galley with me if you want. I don't need to see Velkan go under the laser."

"I'm a good nurse." Buir tweaks a smile. "Not much of a mortician. I'll stay here in case Trattora needs me."

Ghil nods and heads back up the stairs.

Doctor Azong spends the next thirty minutes adjusting images and running calculations on her screens before turning on the robotic laser. My gut churns with renewed doubt. What if she's not as good as she says she is? What if she botches this completely and severs an artery? My emotions rise and fall as the minutes tick by and the faint humming of the laser grows more invasive in my mind.

After a while, Buir curls up on a nearby tarp and closes her eyes. I sit down on a crate and finger the laser gun Ghil gave me, toying with conflicting thoughts ranging from berating myself for ever going into Doctor Azong's practice in the first place to picturing a free Velkan at my side as Cwelt's High Husband.

"The procedure is finished." Doctor Azong pulls off her mask and rubs her eyes.

I jump to my feet and hurry over to the van. Velkan sits up on the gurney. I stare in disbelief at the left side of his neck. *Flawless*, not even a patch of discolored skin betrays the fact that he wore an implanted holographic serf tattoo for most of his life.

"It's gone!" I whisper to him.

He rubs his hand over his neck, frowning. "Doesn't feel any different."

I look around for a mirror and then pull one down from the ceiling on an adjustable arm.

Velkan stares into it, twisting his head from one side to the other as if he's afraid the tattoo has simply moved. His lip trembles. I choke up inside at the sight. It's dawning on him that he is truly free at last, no longer marked as a serf and no longer condemned to a life of slavery at the mercy of his owner. Tears glisten in his eyes. "You took a huge risk for me, Trattora. Now that I'm free, I'm going to help you trace our bracelets and liberate Cwelt."

I nod, blinking back my own tears.

"You did a good job," I say to Doctor Azong, begrudgingly. "I'll get Ghil to come down here now. Maybe this will persuade him to trust you with his face."

Ghil is equally as impressed with the removal of Velkan's tattoo as the rest of us, but still wary of undergoing the more involved facial reconfiguration required to permanently alter his appearance.

Doctor Azong shrugs. "In that case, I can give you some lenses to fool any optical scanners that pick you up—a temporary fix, they won't last long."

Ghil takes the box she hands him and stuffs it into his pocket.

"I'll give it some thought," he says, gruffly, before walking over to drag the androids inside the van. "In the meantime, I reckon we should ask Doctor Azong to tell us more about her connections in the dark market so we can unload that dargonite."

Doctor Azong darts a glance to me and then back to Ghil again. "I can find you a buyer. Dargonite is a hot commodity right now."

"How can we trust you not to betray us to Minders?" I ask.

"What would I tell them?" She arches a reproving brow at me. "That you killed my androids while I was conducting a search for dargonite on board the ship I was performing an illegal dermal sculpting procedure on?"

Ghil rubs his jaw thoughtfully. "If you set up a deal for us, we'll cut you in at five percent."

Her eyes glint greedily. "Five percent of how much?"

Ghil's face hardens. "Of more than you know what to do with. Take it or leave it."

She gives a sharp laugh. "Give me a couple of days and I'll see what I can come up with."

Quick as a flash, the blade of Ghil's knife is under her chin. He moves it higher until her head tilts back and he is looking into her dark eyes. "You have until tomorrow morning by ten. Double cross us again and next time your head will roll."

Fear ripples across her flawless features. She gives a shaky nod.

"Now get back in your van and take your wretched robot mob to recycling."

Velkan opens the front door and gestures to her to climb in. I cast an admiring glance at him. Even his stance seems different to me somehow; he's holding himself like a free man, with a sense of dignity that is lost to those held too long in servitude.

After Doctor Azong's van exits through the security gate and disappears down the street, we gather around in the cargo bay to discuss our next move.

"We can't do much of anything until we cash in that dargonite," Ghil says. "We'll have to wait and see if Doctor Azong comes through for us."

"We have some time to kill before then," I say. "I want to

track down that address Roma gave me for the pawn emporium."

"And we still need to shop for clothes," Buir reminds me.

Velkan and Ghil exchange discomfited looks.

"She's right." I run a critical eye over them. "You can't walk around Aristozonex in grease-stained overalls. We need to look the part."

"What part is that exactly?" Ghil asks.

"Wealthy traders," I reply. "That's what we'll be before too long, so we might as well practice. Come on, let's *all* go into town." I hand Velkan the new CipherSync Sarth got for me. "This is yours now."

Our first stop is at a glittering clothing mall where we step inside full body scanners that zap our measurements and then ply us with a digital catalog of iridescent skintight jumpsuits and matching BodPaks—body-hugging pouches of various shapes and sizes for carrying personal items around in. I stare in bewilderment at the array of options to choose from.

"Are you seeing this?" Buir says. "Some of these suits monitor blood pressure, temperature, even emotions. And this one cools or heats according to your body's requirements."

"I'm still stuck on the prices. One suit each," I stress. "I don't have that many credits on my CipherSync."

Ghil grunts and pulls up his sleeve to consult his own CipherSync. "I can help. Been putting a bit away here and there." He turns to Buir, somewhat flustered. "Get what you want."

She smiles back at him. "Thank you, Ghil, that's very generous of you."

We end up purchasing three outfits each, figuring that should be enough to tide us over for a few meetings with prospective buyers, and anything else we need to look presentable for. I stash my bracelet, along with my dargonite, in my new BodPak. I can't hide anything under a skintight jumpsuit.

"All right," I say, when we head back out into the street all decked out in our strange new outfits and coordinating BodPaks. "Now we need to figure out how to track down that address."

Ghil raises his hand and hails a driverless vehicle. "The LevCab will take us there."

When we climb in, he peers at the address displayed on my CipherSync and reads it aloud to the vehicle.

"Locating tango, thirty-nine, alpha, victor, zero," an electronic voice chimes out. "Destination set. The Syndicate invites you to sit back and enjoy your journey."

I stare transfixed through the tinted window as we rise above the pristine inhabitants of Aristozonex strolling in and out of the dazzling store fronts and elegant eateries lining the streets. Health centers proclaiming the rejuvenating benefits of their heliospheric services, and casinos offering the chance to rack up millions of credits in celestial blackjack, loom large on every corner. Opulent hotels advertising rooftop bioluminescent pools and rapid drone transportation to the theater district are scattered throughout. Students stream out of a large EduPlex, clutching DigiPads and chatting to one another.

All too soon the electronic voice announces, "You have arrived safely at your destination, courtesy of the Syndicate."

"Looks kind of high end for a pawn emporium," Velkan remarks, climbing out of the LevCab.

"There are plenty of casinos here," Buir points out. "I bet the pawn business makes good money."

Ghil snorts. "That's 'cause gambling's about the only thing left on Aristozonex that involves risk."

"I might be able to get more information if I go in alone," I say. "Why don't you wait for me at that cafe across the street?"

Velkan frowns. "Sure you don't want me to come along?"

"Let's see how I do on my own first."

Inside the pawn emporium, I glance around at the vast array of jewelry, relics, clothing and antiques. A hologram overhead boasts wares from every planet in the Syndicate, and beyond. I make my way to the back of the store, feigning interest in various items along the way until I reach a jewelry counter. I lean over the glass and scan the contents displayed inside on the off chance that I'll spot a bracelet like mine.

"Can I be of assistance?" a young woman with a shiny black bob and a heavy fringe that frames sharp eyes asks.

"Yes." I smile broadly at her. "Roma sent me."

The woman curls one brow upward and looks me over with an air of mild surprise. Despite her flawless skin, her unfortunate combination of features fail to complement each other; eyes too far apart, pinched nose too narrow above her pale lips. "I'll fetch my father," she says.

My heart beats a little faster. Evidently, *Roma* is code for something more important than your average transaction. My palms begin to sweat and I sense my new jumpsuit adjusting temperature to compensate. I could have used one of these out hunting on cold days in Cwelt—much more practical than a shamskin.

A burly man with a goatee and dramatically arched black brows walks up to me. "I'm Stefanov," he says with a quick curve of his lips. "I understand Roma sent you."

"Yes, she said you might have some information for me about a bracelet." I pull out the chain from my BodPak and hold the bracelet out for him to see.

He pulls a laser loupe out of his pocket and examines it from several angles before straightening up. "It's a fascinating piece, I'll give you that. No Syndicate stamp, so it wasn't crafted on Aristozonex or any of the other Syndicate planets."

"Roma mentioned you sold one just like it a few months back."

His eyebrows peak and he folds his fingers in front of him. "It was exactly the same, except for the name engraved on it."

"What was the name?" I ask, breathlessly.

"It was unusual, I remember that." He pulls out a DigiPad and scrolls through it. "Here it is, *Ayma*."

My heart thumps so hard it hurts. The name means nothing to me of course, but somehow Ayma is connected to my past, like Velkan. "Can you give me the seller's address? I'd like to find out more about the origin of my bracelet."

Stefanov purses his lips. "I'm afraid an address won't do you any good."

"Why not?"

He looks at me with a bemused expression. "The bracelet was stolen."

Chapter 23

"You mean ... the person who sold it to you stole it?" Hope deflates faster than I can catch a breath.

Stefanov shrugs. "It looked legit at the time, but it showed up on the hot list a few hours after I bought it."

Everything inside me shrivels. How can I possibly trace a stolen bracelet on Aristozonex? It was naive of me to think this was ever going to be as simple as asking for an address. I run my fingers over my temples trying to figure out some way to trace the bracelet back to its owner. "Tell me about the hot list. How does it work?"

"As soon as someone logs a theft on their CipherSync, the item is uploaded to the hot list on the stellarsphere and distributed to Minder Depots everywhere."

"So, the Minders would have an address for whoever logged the theft?" I say.

Stefanov tweaks an eyebrow upward. "They won't divulge that kind of information."

"They might if the price is right."

Stefanov narrows his eyes at me. "You couldn't even afford to pay Roma her asking fee. You certainly won't be able to afford to bribe a Minder."

I take a step toward him and lower my voice. "And what if I've come into a small fortune since I saw Roma?"

His eyes glint as he processes my words. "All the credits in the galaxy won't do you any good if you don't know which Minders can be bribed. There are those so loyal to the Syndicate, they wouldn't flinch if you offered them five hundred thousand credits."

"How about a million?"

Stefanov rubs his thumb meticulously over his goatee for a moment or two. "I may have a contact." He flicks a glance over at his daughter who is busy assisting a customer. He lowers his voice. "But that kind of information is expensive."

"How much?"

"Two hundred thousand credits."

I hesitate, not because I can't afford it, but because I know I'm being ripped off. But I'm desperate to get my hands on the information. And being desperate makes me susceptible to an outlandish deal. "Done," I say, in a resigned tone.

Stefanov's lips twitch into a satisfied smile that doesn't add any warmth to his eyes. "Naturally, payment is expected up front."

I give a curt nod and slip my hand inside my BodPak. My fist closes around a nugget of dargonite. "Do you have someplace private where we can complete the transaction?"

He laughs. "Is your CipherSync on the hot list too?"

"No." I pull out my fist and open it a crack in front of him. "But this is."

His eyebrows rise into two stiff peaks. "Follow me." He turns abruptly and leads me through the back of the pawn emporium and into an elevachute. We descend several floors into a basement of sorts and walk along a dark passageway to an unmarked doorway. Stefanov keys a combination into the control pad and gestures me inside. The door slides shut behind us with an ominous click. I'm trapped in another windowless room with a stranger for the second time in twenty-four hours. I only hope I've made the right decision this time. My heart keeps racing ahead of my brain, and I've not been as cautious as I should be.

"Let me see that dargonite," Stefanov says.

I hand over the nugget and shift from one foot to the other while he examines it under a large magnifier and composition analyzer. "It's the real deal," he pronounces after a few minutes. He sinks down in a chair and holds the nugget out in front of him as if scarcely believing what he's seeing. "Never held a nugget of dargonite before. Where did you steal this from?"

I open my mouth to protest but catch myself just in time. Maybe it's better he believes that for now. "Some place far from here. And it's worth a lot more than two hundred thousand credits. So now that you've verified its authenticity, I need the name and address of a Minder who can get me the information I need."

Stefanov tightens his fingers around the nugget. "How much dargonite do you have?"

I hesitate, reluctant to give away too much. "Enough to pay the Minder."

"Risky to offer him dargonite." Stefanov pins me with a

penetrating gaze. "And unnecessary. I can front the costs of bribing him with credits if you are willing to give me another nugget as collateral. I know people who would be very interested in paying market value for it."

I chew on my lip, mulling over the offer. It probably isn't wise to alert a Minder, even if he is dirty, to the fact that I have dargonite in my possession. And I can't entirely trust Doctor Azong to come through for us. I like the idea of Stefanov lining up a second potential buyer, but I don't trust him either.

"All right." I push another nugget of dargonite toward him. "But I want to meet your buyer and be in on the negotiations."

Stefanov gets to his feet. "Meet me back here tomorrow night. Come alone."

"And the information on the Minder?"

"His name's Brivardo." Stefanov consults his CipherSync. "I'll transfer the contact information right away and let him know to expect you within the next hour or two."

I pull up my sleeve and set my CipherSync to receive mode.

Stefanov eyes my device disparagingly. "Antiquated for someone flush with dargonite."

I glare at him. "I can't shop with nuggets."

He holds his palms out apologetically. "I simply meant that we carry an excellent selection of newer models if you're interested."

I consider it briefly, but it's dicey buying something that Stefanov could potentially fit with a tracking device that would lead him straight to our ship. Once we unload the dargonite, we can upgrade everything, including our weapons, with state-of-the-art replacements. "Thanks, but after our deal goes down I intend to hit the high-end shopping district. I'm sure you understand."

Stefanov lets out a chortle. "Just don't spend it so fast that you come crawling back to the pawn emporium trying to cash in your purchases."

Once he finishes transferring the credits and the contact information for the Minder, he takes me back upstairs and escorts me to the door. "If you're late tomorrow night, the deal's off. I get skittish easily."

"I'll be here," I say.

I feel his eyes burning a hole in my back as I cross the street to the cafe where the others are waiting.

Velkan half rises out of his seat, his eyes searching mine.

"Well?" Ghil demands.

"It's complicated." I pull up a chair. "And I'm parched from all that negotiating."

"Here, try this." Buir pushes her drink across the table to me. "If you like it, I'll order another one."

I take a sip and gasp. It's sweet and velvety, but with a kick that sends a spark through me and sharpens my mind instantly.

"What is this stuff?" I ask, peering into the glass.

"Elektra Chai," Buir says. "Full of revitalizing ions."

"If you think that's good, you should try my Molten Mocha for a volcanic energy surge." Velkan tilts his mug and peers into it. "Actually, only the dregs are left. You'll need to order your own." He grins at me, tossing his hair over his shoulder. "I can vouch for it."

Ghil waves a dismissive hand. "Forget those fancy-pants drinks. Order yourself a Propulsion Expresso. You'll be fully charged for three straight days."

I shake my head. "All right, I'll try one of each. Now let me bring you up to speed on what happened in the pawn emporium."

"Go ahead," Ghil says, entering my order on the digital interface at our table.

"The owner is a man called Stefanov. He says he sold a bracelet just like mine a few months back. Problem is, it showed up on a hot list of stolen items so he doesn't have an address for the owner."

Velkan groans. "We actually get a lead and then it goes nowhere."

"Not so fast," I say. "The person who reported it stolen had to log an address in the Syndicate database for the Minders' investigation."

"No! Absolutely not." Ghil pulls self-consciously at the cap covering his ears and forehead. "We're not involving Minders." He glances over his shoulder and then turns back to me. "I'm a fugitive here, remember?"

"Stefanov gave me the name of a Minder who can be bribed," I say. "And he loaded my CipherSync with credits. I'll handle the negotiations. You don't have to show your face."

A refreshment drone delivers my drinks to the table. I take a sip of the Molten Mocha first and gasp, giddy with the sensations on my tongue and darting through my bloodstream.

"I don't know," Ghil says. "If there's one thing I've learned about crooks, it's that if you can buy them, so can everyone else. What if this Minder sells us out?"

"The Syndicate isn't paying him much if he's supplementing his income with crime. He'll go with the highest bidder," I say. "And that would be us."

Ghil takes a swig of his expresso and lets out a guttural sigh. "Let's hope you're right about him not ratting us out. If the Syndicate finds out you tried to bribe a Minder, we'll be on the next ship to the penal colonies."

I lean across the table. "They're not going to find out. No one can resist the lure of dargonite."

Ghil throws me a disgruntled look. "Well, you're about to put that theory to the test."

Velkan turns to me. "I'll go with you to the Minder Depot."

I shake my head. "Stefanov told his contact I would be alone. I don't want him getting spooked and backing out."

"Send me the depot address." Ghil taps on his CipherSync.

Velkan furrows his brow. "If you're not back in two hours, I'm coming after you."

I transfer the address to Ghil's CipherSync and then take a quick swig of my Propulsion Expresso. My eyes bulge. Every nerve ending tingles and heat rushes through my limbs. "How do you drink that stuff, Ghil?" I gasp.

He shakes his head and reaches for the mug. "Swirl and swallow. Nothing to it."

"In that case, you can have mine too." I get to my feet. "See you all back on board."

I hail a LevCab and read out the address Stefanov gave me. An electronic voice repeats my destination and then the LevCab elevates above the city streets and proceeds along a laser lit path tunneling through oval openings in high rise buildings thousands of feet tall. Fifteen minutes later, we pull up outside a smoked glass building wrapped in the Syndicate flaming planet insignia. I swallow hard and walk purposefully through the foreboding entry. I smile with relief at the human behind the counter. Interesting that they don't employ androids for the position. Probably too much risk of someone overriding their chips and infiltrating the Minder Depot. "I'm here to see Minder Brivardo," I say, eying the woman's name tag, *Minder Clerk Daphnist*.

"Do you have an appointment?" she asks.

"No, it's a personal matter. I was hoping he could spare me a few minutes."

A faintly irritated expression comes over the clerk's face. "I'm afraid you'll need to make an appointment."

"Tell him Stefanov sent me."

The clerk tightens her lips and then activates her CipherSync. "Minder Brivardo, there's a woman here to see you without an appointment. She says Stefanov sent her." She listens for a few seconds. Her brow furrows. "Yes, absolutely."

The clerk gets to her feet and buzzes me through the security door. "Follow me, please."

She leads me down a corridor and gestures me into a brightly lit office at the rear of the building. "Wait here. Minder Brivardo will be with you shortly."

Minutes later, a spindly man with an overly-chiseled jaw that doesn't match his paltry physique pads into the room.

I get to my feet and he motions to me impatiently. "Sit. Sit. What can I do for you?"

I smile coyly at him. "Thank you for seeing me Minder Brivardo."

"Stefanov sent you?" He peers at me expectantly.

I nod. "I need some information."

He taps the tips of his fingers together, his eyes darting around the room. "What kind of information?"

I pull out my chain. "A bracelet like this was reported stolen a few months ago." I pause, and let out a heavy sigh. "It belonged to an old friend of mine. We lost contact a long time ago. I would do anything to find her again. When I saw the bracelet on the hot list, I knew right—"

Minder Brivardo makes an irritating clucking sound. "Save your spiel. I don't care why you want the information. I keep telling Stefanov this isn't worth it anymore for the pittance he pays me. I take a huge risk every time I access confidential files. The Syndicate sent a record number of people to the penal colonies on the outer rim last month. And for lesser crimes than selling personal information. I can't help you."

"Forget Stefanov." I look him straight in the eye. "I can afford to compensate you well."

His eyes gleam with an interest that wasn't there a moment earlier. "How well?"

"Five hundred thousand credits."

He snatches up a tissue from a dispenser on his desk and mops his forehead.

I lean forward in my chair. "Or one million credits if I walk out with the information now."

Chapter 24

A charged silence fills the room. I can tell by the quiver of Minder Brivardo's nostrils that he's processing the enormity of what I offered him, and weighing it against the risks involved. It doesn't take him long to come to a decision.

"Wait here." He gets to his feet. "I'll see what I can do."

As the minutes drag by without any sign of him returning, a thread of unease weaves its way into my thoughts. What if he turns me in after all? What if Stefanov misjudged his allegiance to the Syndicate? Or maybe Stefanov gets a cut for turning over criminals to him. My heart begins to race. Just when I've convinced myself I should leave before I'm arrested, the door slides open.

Minder Brivardo slips inside and the door closes again behind him. He beckons impatiently with his fingers. "Turn on your CipherSync. I have an address."

I activate receive mode. "Is it far from here?"

He hefts a brow upward. "Might as well be on the next planet. You won't get near it without security clearance."

I frown. "Why's that?"

"Your friend lives in the Syndicate military quadrant."

I run a hand through my hair digesting this new information. This is a complication I didn't anticipate. And one I have no idea how to address.

"And before you ask about falsified military clearance," Minder Brivardo says, raising one hand up to me. "I don't touch that. You're on your own." He peers at his CipherSync and then looks up, eyes gleaming. "The address information went through. You can transfer the credits now."

I nod and tap the screen on my CipherSync to activate the transfer.

Minder Brivardo wets his lips and stares hungrily at his own CipherSync. Moments later, a voracious smile spreads across his face. "Excellent. The address I gave you will disappear from your tablet after an hour. And remember, this conversation never happened."

I smile across at him. "So long as *you* remember that if your information is bad, I'll be back to pick up this conversation where we left off. Beginning with the part where you told me you'll be sent to a penal colony if the Syndicate finds out you're siphoning information out of their system and selling it to the highest bidder."

Minder Brivardo pales. "You need to leave now."

I incline my head slightly. "Thank you for your time. It was most enlightening." I exit the room, leaving a jittery-looking Brivardo to wonder if Stefanov really sent me at all.

By the time I arrive back at the Zebulux, the deep, orange glow of evening has settled over the ship and pinpricks of starlight dot the sky. I make my way inside and close up the cargo bay before heading upstairs to the dining room.

The others are gathered around the table finishing a meal, which I can tell by a fleeting glance was definitely not one of Ghil's concoctions.

"Did you get the address?" Buir asks.

"Yes." I sink heavily down on the bench next to Velkan.

"What's wrong?" He frowns at me.

I rub my face wearily. "The address is in the Syndicate military quadrant. We can't get in there without security clearance."

Ghil shakes his head. "We aren't even going to try. The Supreme Leader lives in the military quadrant. It's the most heavily fortified area on Aristozonex."

"So now what?" Buir asks.

"Maybe we can't get in," I say. "But the inhabitants have to come out at some point."

"What good does that do us?" Velkan asks. "We don't know who we're looking for."

"Actually, we do." I look around at the others. "Stefanov told me there was a name engraved on the bracelet, *Ayma*."

Ghil throws me a skeptical look. "Brilliant, all we have to do is accost everyone leaving the military quadrant and ask them if they're Ayma." He throws up his hands in disgust.

"We won't be accosting anyone," I say. "We'll figure it out by a process of elimination."

"And how does that work exactly?" Ghil grumbles.

"For starters, Ayma is likely a female name because it ends in the letter "A," like my name. My guess is she's around my age, as she has a bracelet just like mine and Velkan's—and if that's the case, she attends the EduPlex. That's where we need to go to find her."

Velkan folds his arms across his chest and considers it. "Might be worth a try. We have nothing better to do anyway while we're waiting on Doctor Azong or Stefanov to find us a buyer."

"We don't all need to go to the EduPlex," I say. "I don't want to scare her off. You and Ghil can stay here in case Doctor Azong or Stefanov try to make contact. I'll take Buir with me."

Ghil shrugs. "I'm too old to pass myself off as a student anyway."

I give a sheepish grin. "Maybe with a little dermal sculpting …"

He laughs and gets to his feet. "I'm off to bed. Tomorrow's a big day." He winks as he disappears out the door. "Got to look good for our buyers."

Early the next morning, Buir and I hail a LevCab and direct it to take us to the EduPlex. There are already a few teenagers milling around on the sloping lawn outside the imposing glass building by the time we get there. To my dismay, they are wearing a uniform of electric blue jumpsuits with the EduPlex insignia across the back. "We won't be able to go inside unless we can find some way to blend in," I say to Buir.

"Maybe we won't need to," she replies. "Let's ask those students if they know anyone called Ayma."

I half-raise my hand to splay it in greeting before I catch myself. Instead, I walk casually over and plaster on a smile. "Do any of you know Ayma, by chance?" I ask them. "She left her CipherSync at a cafe around the corner."

The students exchange a loaded look. The taller one raises a skeptical brow at me. "One of her security detail would have picked it up if she'd left something behind. Can't be hers."

"So you do know her?" I ask, trying to temper my excitement.

The teenager narrows his eyes at me. "Everyone knows Ayma."

"We're visiting traders," Buir pipes up. She smiles coyly at the teenager. "The address on the CipherSync is in the military quadrant."

The teenager gives a quick shrug. "Yeah, that's where she lives. She should be pulling up here anytime." He points to the curb. "Over there, she has a reserved spot."

Right on cue, a sleek, charcoal LevAuto hovers around the corner and settles silently into the designated spot. A tall olive-skinned man steps out, scans the area, and then adjusts his CipherSync before communicating something to another party. The side door slides upward and into the roof of the car. A girl around my age steps out, her glistening ebony ponytail swinging to and fro. Her eyes scour the grassy banks in front of the EduPlex. A moment later, her face lights up and she waves at a blonde girl who jumps up and walks toward her.

I take a breath and step between them. "Ayma," I begin.

Powerful arms grip my shoulders and haul me to one side. "Who are you?" the olive-skinned man demands. "I've never seen you here before."

"I'm new." I wriggle out from his grip and dart back over to Ayma, yanking my bracelet out from my BodSak. "Do you recognize this?" I manage to blurt out before I'm zapped and pinned to the ground. Buir screams and dashes over.

I glance up at Ayma, wincing at the pain in my left arm, still clutching my bracelet. "You had one just like it," I gasp. "It was stolen."

Ayma's intense, violet-blue eyes widen. "Let her go, Warrion." She fastens a look on me that says if I step out of line, she'll turn Warrion loose to finish what he started.

Warrion releases me and pockets whatever weapon he used to zap me with, scrutinizing me the entire time.

Ayma holds out a slender hand and pulls me to my feet. She reaches for my bracelet and examines it with trembling fingers. "Where did you get this?" she asks in a strained voice.

"I've had it since I was adopted as a baby. I don't know which planet it came from." I lean toward her. "Please, do you know anything about it?"

She lowers her eyes, her breathing ragged. After a moment, she casts a quick glance over her shoulder at Warrion and then turns back to me. "Meet me tomorrow at the Syndicate military quadrant. I'll leave passes at the control station for you and your friend." She chews on her lip for a moment. "I know where the bracelets came from, but we can't talk here."

My heart lunges in my chest at her words. I open my mouth to beg her to tell me more, but she's already striding off in the direction of the EduPlex. Warrion glowers at me as he closes in behind her.

"I don't like that Warrion," Buir says in a hushed tone. "It may not be safe for us to go to the military quadrant."

"We don't have a choice," I say. "Ayma knows where the bracelets came from."

Back at the Zebulux, we fill in Ghil, and Velkan on everything that transpired at the EduPlex.

"Velkan should go with you tomorrow," Buir says. "This is about him too."

He throws her a grateful look but waits for my decision.

I nod. "Agreed. Velkan and I will head out there first thing tomorrow."

Ghil consults his CipherSync and then rubs a hand over his jaw. "I hate to be the one to point this out, but it's already after ten o'clock, which makes Doctor Azong officially a no-show."

"We could give her another hour," Velkan suggests.

"Or we could swing by her practice and put some pressure on her," I say.

"We can't all go," Buir says. "Someone needs to stay here in case she shows up."

"I'll stay," Ghil volunteers. "Even with those fancy lenses Doctor Azong gave me, I'm taking a risk every time I leave the ship."

"I'll stay with you," Buir says. "We can work on our new menus."

Velkan and I exit through the security gate and make our way back out of the docking area and past the gaudy holographic billboards. Within minutes, we reach the discrete glass building housing Doctor Azong's dermal sculpting practice. The foyer is deserted apart from the android receptionist who lifts her head and calls out brightly, "How may I be of assistance to you today?"

"I need to see Doctor Azong," I say.

"Doctor Azong is incapacitated."

"It's urgent," Velkan says.

"Doctor Azong is incapacitated."

I lean over the counter and glare at the android. "If you say that one—"

"Doctor Azong is incapacitated."

I reach across the counter, grab the android by the hair and shove her as hard as I can.

"What did you do that for?" Velkan asks.

"I've been wanting to do that ever since my first visit. That thing is obviously malfunctioning, and even if it wasn't it is now."

"So, where's Doctor Azong's office?" Velkan asks, looking around.

I grab his hand. "This way!"

I lead him through the archway and back to the conference room.

"There's no one here," he says, turning to go.

"Not so fast." I reach under the table to find the hidden control panel. The door to the secret office slides open with a gentle whoosh. I step inside and shrink back in horror. A dark pool of blood is creeping out from underneath the doctor's desk.

Chapter 25

I tread tentatively around the desk and stare in disbelief at the body lying on the floor.

"It's Doctor Azong," I say in a shocked whisper.

I take a step toward her, but Velkan reaches for my arm. "Don't touch her. We need to get out of here before we're implicated in this."

I turn to him, perturbed at his grave tone. "You don't think her death had anything to do with us, do you?"

He furrows his brow. "Too much of a coincidence. Maybe the buyer she talked to decided he could do better by coming to us directly."

Fear whirls in my mind. What if the buyer is already en route to the Zebulux? "We'd better head back to the ship and make sure Buir and Ghil are all right."

I turn to go and freeze when I see the android receptionist standing a few feet away, her rigid gaze fixed on me. Something about her stance feels wrong. Or maybe it's a vibe I'm getting. There's nothing detectable on her blank face, no indication of her programmed state of mind, but all my hunting instincts kick into gear. I can read an animal in the way it holds itself, tell at one glance when it's unaware that it is being stalked, or gauge by a single tremor of a taut muscle when it's about to pounce. My gaze travels to her right hand as she slowly raises a laser gun. "How may I be of assist—"

"Get down!" I yell to Velkan. I dive behind the desk for cover, shaking all over.

Velkan rolls in next to me. "That thing must have killed Doctor Azong," he whispers.

I put a finger to my lips. We can't see anything from here, but I hear methodical footsteps moving in our direction. I close my eyes and pinpoint the android's position. On the count of three, I leap out in a low crouch and grab her by the ankles, toppling her in one fell swoop. The gun falls out of her hand and I kick it as far out of her reach as I can. Velkan scrambles up beside me and flips the android over, digging at the back of her head for something.

"What are you doing?" I ask.

He yanks something out from under her hair. "A magnetic override chip. Someone wrote a kill order and temporarily repressed her base predictive program."

I stare in disbelief at the android as she calmly picks herself up and brushes herself off. She smiles serenely at us. "I will be at my station should you require any further assistance."

My heart thuds wildly in my chest. "She just tried to kill us," I say to Velkan. "Doctor Azong's buyer must be behind this. The dargonite is the only connection between us and Doctor Azong."

"We need to leave before anyone finds us." Velkan grabs my hand and we hurry out into the main foyer. "Doctor Azong would like you to disinfect the entire area," Velkan calls to the android on our way out.

"Certainly," she replies with a slight tilt of her head.

"Our fingerprints aren't in any Syndicate databases," Velkan says, "but with a murder this close to the docking station, the Minders might decide to extend the investigation to foreign ships in the port."

We keep up a brisk pace, but not in a way that would attract unwanted attention. The inhabitants of Aristozonex never run, other than in designated workout plazas under the supervision of medical droids. Ghil says they are obligated to take a requisite number of steps per day, which are automatically recorded, uploaded to their health history, and monitored for anomalies. I breathe slowly in and out, trying to blend with the pace of those around me. Their footsteps are nimble and smooth, syncing with a velocity set for them on their CipherSyncs, calculated for peak performance without adding undue stress to their bodies.

I glance constantly over my shoulder, fully expecting Brivardo and a squadron of Minders to come bearing down on us at any minute. Once they discover Doctor Azong's body, it won't take long for them to review the cameras and then they'll have our pictures.

Despite my new heat-regulating jumpsuit, I'm drenched with sweat by the time we make it back to the Zebulux. I trudge up the docking ramp on shaking legs. Velkan closes the cargo doors and together we head upstairs to the communal area.

Buir looks up, startled at our arrival.

"Are you all right?" I ask.

She nods, frowning. "What's wrong?"

Ghil sticks his head out from the galley. "Did you find Azong?"

"It's not good news," Velkan says.

Ghil walks out wiping his hands on his apron, his eyes sharp and alert. "What do you mean? Did she turn us in?"

"She's dead," I say.

Buir's eyes widen. "How?"

"Shot by her android receptionist," Velkan says. "Someone installed a magnetic override chip with a kill order on the android's base program."

"Must have been the buyer she was negotiating with," I say.

Ghil folds his arms across his chest and frowns. "What makes you think it had anything to do with the dargonite?"

I look him square in the eye. "Because the android tried to kill us too."

A worried look fills the folds of Ghil's face. "If they know who you are, you're going to need to take extra precautions every time you leave the ship from now on."

I give him a wry grin. "Guess we're all wearing beanies tonight."

"Tonight?" Buir says.

"Stefanov is setting up a meeting with his buyer this evening," I say. "As we're down to one buyer, I don't have much choice but to show up."

Velkan tightens his lips. I can tell he's worried about my safety, but he knows better than to try and talk me out of going. We have to unload the dargonite, and soon. "I'm coming with you," he says in a tone of quiet insistence.

"Stefanov said to come alone."

"Then I'll wait outside." His eyes soften. "In case you need me."

I give a grateful nod. "Thanks."

"Well, what are we going to do until tonight?" Buir asks.

Ghil shrugs. "I got a deck of cards somewhere."

Buir pulls a pout. "That doesn't sound like fun. How about we go downtown and see some more of the sights?"

I look around at the others. "Everyone up for that?"

Ghil scratches the back of his neck. "I'll stay put. I don't mind wandering around close to the ship, but downtown could be sketchy for a wanted man, even with my lenses. About the only place I'd be safe would be in the sewers. The Syndicate has high-tech facial recognition cameras everywhere."

Velkan punches him playfully in the shoulder. "You should have gotten on Doctor Azong's gurney yesterday. You'd have been a whole new man today."

Ghil nods thoughtfully. "I'm still chewing on the idea. Maybe I'll find a remote planet outside of the Syndicate and settle there instead." He gets to his feet, a wistful look on his face. "I'm going to check the engine room and make sure everything is up to par. If this deal goes down tonight, we can take off in the morning and start shopping for a new ship."

"*After* we meet with Ayma," I say. "I'm not leaving here until I find out what she knows about our bracelets."

Ghil purses his lips and throws me his beanie before exiting the room.

I pick it up gingerly and dangle it in front of me.

Buir looks at it with disgust. "You're not really going to wear that thing, are you?"

"No." I toss it on the table. "I'm not a fugitive. Whoever's looking for me won't be looking downtown."

Our LevCab takes us several hundred feet up in the air and follows a laser-lit pathway that cuts through the center of a glittering shopping emporium that's so beautiful it takes my breath away. Buir and I gasp out loud at the crystal-like fountains sparkling through the glass.

"Look at the height of some of these buildings," I say. "How do they keep them from toppling over?"

"Ghil tells me they're made of plutonglaze glass," Velkan explains. "It self-regulates temperature and light, and monitors weather conditions so if a solar storm comes in, the building's shield system is activated."

"I've never heard of it," I acknowledge. "But then our educational reference materials on Cwelt are all over fourteen moons old."

Velkan smiles. "It's a recent development."

"How does the shield work?" Buir asks.

"A chemical is released into the glass to fortify it," Velkan explains. "It pretty much turns the building into an iron fortress in minutes. The effect lasts for several days. It can also be manually activated in case the building ever comes under attack."

"I wonder if dargonite could make the glass invisible." I turn to Velkan. "Just think of the possibilities. Aristozonex would cease to exist for any attacking spacecraft."

"You're right," he says, frowning out the window. "No wonder the Syndicate is seizing control of the dargonite mines. There's no telling what uses dargonite could be put to, but if it falls into the wrong hands—" He breaks off and throws me an apologetic look.

"You mean Maulers," I say.

He rubs his hand slowly over his jaw. "*Especially* Maulers. If they discover the dargonite on Cwelt, they'll fortify their position. One warship may not be enough to liberate your people by the time we go back."

I drop my gaze, digesting the truth of his words. Even if he is right, I still have to try. I won't leave my people to their fate. I promised Meldus I would save them when I sat by his burning pyre for those long hours.

The LevCab slows to a halt and descends into the drop-off location downtown. I dismount with the others and look around awestruck. The walls of the buildings here shimmer like colorful waterfalls. Holographic projected billboards advertise everything from the latest Artificial Intelligence home appliances to weightless beds guaranteeing unparalleled sleep rhythms.

"Look!" Buir points at a hologram of a mouthwatering dessert. "I want to try one of those!"

"Infused ice cones." Velkan laughs. "Ghil sometimes sneaks one onto the ship for me. They do weird things to your tongue and the roof of your mouth, but they're good."

We cross the street, and after some deliberation, I order a milky way cone. The first lick sends a fizzy tingle all through me, electrifying my tongue with a barrage of sensations and flavors. "Yikes! This is amazing!" I gush.

Buir nods and moans with pleasure. "How did I exist all this time without these?"

We spend the rest of the afternoon wandering through exotic

shopping emporiums, examining the wares and guessing what some of the items are. Everything is a novelty, from the AI guided toy hovercraft for kids to the vast array of personal android assistants specializing in everything from childrearing to housekeeping.

"We should get going," I say with some reluctance. "I can't be late for the meeting with Stefanov and his buyer."

"I'll take a LevCab back to the ship," Buir says.

"Are you sure you're okay traveling back alone?" I ask.

"Positive." She splays her hand good-bye. "Much more relaxing than traveling by LunaTrekker."

Velkan and I watch her climb into a LevCab before hailing one of our own. Once we are airborne, Velkan turns to me. "If anything seems off about the buyer, just walk away. We don't know if we can trust Stefanov, and after what happened to Doctor Azong, we can't afford to take any chances."

"Stefanov isn't going to double-cross me," I say. "He wants in on the deal. He knows that even a cut of this sale is more than he'll make for the rest of his life."

Velkan takes my hand in his and rubs his thumb gently across my palm. "Promise me you'll be careful."

"That tickles." I snatch my hand away.

"How about this?" Velkan says, leaning in to kiss me.

I close my eyes and melt into the softness of his lips, wishing the moment would never end.

All too soon, Velkan pulls away. "LevCab's going down," he whispers. "I could make it go up again."

I laugh. "Another time."

Velkan brushes the back of his hand over my curls. "Your hair is beautiful, but do you want to know the real reason I call you *Girl of Fire?*"

I give a self-conscious shrug.

"It's because you have fire in your belly. You're not afraid to right wrongs and go after the truth. No matter the cost."

"Or maybe I am afraid, but I choose to act anyway."

"That's what fire in your belly is," Velkan says, as he reaches for our BodPaks.

I pay our fare and we climb out. Our mood quickly turns somber as we approach the pawn emporium.

"Where will you wait?" I ask.

Velkan gestures at a cafe two doors down. "I'll be at an outside table. If you're not back in an hour, I'm coming to find you." He pulls me toward him in a crushing hug that tells me he dreads the thought of anything happening to me.

"I won't be long." I draw away with reluctance.

He nods good-bye and watches me walk up the steps to the front door of the pawn emporium.

Stefanov is waiting for me inside, a reproving look in his eyes. "You were supposed to come alone."

"Does it look like anyone's with me?" I retort.

"You took your sweet time saying good-bye to your companion," he grumbles. "Follow me. The buyer is waiting on us downstairs."

He leads me to the elevachute, and we descend into the basement and take the same route as before until we come to his private office. The door slides open, and I step inside.

"There's no one here," I say, a feeling of unease mounting by the second. I spin around just as Stefanov locks the door behind us.

Chapter 26

"My buyer is here but prefers to remain anonymous." Stefanov motions to a four-panel antique carved screen partitioning off the back corner of his office. "I'm sure you can appreciate the need for discretion in a transaction of this sort."

I stare at the screen, my heart racing. I can just about make out the faint outline of a person behind it. The enormity of the risk we are taking hits me. If we are caught conducting a dargonite deal on Aristozonex, I will never see the light of Cwelt again.

Stefanov pulls a chair out for me at his desk. "You will remain on this side of the room at all times. I will handle the negotiations. After the terms have been hashed out, you will leave first. This meeting never happened. Do you understand?"

I fix a stony gaze on him. "How do I know this isn't a setup?"

Stefanov smirks. "You don't. You just have to trust your gut that I'm too greedy to let this opportunity slip through my fingers." He walks across to the screen, leans around it and says something to the buyer in a low voice.

"How much dargonite are you selling?" he asks me when he reappears.

"Sixty Syndicate shekels," I blurt out. I never even thought to weigh the dargonite, but sixty seems like a high enough number to spark some interest.

"Where is it located? My buyer wants to see it first."

"It's here," I say, and then immediately regret it. After what happened to Doctor Azong, I should probably be more cautious about the details I divulge before I've secured a deal.

Stefanov elevates his brows. "How did you get it past customs?"

"It's in a safe location," I retort. "That's all your buyer needs to know. Now let's talk numbers. How much is your buyer willing to pay per shekel?"

Stefanov retreats behind the screen and I hear a muffled conversation, but even straining to listen in, I can't figure out what they're saying. When Stefanov reappears a few minutes later, he throws me an exhilarated look. "Full market value. Three million credits per shekel."

I blink, uncertain how to respond. *Three million.* Did I mishear him? I frown at the screen while I try to calm my racing heart.

Stefanov takes a step toward me, a flush creeping up his neck. "Three million isn't enough? Are you out of your mind? Even allowing for my cut, you will have more than enough to lead a very comfortable life anywhere in the Syndicate."

I brush my fingers across my jaw as if contemplating the offer. Truth be told, I'm reeling from the ramifications. If sixty shekels can fetch one-hundred-and-eighty million credits, what would a whole mine be worth? Cwelt could quickly become one of the wealthiest planets in the galaxy. But we'd need a partner. I lift my head and look Stefanov square in the eye. "Ask your buyer if he is interested in negotiating a deal for mining rights."

Stefanov casts a skeptical look at me. "*You* know of a dargonite mine outside the jurisdiction of the Syndicate?"

"Just ask your buyer."

Stefanov shrugs and sticks his head behind the screen again. When he reappears this time, he gives me a self-satisfied smirk. "My buyer is equally doubtful that you've located a dargonite source on a planet willing to sell off mining rights."

I assume my most regal High Daughter expression. "I *own* the rights."

A flicker of disbelief, followed by curiosity crosses Stefanov's face. His eyes flit briefly to my hair. "Where is this planet?"

"That's irrelevant for now," I say. "First, we need to come to some agreement."

Stefanov rubs his jaw thoughtfully. "My buyer wants to see the dargonite before any mining rights deal is struck. How about tomorrow morning?"

I hesitate, wondering if it would be better to invite the buyer on board the Zebulux or bring the dargonite here. Transporting it would be an issue. Trying to hide sixty shekels of rock while we travel through Aristozonex in body-hugging jumpsuits poses quite the challenge. And until the credits have been transferred to my CipherSync, I'm leery of letting the dargonite off the Zebulux anyway.

"All right, but it needs to be today. I have other business to attend to in the morning."

Stefanov nods and gestures to the door. "Wait for us upstairs. My buyer wants to discuss something with me in private."

I get to my feet and exit the room, already second-guessing my decision to allow another stranger on board the Zebulux. But what choice do I have? A legitimate buyer wouldn't demand anything less than to inspect the goods before releasing that amount of credits.

Inside the elevachute, I lean back against the wall, my legs weak beneath me. It's really happening. We're about to sell a couple of buckets of dargonite for an astronomical sum. After that, we can procure a warship and go back to liberate Cwelt.

I exit the elevachute on the ground floor and make my way to the front of the pawn emporium. Stefanov's daughter eyes me warily from beneath her glazed bob.

"I didn't introduce myself earlier," I say, clenching my fist so I remember not to splay my hand. "I'm Trattora."

The girl sizes me up for a moment before beckoning me closer. "Look, I don't know what it is you're selling," she whispers, "but I don't like the look of your buyer's bodyguard."

"What did he—" I trail off mid-sentence at the sound of footsteps approaching.

"We're ready," Stefanov says, walking up to me. Behind him, a hooded figure in a full-length shimmering silver cloak comes into view accompanied by a larger hooded figure in a full-length black cloak. *A bodyguard?* A flicker of apprehension goes through me when I notice they are both wearing face masks. Maybe I shouldn't have let them see my face either. Not trusting myself to speak, I give a discreet nod in their direction. Neither one acknowledges me, which I take as a sign that they'll be communicating strictly through Stefanov.

Stefanov turns to his daughter. "Leeta, if I'm not back in two hours, you know what to do."

Her eyes dart to the buyer and then back to her father. "Where are you going?"

"We won't be long." He gestures to me. "We're accompanying the seller to inspect the cargo."

Leeta throws me a long, foreboding look. Unnerved, I turn away from her piercing stare and walk toward the exit. Was she trying to warn me about something?

I hurry down the steps to the curb. "I'll let my friend know we're leaving and hail a LevCab," I call back to Stefanov.

"That won't be necessary," he replies. "We can take my vehicle."

I turn to wave Velkan over but he has already left the cafe and is heading our way. He throws a dubious glance at the two hooded figures when he walks up. "Everything all right?"

"The buyer wants to see the dargonite," I whisper.

Velkan rubs a hand across his jaw. "Ghil's not going to like this. Bringing strangers on board is risky. Remember what happened with Doctor Azong?"

"Easier this way than trying to bring the dargonite into Aristozonex."

Velkan looks unconvinced, but he doesn't argue with me.

We follow Stefanov and the two hooded figures to a parking structure at the end of the block. I look around the gleaming empty space wondering where the LevAutos are parked. Stefanov scans his CipherSync at the counter under the courteous gaze of an android attendant, and a moment later the wall behind us slides open. A sleek mushroom-colored vehicle floats out through the opening and parks alongside us.

Stefanov gestures to the buyers to take the front row of seats.

Velkan and I climb in after them and seat ourselves in the back, allowing Stefanov to sit in the row between us.

"Where to?" Stefanov calls over his shoulder.

"The docking station," I say.

"Traders. I thought as much." He gives a command to the vehicle and then leans forward to say something to his buyer.

"I'm thankful not to be sitting next to the silent assassin in the black hood," Velkan whispers in my ear.

I smother a laugh. "Not funny. Those masks spook me."

"They're not taking any chances on us being able to identify them," Velkan says. "That's a good indication how dangerous it is to be caught trading in dargonite."

"If I sell the mining rights, we could become one of the wealthiest planets in the galaxy."

"Assuming we can run the Maulers out of there," Velkan points out.

I grimace. "Which is another good reason to sell the mining rights—the buyers will be motivated to help us eject the Maulers."

"We're almost at the docking station," Stefanov says. "Which ship are we headed to?"

"The Zebulux, berth 017-AG2," Velkan replies.

Minutes later we pass through the security gate and pull up outside the Zebulux.

"I'll open the cargo door," Velkan says, climbing out. He walks around to the side of the hull and enters the code on the control panel.

Once the door is fully retracted, Stefanov commands his

vehicle to pull inside the cargo bay.

"I'll wait here with the buyers while you fetch the dargonite," Velkan says to me when I get out. "Let Buir and Ghil know what's happening; they can help you bring it down here."

I give a reluctant nod. I don't like leaving him here alone, but one of us has to retrieve the dargonite.

Ghil's face hardens like steel when I tell him I brought more strangers on board.

"They mightn't be real buyers!" he yells, pacing in front of me. "They could be Minders rounding up fugitives for all we know."

"Calm down, Ghil," Buir scolds. "If they were Minders, they would already be searching the ship. First things first. If they want to inspect the dargonite, we need to fish it out of the mush and rinse it off."

Ghil traces his fingers nervously back and forth over his lips. "We won't turn it all over, just in case. They'll be none the wiser, that way we'll have a cushion if things go south."

I frown. "I told them we had sixty shekels of dargonite to sell."

"Good." Ghil gives an approving nod. "That's less than what's in there."

"Let's make this quick," I say. "I don't want to leave Velkan by himself for too long."

Buir fetches a sieve from the galley and starts fishing around in the mush for dargonite nuggets. As soon as she retrieves them she tosses them into the sink and I hurriedly wash them off. When I'm done, Ghil loads them into two buckets. It takes us less than ten minutes to pull out and clean off enough dargonite to be convincing.

"You don't have to come with us, Ghil," I say. "They might have seen your face on the wanted holographs."

He furrows his brow. "If they're legitimate buyers, the last people they're going to involve is Minders. I reckon I'll be safe enough with crooks."

I lead the way along the utility hallway and down the stairwell into the cargo bay. Ghil lumbers after me, the weight of the buckets dragging him down, but he stubbornly refuses my repeated offers of help. Buir brings up the rear, carrying some cups and a pitcher of infused water.

Ghil plops the buckets down in the center of the cargo bay and takes a long, hard look at the buyer and his bodyguard. "What's with the masks?" he grumbles. "Don't you trust us or something?"

The tall man in the black cape steps toward him and cocks his head in a menacing manner. "Not anymore, brother."

Chapter 27

A ripple of disbelief traverses Ghil's face before he kicks into gear. He storms across the floor and rips the mask from Crank's face. "Are you too spineless to walk in here and show your face?" he yells.

Crank tightens his jaw, his eyes flashing a dangerous display of emotions. "You betrayed me."

Ghil shoves Crank in the chest, but he doesn't budge.

Stefanov edges slowly backward. He looks like he might be getting ready to make a run for it.

"*You* betrayed *me*," Ghil growls. "You struck a deal with Sarth to auction off one of our crew without telling me. Is that the kind of loyalty you show your own blood brother?" He turns and narrows his eyes at the hooded figure to Crank's left, comprehension flooding his face. "Sarth!"

She reaches up and deftly removes her mask, a cunning smile tugging at the corners of her lips. "Hello, Ghil. I believe you've got something that belongs to me."

The thud of my heartbeat grows louder in my ears. How did she find us? I can't let her rip everything away from us now that we've almost accomplished what we came here to do.

"You left us no choice but to flee," I say, stepping between them. "You can have your wreck of a vessel back, just as soon as we're done with it."

Sarth tilts her head at me in a mocking manner. "For someone as bright as you are, you're a tad forgetful. The cardinal rule on the Zebulux is that I own everything on board." She gestures disparagingly at Velkan. "Even your serf boyfriend."

"That contract ended," I retort. "Show her, Velkan."

He walks up to Sarth and turns his neck to one side.

She narrows her eyes. "Dermal sculpting to hide a serf is a Syndicate felony. I could turn you in for identity fraud."

"But you won't," I say, with as much conviction as I can muster, "because then we'd inform the Syndicate about the illegal human auctions you participate in on Diretus, and your illicit trade with the body poachers, and even the deal you tried to make to get a hold of the dargonite. You'd spend the rest of your miserable life in a penal colony on the fringe."

Sarth wets her lips. "I had nothing to do with your auction. I had too much to drink and passed out. Someone rifled through my belongings and took my CipherSync and everything else in my pockets, including the lock of your hair." She pauses and studies me for a moment as if trying to assess whether I'm buying her story. "I came here today to deal, not for revenge. We can sell the dargonite to one of my contacts in the dark market, split the proceeds and go our separate ways. I'm even willing to give up those mining rights you promised me."

"Why should I believe you?" I say. "You probably planned all along to auction me off once we reached Diretus."

Sarth nods across to Crank. He pulls out a small leather pouch from beneath his cloak and tosses it to me.

I glance at it hesitantly. It weighs almost nothing. "What is this? If you're trying to buy me off, it won't work."

"Open it!" Sarth snaps, impatiently.

I pull the drawstring and tip the contents into the palm of my hand. My eyes widen. I grit my teeth and let the bloodied finger fall to the ground. Buir glances down and screams. My stomach churns at the sight of the crusted blood on the graying flesh. I glare at Sarth. "Is this some kind of joke?"

Crank crosses his thick, tattooed arms across his chest. "Consider it a small gesture of apology from the guard who dared to steal from Sarth." He hefts a hairy brow upward. "I can connect you to his cell for a live confession if you want."

I shake my head vehemently, abhorred by the thought of what the guard must look like after being tortured by Crank and his henchmen. It still doesn't prove Sarth's story—Crank could torture a guard into confessing anything—but if they're lying, they've gone to elaborate lengths to make sure we'll still be willing to deal with them.

I frown down at the floor, a troubling thought brewing in my head. Could Sarth have been responsible for Doctor Azong's death? She may well have found out that we had been in contact about a buyer. And if that's the case, she tried to kill me too. Everything in me recoils at the thought of conducting a deal with Sarth, but I need to string her along, at least until I can find another buyer. "All right. Find us a buyer, and we'll split the proceeds of the dargonite with you. Until then, the Zebulux remains in our possession."

Crank and Sarth exchange a fleeting glance. "Done." Sarth rubs her hands together briskly. "Crank and I will meet with my contact tomorrow morning and get back to you by noon." Her eyes scan the cargo bay as she turns to leave. "By the way," she says. "It's ninety-eight shekels of dargonite. Make sure it's all accounted for."

I hold my breath until she and Crank disappear down the ramp. At some point, Stevanov wisely made his escape. Velkan immediately closes the cargo door and we gather round in a subdued circle.

Ghil stares at the LunaTrekkers, a glazed look in his eye.

"You know Crank better than any of us," I say to him. "Do you think he was telling the truth?"

Ghil's shoulders heave up and down. He shakes his head and turns to face us. "They're lying through their teeth. They're here for the dargonite, and they'll say anything to get their hands on it."

"You don't think they'll find us a buyer?"

Ghil lets out a scoffing laugh. "They'll find *themselves* a buyer. If they do set up a meeting, it will be a trap, guaranteed."

"Now what are we going to do?" Buir asks.

"Find our own buyer," I say.

Buir raises her brows. "How? We don't have any contacts here."

"I'm not sure," I say. "Maybe Ayma can help us."

An alarmed look flits across Velkan's face. "*Ayma?* If she lives in the military quadrant that means her family is part of the Syndicate hierarchy. We can't even hint at this to her!"

"She's from wherever we're from." I fix my gaze on Velkan.

"She might be willing to help us."

Velkan shakes his head. "We'd be taking a huge risk."

I tweak a smile at him. "All I've done since you landed on Cwelt is take risks."

He laughs, sending a tingle down my spine. "Some risks are worth taking."

Buir groans and rolls her eyes. "Really? Sarth and Crank are plotting to steal the dargonite and do away with us, and you two are flirting."

"Negotiating would be a better word," I say, tearing my eyes away from Velkan's smile. "We'll head to the military quadrant right after breakfast. If Ayma won't help us, I'll talk to Stevanov again. He has contacts in the dark market."

"I'll stay with the Zebulux," Ghil says, heading for the stairwell. "My mugshot can't show up anywhere near the Syndicate military quadrant."

"I'll stay with you," Buir says. "Ayma is only leaving two passes at the security gate anyway."

Ghil gives an appreciative nod and continues up the stairs.

Velkan accompanies Buir and me to Sarth's quarters.

"Are you going to be all right without us tomorrow?" Velkan asks Buir.

She arches a brow at him. "You've seen how Ghil handles those knives. What do you think?"

Velkan gives a wry grin. "Not much use against a plasma gun."

"Don't worry, we'll be back before Sarth and Crank get here," I say. "Anyway, they can't take weapons past the port security into the docking station."

I splay my hand good night to Velkan and watch him walk down the hallway to his bunk room.

Buir falls asleep almost right away, but I lay awake for several hours, thinking about Ayma and wondering how much she knows about the origin of our bracelets. I'm glad Velkan's coming with me tomorrow. Whatever Ayma divulges, it involves him too and, good or bad, I want him there to share that moment with me.

The next morning, Buir shakes me out of a deep slumber. "Are you ever going to get up?"

I rub my eyes. "What time is it?"

"Almost eight."

"What?" I jump out of bed and weave my hair into a quick braid. "You should have woken me earlier!"

"I left breakfast for you in the galley," Buir says.

"I'll eat later. Gotta go."

Velkan is already waiting downstairs in the cargo bay. "Rough night?" he asks, eyeing me with concern.

I shrug. "I couldn't get to sleep. I kept wondering what news we'll get today."

He gives a sympathetic smile. "I didn't sleep much either. I kept imagining all the possibilities."

"Don't get your hopes up. Ayma seemed uneasy about the prospect of telling us where the bracelets came from."

Velkan tosses a skein of hair over his shoulder and strides toward the door. "Time we found out."

The military quadrant is awash with activity; a steady stream of sleek, black vehicles entering and exiting. Holographic messages with unintelligible strings of code flash intermittently overhead. Masked soldiers, dressed in black, guard the entryway, guns at the ready. As we walk toward the security gate, several drones fly overhead and circle us like annoying flies.

"What are they doing," I ask.

"Taking DNA readings and running them through their criminal database," Velkan says in a low tone. "Don't worry, we're not in there, *yet*."

A shiver runs across my shoulders. Despite Velkan's reassurance, I can't help wondering if anything has been uploaded to incriminate us in Doctor Azong's murder.

When we reach the security booth, an electronic voice ripples through a speaker, "state the purpose of your visit."

"We're traders from the Zebulux," I say. "Ayma invited us here to discuss some ... business opportunities."

A camera whirs and takes our picture. "Checking," the voice says.

"They're uploading our scan to Ayma to verify who we are," Velkan whispers to me. "She's not going to recognize me."

"Doesn't matter," I say. "As long as she recognizes me, she should verify us."

As the minutes tick by, I shuffle my feet impatiently. I've gambled everything on the bracelets meaning as much to Ayma as they do to me. If I'm wrong, Velkan's time as a free man will have been short-lived.

I breathe out a sigh of relief when the words, *identification confirmed,* flash over the security gate. Seconds later, a dispenser on the counter spits out two ID passes.

I reach for them and hand one to Velkan, glancing around.

"Where do we go from here?"

Velkan opens his mouth to respond just as a sleek black LevAuto pulls up. The door slides soundlessly open. I look at Velkan and shrug. "This must be for us."

He blows out a heavy breath. "I hope we're not about to make a grave mistake."

"I trust Ayma," I say, climbing in. "She recognized that bracelet and it meant something to her."

We ride in silence as the vehicle hovers over the immaculately appointed residences inside the military quadrant. The homes gradually grow more opulent the farther we move away from the security gate. I turn to Velkan and give a nervous smile. "I guess her family really is important."

"Let's hope it works in our favor." Velkan runs the tip of his finger self-consciously over his neck where his holographed tattoo had been.

Minutes later, our vehicle comes to a stop a short distance from a gleaming glass building on a tubular foundation that sprawls over a gently sloping lot. The entire upper level of the residence comprises a large hangar full of luxurious private shuttles. A laser security dome encloses the entire building, allowing no unauthorized flights in or out. My breath catches in my throat at the fortified guard station and plated gate standing between us and the palatial residence. Four or five armed guards are congregated outside the station, and there could be any number of them inside. "Let's hope they're not here for us," I whisper.

"Not likely," Velkan replies. "If Ayma's parents are high-ranking officials, this place is probably swarming with guards at all times."

We wait in the back seat of the vehicle for what seems like an agonizing length of time before the plated gate lowers into the ground and our vehicle pulls forward again. I let out my breath and lean my head against Velkan's shoulder. "My good feeling about Ayma was beginning to waver there for a minute."

"I'm still not sure we can trust her," he says, grimly. "Easier to interrogate us once we're inside."

The LevAuto hovers up the driveway and stops outside the front door. As we're climbing out, Ayma appears at the top of the steps. I'm struck by her beauty, the smooth contours of her fine jaw and high cheekbones, dark lashes unfurled like spider legs, deep red lips, and that ebony hair, now loose and sweeping her shoulders like the night sky. I glance across at Velkan, fighting back a pang of jealousy, but he's more focused on the guards who have appeared like silent shadows out of every nook and cranny.

"Welcome." Ayma motions us inside with an authoritative flick of her wrist. We follow her into a spacious entryway with a floating spiral staircase in the center. She dismisses the guards and leads us into an office at the end of a short hallway. "Take a seat," she says, as the door slides shut behind us.

We sit down on a luxuriously soft couch that instantly molds to our bodies. Ayma pulls out a DigiPad and taps on it, her fingers flying rapidly over the screen.

"What are you doing?" I ask.

"Scrambling the surveillance," she says, before plopping down in the couch opposite us. She sighs. "Every breath I take is recorded and analyzed."

"So how do you get around it?" I ask curiously.

She grins across at me. "Technology is my language. I enjoy the challenge of outwitting every reconnaissance device they come up with."

"Are you sure no one can hear us?" Velkan asks.

"Positive." Ayma straightens up and fixes her gaze on him. "Do you have a bracelet too?"

Velkan nods. "It was on my wrist when my master, Sarth, found me." He glances uncertainly at me. "I ... used to be a serf."

Ayma arches a brow. "Not anymore I see." She turns to me. "What about you?"

"The traders who sold me to my parents said I was wearing the bracelet when they found me."

"Me too," Ayma says softly. "My bracelet was stolen from me in the EduPlex a couple of months ago. It showed up in a pawn emporium a few days later."

I shift forward in the couch. "You said you knew which planet the bracelets come from."

Ayma gives a sober nod. "Mhakerta. A remote planet in the Netherscape."

My heart begins to beat a little faster. "Have you been there? To search for your birth parents?"

She shakes her head. "No one travels there anymore."

"Why not?" Velkan asks.

"Because Artificial Intelligence seized control and enslaved the humans."

Chapter 28

The blood in my veins turns to ice. I stare at Ayma, dumbstruck. "How do you know that?"

She reaches into her pocket and pulls out a small bracelet exactly like mine. "Watch this," she says, tapping on it. I gasp in disbelief when a sequence of lights flickers across the band.

"It took some time, but I figured out how to reactivate it, and I was able to unlock the coordinates that were coded inside." Ayma hands it to me to take a closer look. "When I located the planet, I hacked into their mainframe. Mhakerta is controlled by a self-actualizing software program that calls itself Preeminence."

Velkan rubs a hand across his jaw. "So how did we escape?"

A beat of sadness strikes Ayma's expression. "From what I can gather from deleted lab logs, we were evacuated by our birth parents." She sighs. "I don't how or why exactly, but they were afraid of what Preeminence was planning to do to compound its intelligence. Mhakerta has been in complete isolation from the outside world for almost two decades. Inter-planetary travel was restricted several years before we were born."

My mind races at a dizzying speed to piece together what Ayma is saying. "So, you're saying that our birth parents are essentially trapped on a planet run by a malicious software program."

She twists her lips. "If they're still alive."

"Did you learn anything else from the bracelets?" Velkan asks.

Ayma shakes her head. "Only that there were five of them."

I frown. "And two are still unaccounted for."

"There's no way to tell for sure if they ever left Mhakerta," Ayma says.

"How are you able to glean all this information?" Velkan asks.

Ayma curves her lips into a mischievous smile. "Lots of practice hacking. I get a kick out of playing the rebel. The Syndicate has invited me to join their military security division once I graduate. They discovered I'd been browsing around in the backend of their top clearance stealth fighter project for years unbeknownst to them. They decided it would be better to have me on their side."

"You've been hacking into Preeminence too," I add.

A serious look comes into Ayma's eyes. "It's extremely sophisticated. Took me months to figure out how to get in and out without leaving a trail."

"But it can be done," I say.

She shrugs. "No one could enter their airspace if that's what you're thinking. Preeminence's robotic air defense system is impenetrable from everything I've seen."

I sit quietly for a few minutes, my insides churning like a solar storm. I feel lost, and helpless, inadequate even to begin to process everything Ayma is saying. I don't know how to move forward once I sell the dargonite. I'm torn between helping the parents who raised me and saving my birth parents who are trapped by some psychotic, self-actualizing software program. "We have to do something," I say. "I can procure a ship if you can find a way in."

Ayma angles a brow. "And then what? How are we going to take down their robotic military with one ship?"

"Can't you overwrite the software?" Velkan asks.

"It's not that simple." Ayma frowns. "Preeminence is more powerfully encrypted than anything I've ever seen. It possesses an exponential intelligence that I've never encountered before, and it builds on it constantly from one day to the next."

"The longer we delay the more difficult it will be to infiltrate," I say.

Ayma grimaces. "Impossible would be a better word."

I arch my brows. "So much for being a technology whiz."

A flash of anger lights up her eyes. Something shifts in her expression. "I suppose I could take a stab at it."

"Is there a way we could locate the other bracelets?" I ask.

She rubs a polished fingertip over her lips. "I tried tracking the trajectory, but the other bracelets must have malfunctioned. Either that or ... the children didn't make it."

I bite my lip. The enormity of what our birth parents did to save us hits me all at once. They knew the huge risk involved, but the alternative must have been more horrific. My heart aches for them and for all the people of Mhakerta.

"Harsh as it sounds, we can't waste time trying to track them down right now," Velkan says. "We need to stay focused on what we came here to do; sell the dargonite, maybe even mining rights, and procure a warship."

Ayma's eyes widen. "*Dargonite*? Where did you get dargonite?"

I take a deep breath, hoping my instincts about her are right. We may have found some common ground when it comes to our bracelets, but Ayma's father is a high-ranking member of the Syndicate, and trading in dargonite is a felony.

"It came from my planet, Cwelt," I say. "It's under siege by Maulers. We escaped on Sarth's oremongering vessel. When she tried to sell me in an auction on Diretus, we abandoned her and fled in her ship." I slide forward to the edge of my seat. "We need your help to find a buyer on the dark market. We have to purchase a warship and fly back to Cwelt to rescue my people before it's too late."

Ayma wrinkles her forehead. "I don't know anything about the dark market."

"If you can hack into the mainframe, surely you can hack into the stellarsphere and find it," I say.

"You realize you're asking me to commit a crime punishable by banishment to the penal colonies, execution even?"

"It's the only hope I've got of saving the only parents I know," I reply. "Surely you can understand that."

Ayma's features soften. She's quiet for a moment and then she nods. "I'll nose around a bit and see what I can find. You'll have to be patient. Crime's not my specialty."

I grimace. "Wasn't mine either, but I'm learning on the job."

Ayma gets to her feet and stretches. "Do you want something to drink?" She walks over to a dispenser behind the desk. "Pink Solarade, Infused Crantoidberry, Elektra Chai—"

"Ooh, yes! I'll have the Chai, please," I say.

"Crantoidberry for me," Velkan says.

Ayma taps the dispenser for our selections and brings them over. "Here you go," she says, handing our drinks to us. "If you want, I can show you around. There's no one home."

"Sure," I say, glancing across at Velkan.

Velkan gives a quick nod. "Just so long as we're back before noon."

Ayma opens the door. "I'll have my LevAuto take you back to your ship when we're done."

"Where are your parents?" I ask as we follow her out of the office.

Ayma presses her lips together. "Working."

"What do they do?" Velkan asks.

"My father's the Syndicate Fleet Commander and my mother is a judge on the Supreme Chancery—the ruling body of the Syndicate. They're never home."

A smile twitches on Velkan's lips. "No wonder you've had so much time to hone your hacking skills."

Ayma flashes him a brilliant smile in return, and another tiny pang of jealousy goes through me. She's stunningly beautiful, and I suspect it has little to do with the fact that she can afford the best dermal sculptors on Aristozonex.

She leads us out the back of her home into a lush garden filled with manicured plants of every shade of green and vibrant flowers exuding intoxicating scents. Birds flit past us, chirping and warbling, as they make their rounds of the nectar-laden blossoms. The garden sweeps down to a circular pool reflecting the sun like a crystal eye.

"I've never seen anything so beautiful," I say, trying to drink it all in. "Cwelt seems like a desert in comparison."

Ayma shrugs. "All bioengineered. A designer draws up what you want and you upload the plans. Everything is fabricated at the ornamental garden plant and delivered by drone drop. No maintenance involved."

"You mean ... it's not real?" I ask, frowning.

Ayma throws me a bemused look. "Of course, it's real! Although, holographic settings are becoming popular. Some people prefer the flexibility of changing out their environment from time to time—holographic settings are more economical too."

"Is the pool real?" Velkan asks.

Ayma grins. "Want to go swimming?"

Velkan shakes his head. "I don't know how."

"You don't have to," Ayma says. "The suit does all the swimming for you."

"We should really get going," I say.

"Some other time then." Ayma takes a quick sip of her Crantoidberry. "I'll have my LevAuto pick you up at the front door."

"How will I contact you again?" I ask.

"I'll give you access to my private account." She taps on her CipherSync. "Don't divulge these contact details to anyone. I'm supposed to use the registered account, but everything on it is closely monitored."

"Let me know as soon as you find a buyer," I say.

I climb into the vehicle after Velkan and sink back against the plush seating. "This is a whole other level of luxury than LevCabs," I say.

"No kidding." Velkan stares out the window with a contemplative look on his face.

"I suppose you're wondering why out of the three of us you ended up the serf." I say.

He turns to me and grins. "Actually, I was thinking about Ayma."

I stiffen, my smile freezing in place.

"When I met her, it felt like I already knew her," Velkan continues, his brow knotting. He looks straight at me. "There must have been some connection between the three of us on Mhakerta."

My muscles relax a little. Maybe he wasn't thinking about her in *that* way. He's curious what the connection between us is. "Our parents might have known each other," I say.

"I wondered about that too," Velkan replies. "If they worked in the scientific sector, they might have realized what was happening and decided to evacuate us before Preeminence sealed Mhakerta off from the outside world."

"Expelled from our planet of origin," I muse as we come to a halt outside the docking station.

"Something like that," Velkan says.

We climb out and make our way over to the security gate. Velkan scans his holographic reentry stamp first.

"Access denied," an electronic voice announces.

He quickly scans it again, but the voice repeats the same message.

Fear spikes inside me. I throw a darting glance around the station, searching for Minders. Did someone turn Velkan in as a serf in hiding? Surely not Ayma?

Velkan frowns. "Try yours."

I step forward and wave my hand over the interface.

"Access denied."

My blood chills. "Someone must have ratted us out," I whisper to Velkan.

"Let's find out." He grabs my hand and marches up to the control booth.

"How may I be of assistance today?" an android asks.

"We need our holographic entry stamps reactivated," Velkan says. "We're trying to get back to the Zebulux and for some reason, we're being denied access."

"Checking." The android studies the screen in front of him before shifting his features into an expression of regret. "I'm sorry. The Zebulux departed port an hour ago."

Chapter 29

My first thought is that the android is mistaken, but then they never are. Almost immediately a sinking feeling drags me down a shaft of despair.

I turn to Velkan and see the same stricken look on his face.

"Sarth!" he says, his voice thick and faltering.

My stomach roils in response. "Do you think Buir and Ghil are on board?" I whisper.

He swallows hard but doesn't answer me, sending my mounting trepidation spiraling into full-blown panic. "What about the crew?" I ask the android. "Did they depart with the ship? And don't tell me you're checking, just tell me where they are."

"Checking."

I shut my eyes and take a deep breath, conjuring up the two most likely scenarios, both of which are horrendous. Sarth and Crank kidnapped Buir and Ghil, or they killed them. Buir and Ghil would never leave of their own accord without us.

"No further information available," the android replies, fixing a frosty gaze on me. "Next in line."

I narrow my eyes at the android, but Velkan places a restraining hand on my arm. "Let's get out of here," he whispers. "We don't want him alerting a Minder."

I turn away from the booth, my thoughts swirling in a storm of emotions. I gulp back a sob jammed halfway up my windpipe.

"It's going to be all right, Trattora." Velkan guides me through the crowd as I blink back tears.

"How can you say that?" I snap back. "I've lost everything that matters to me; my best friend, the dargonite, the ship—any hope I had of saving Cwelt."

He turns to look at me, his tender eyes moist with his own pain. "I'm still here, and I'll do whatever I can to help you."

Tears trickle freely down my cheeks. "I know, and you matter too, it's just …"

"You don't have to say anything, I understand what it is to speak from a place of pain."

I wipe the tears from beneath my eyes, his quiet strength helping me calm my thoughts and think more clearly. "We need to find out if Buir and Ghil are still on board. That android knows exactly how many people departed on the Zebulux. There must be some reason he isn't telling us."

"Maybe." Velkan casts a quick glance around the station. "But someone else might be willing to tell us, with a little persuasion."

"Like who?"

"Follow me," he says, making his way over to an elderly uniformed man seated next to a booth with a view screen inset.

"What's he doing?" I ask.

"Trash detection," Velkan replies. "He scans everyone going

in and out. If anyone knows what goes on here, it's him."

"He's the first old person I've seen since we docked," I say.

Velkan grimaces. "Trash detection is a form of community service for offenders, one step above being sent to a penal colony. He's ineligible for dermal sculpting due to his criminal record."

Velkan walks casually up to the man and gives a polite nod. "Busy here today."

The man lets out a snort of disgust. "These foreigners don't use the trash vaporization chutes before exiting the station like they're supposed to. Next thing you know, something crawling with germs falls out of their pocket on Aristozonex and the Sanitation Unit is on my case."

Suddenly, the screen lights up and beeps. The elderly man flicks a switch with a metal finger and deploys a recycle drone which shoots out and hovers over the offending party. *Please step away to the vaporization chute. Please step away to the vaporization chute. Please step away to the vaporization chute.*

Velkan gives a sympathetic shake of his head. "It's not as if there aren't enough holographic postings of the rules."

The elderly man curls a wrinkled lip at Velkan. "Half of these traders from primitive planets can't read."

I open my mouth to give him an earful but Velkan's grip on my hand tightens, warning me not to dampen any rapport he is building.

"Yeah, you never know who these ships are bringing in," Velkan replies. "I bet you get all kinds."

The man throws a furtive glance over at the security gate and then leans across to Velkan. "Just this morning, Minders dragged a Syndicate fugitive off one of those foreign vessels that's been parked here for the past couple of days."

"A fugitive!" Velkan shakes his head, feigning disgust. "How did they know he was on the ship?"

The man's eyes crinkle with delight at an interested audience. "Word is he stole the ship from the captain and she tracked him here. Mean-looking woman in a silver cloak, and her engineer was a beast." The man laughs, low and rumbling, wagging his metal finger at us. "The last ship that fugitive will see will be the one that hauls him off to the penal colonies."

"I think I saw that captain and her engineer earlier." Velkan paints a puzzled look on his face. "Didn't they have a young girl with them, probably crew?"

The elderly man frowns, a look of displeasure crossing his face at the possibility that he missed something. He extends his metal finger and scratches the back of his neck. "I don't recall seeing her."

Velkan shrugs. "I'm probably thinking of someone else. Hard to keep track with all these people coming and going."

The screen lights up and beeps again and the elderly man's interest switches to the offending trader. "Hey!" he yells, flicking a switch to deploy another recycle drone. "Don't you know what a trash vaporization chute is?"

Velkan gives me a subtle nod and we slip away into the crowd.

"Buir must be on the Zebulux with them." My voice trembles so hard the words come out slurred.

"We don't know that. Maybe she managed to escape and hide somewhere in the docking station," Velkan says. "Or on one of the other ships. We'll figure out a way to get back inside the station. But first, we have to find Ghil before he's conscripted. If he can tell us where Buir is, that will save us time looking for her."

"Minder Brivardo will know where they took Ghil," I say. "We can bribe him with the rest of the credits Stefanov loaded on my CipherSync."

We hail a LevCab and ride in silence to the Minder Depot. I'm not sure how happy Brivardo's going to be to see me again so soon after exchanging parting threats. He's leery of the increasing risk of selling classified information, and if I arouse suspicions at the station by showing up again too soon, we could both end up being investigated.

My heart thuds as we pull up outside the station. "Wait here," I say to Velkan. "As soon as I find out where they're holding Ghil, I'll be back."

"Offer him however many credits it takes," Velkan says, holding my gaze.

I nod. "After everything Ghil's done for us, I won't let him down when he needs me most."

Velkan squeezes my fingers softly as they slip through his. I climb out of the LevCab and make my way inside the building, savoring the comforting touch of his hand. If this doesn't go well in here, at least there's one person who will come looking for me.

"I'm here to see Minder Brivardo again." I smile down at the surly clerk. "A follow-up to my last meeting. Tell him it's Trattora."

The clerk repeats what I said into her CipherSync in an irked tone. After a minute, she gives me a curt nod. "He'll see you. You know where to go."

"Thank you."

She buzzes me through the security door, and I walk briskly down the corridor toward Brivardo's office, my pulse drumming in my temples.

He looks up nervously when I come in, half rising out of his chair. The door slides closed behind me. "Sit, sit. Why are you back? You didn't discuss our meeting with anyone, did you?" He mops his brow with the cuff of his uniform, blinking rapidly. "Do you suspect you're being surveilled?"

"I need more information," I say.

"I gave you everything I could access on that case." Brivardo lowers his voice. "It was classified. That bracelet was stolen from the Syndicate Fleet Commander's house."

I shake my head. "Different information. A fugitive was arrested today at the docking station. I need to know where they took him."

Brivardo scratches his temple, clearly agitated. "Why do you care about a fugitive?"

I hesitate. It's too risky to tell him the truth. If he knows I was involved in harboring a fugitive, he might be tempted to turn me in for the reward. I need to use his greed against him. I lean across the desk. "He boasted to another captain in the dock that he knows of a dargonite mine on a planet outside the jurisdiction of the Syndicate. Naturally, I'm interested. You?"

The covetous flicker in Brivardo's eyes is unmistakable. "How do you know he was telling the truth?"

"That kind of talk gets you arrested around here. It's not the kind of thing people typically lie about."

A sheen of sweat appears on Brivardo's forehead. I can tell he's wrestling with the decision.

"Are you in?" I ask. "You get paid up front for the information, fifty-fifty split on the back end if we locate the mine."

"What makes you think he'll tell you where it is?" Brivardo asks.

"Not tell me, *show* me." I arch a brow at him. "My crew is going to help him escape." I'm not sure if Velkan technically counts as crew, but it sounds better than admitting to Brivardo that Velkan is all the help I have left.

Brivardo furrows his brow. "You've a ship lined up to get him out of here?"

"Yes," I lie. *Had* a ship. That part I need to figure out all over again.

Brivardo drums his fingers on the desk. "You realize this decision could cost me my life."

"Or leave you set for life," I point out, with a seductive grin.

He stands and paces like a caged animal that smells a hunk of meat just beyond its bars. "Fugitives are permitted visitors up until six hours before their conscription vessel departs. If he was arrested this morning, you'll need to head straight to the address I give you if you want to see him. He won't be there tomorrow. Conscription vessels always leave for the penal colonies at night—keeps the protests down."

"So, you're in?" I say, sliding my chair out.

Brivardo eyes me warily. "Credits first. This information is double the price."

"Two million credits?" I stare at him, outraged.

He shrugs. "Take it or leave it."

I tighten my lips. He knows I have no choice. Telling him a dargonite mine was at stake probably upped the price.

I transfer the credits, and Brivardo checks his CipherSync. A twisted grin spreads across his sweating face. He beckons me closer. "The holding depot for convicts earmarked for conscription to the colonies is three blocks from here, *219-073-186 Harvest Moon Boulevard.*"

"*219-073-186* Harvest Moon Boulevard," I repeat, getting to my feet.

"Wait!" he says. "When do I get my split on the mine?"

"I'll be in touch," I say. "First, I need to find the fugitive."

Brivardo gives a nervous nod. "I'll be waiting and I better hear from you soon."

I exit the Minder Depot, relieved to see Velkan waiting for me on the corner. He hurries toward me—a questioning look in his eyes.

"I got an address," I say. "But the conscription vessel leaves tonight. Ghil only has a couple more hours to see visitors before they cut him off."

"How are we going to get him out of there?" Velkan asks.

I let out a heavy sigh. "I don't know. I'm still working on that, but at least we can ask him what happened to Buir."

We take off down the street at a brisk trot, trying desperately not to break into a run and attract unwanted attention to ourselves. I'm still not sure what we're going to say to Ghil. It's not like we have a plan to save him or anything. But knowing him as I do, I'm hoping he might have an idea.

Security at the conscription holding depot is tight. We are ushered through two different body scanners before we are permitted to go inside the building. Armed androids dressed in scarlet jumpsuits are stationed at six-foot intervals throughout the foyer. We take our place in line at the security booth behind a woman clutching a toddler by the hand and sobbing profusely. I wonder what crime her family member committed to be dealt such a severe punishment.

When we reach the booth, Velkan steps forward. "We're here to see the fugitive that was arrested at the docking station, berth 017-AG2." He raises his brows apologetically. "Former employee. Shocking situation."

The human guard casts a bored glance at us and then turns to his screen and swipes his fingers rapidly through several lists. "CipherSyncs," he snaps.

Velkan and I obediently hold out our wrists.

"You have a ten-minute pass with the prisoner. When your CipherSync beeps, your time is up. Second corridor on the left, fourth detainment cubicle down."

Heart pounding, I lead Velkan past the android guards and down the corridor. I come to a stop outside an eight-by-eight foot brightly-lit cubicle. The entire viewing wall is glass with an entry door and built-in comm system at varying heights, some low enough for small children to talk through. My stomach knots when I think of the woman and toddler in line in front of us.

Lying on a narrow bed buried under a white blanket is an unconscious figure.

"Ghil," I say to him through the comm system.

Velkan steps up beside me and stares into the cell. "He sleeps hard. You need to yell."

"Ghil!" I call out insistently.

The figure doesn't flinch.

My heart tightens in my chest. "They might have beaten him unconscious," I say, turning to Velkan.

He grimaces. "I'll fetch a guard. Wait here."

Left to my own devices, my thoughts quickly run amok. I can't hear Ghil snoring. What if he's already dead? Panic mounts inside me. What if we never find Buir? The pain of that thought is as bad as the thought of anything happening to my parents.

I look up at the sound of Velkan striding back down the corridor with a guard in tow.

"Visitors!" the guard barks through the intercom as he thumps on the glass with the butt of his laser gun.

There's no response.

The guard throws me a disgruntled look and unlocks the door. He gestures to me to go in. "Don't expect me to touch him," he snaps.

I step inside, walk over to the sleeping figure, and squeeze his shoulder gently. My fingers stiffen when I realize it's an android I'm trying to shake awake.

Chapter 30

My heart races up my throat. The hilt of a small dagger juts out from the back of the android's head. *Ghil must have escaped!* Willing myself to stay calm, I straighten up and walk back to the door. I give a halfhearted shrug in the guard's direction. "Forget it. He's out cold." I turn to Velkan and say in a loud voice. "We fulfilled our obligation to his family. Let's get out of here."

Velkan's eyes crinkle in confusion, but something in my manner convinces him to play along.

The guard locks the door behind me without as much as a glance in the sleeping figure's direction.

Velkan and I walk nonchalantly side by side along the hallway back to the holding area foyer. I throw him a sidelong glance. He looks distraught. I desperately want to reassure him that Ghil's all right, but the last thing I need to do is alert the guard to the fact that I'm hiding something.

As soon as we are out on the street, I pull Velkan close. "It was an android," I whisper to him.

Velkan's eyes grow wide. "How did Ghil pull that off?"

"There was a small dagger in the back of its neck, likely

severed the wiring. I don't know how Ghil managed to smuggle a knife in."

"He always keeps a nylon composite knife or two in his boots," Velkan says. "They're harder than steel and equally as deadly, but they don't trigger detectors."

"So how do we find him now?" I say.

Velkan gives me a wry grin. "Ghil's a veteran of living in the shadows. If he wants to be found, he'll find us."

I run a trembling hand over my brow. I'm woozy and confused, still trying to digest the fact that Ghil has escaped. I hope he cares enough about Buir not to disappear for good. I gesture to a Solar Juice Bar across the street. "Let's grab something to drink and figure out what to do."

Velkan orders two Delta waters and carries them out to a table on the sidewalk. He sits down heavily and drains his glass in one long gulp. "I needed that," he says, sinking back in his chair.

I take a sip of my water. "Do you think Ghil might be watching us from some hiding place?"

Velkan throws a furtive glance around. "If he is, he has no way to contact us without exposing himself."

I sigh and set down my glass, just as the holographic billboards on every building flash a synchronized red alert. I look up in alarm. Ghil's face fills the sky above the businesses lining the street. The ticker tape below the image reads, *Escaped Syndicate fugitive, armed and dangerous.*

I quickly bow my head to hide from the cameras the expression of shock and horror I'm certain is plastered all over my face. What if the guards connect Ghil's escape to our visit? I glance tentatively up, but to my relief, the billboards have resumed their advertising and our mugshots don't appear.

"We need to help him," I hiss at Velkan.

"How?"

"If he can't come to us, we'll go to him."

Velkan shakes his head. "Where would he hide in a city like this?"

I look around at the glittering high rises, cameras documenting and tabulating every freeze-frame of life. There is nowhere to run and nowhere to hide on Aristozonex. The Syndicate will find him. I know better than most the mechanics of the hunt. My thoughts drift to my last sham hunt in Cwelt's sacred triangle. It seems like such a long time ago, another lifetime. Before the Maulers came. A wave of pain hits like a hammer when I remember my people hiding in the underground caves.

And then it comes to me. *The sewers!*

I grab Velkan by the sleeve. "Ghil can't show his face anywhere. Maybe he went underground. He said the sewers would be the only place he would ever be safe." I scrape my chair out and get to my feet. "We need to buy lamps."

Velkan looks at me, startled. "You want to go into the sewers?"

"We need to go to him, remember?"

Velkan takes a swig of my Delta Water and then follows me into the street.

"Look for a store that sells hunting supplies," I say.

Velkan chuckles. "People don't hunt on Aristozonex. We need a general dispenser that prints small, miscellaneous items."

I wrinkle my brow. "What are you talking about?"

"Most smaller goods can be printed on demand." Velkan points up ahead. "I see a dispenser on the next corner."

He leads me up the street to a circular booth embedded with screens all the way around, each displaying a rolling assortment of sundry items. A woman standing in front of the screen next to us reaches down and retrieves a toy LevCab from a slot below. She hands it to the delighted child at her side.

"Voice activated," Velkan explains. "It brings up our options and prints our selection."

"Impressive," I say. "Bet it can't print shamskins."

Velkan laughs and turns to the screen. "Display flashlights."

Immediately, an assortment of flashlights in various sizes scrolls across the screen.

"Now we make our selection." Velkan points to an item on the screen. "How about that one?"

I shrug. "Looks fine."

"Item C-12," Velkan says. "Quantity two." He scans his CipherSync and a slot opens beneath the screen, displaying two flashlights on multi-purpose belts.

"Here you go." Velkan grabs one and hands it to me.

I start to strap it on, but Velkan stops me. "Stash it in your BodPak for now. We don't want to attract unnecessary attention." He looks up and down the street. "Now we need to find our way down to the sewers. I haven't seen any manhole covers or vents anywhere."

"I think I know who might be able to help us with that," I say.

Velkan looks at me sharply. "Not Brivardo again?"

"No, our friendly trash detector cyborg."

Velkan raises a brow. "Cwelt may be primitive, but you can be surprisingly brilliant at times!"

"Well, when you're done basking in my brilliance, let's make tracks before he checks out for the day."

Velkan reaches for my hand. "I'm not sure he's technically a cyborg if he only has a metal finger, so you lose a few points for that."

"Don't dock me yet," I retort as we make our way back down the street to hail a LevCab. "He may have more metal parts we don't know about."

To my relief, the cyborg is sitting in the same spot in the docking station as earlier, muttering to himself as people swarm by. Judging by the sour expression on his face, he has only grown more disgruntled as the day wore on. Several recycle drones hover over guilty parties, directing them to the nearest trash vaporization chutes in various galactic languages.

"He doesn't look like he's going to be as receptive to friendly banter this time around," I say to Velkan. "And we don't have time to waste softening him up. Maybe we should just offer him some credits in exchange for showing us how to access the sewer system."

"He's going to wonder why we want to go down there."

"I have an idea about that," I say, tugging Velkan's arm.

He looks doubtful, but he acquiesces with a shrug.

We walk slowly past the cyborg and nod in his direction. A flicker of recognition comes into his eyes, and he waves us over. "Leaving already?"

"Not yet." I smile brightly at him. "We have some research to conduct for the Interplanetary Health Alliance."

The cyborg extends his metal finger and scratches his back, reassessing us. "Didn't take you for scientists," he remarks. "More like tourists from one of them up and coming planets."

"We study viruses and bacteria in human waste," I say. "Not the most glamorous kind of research."

The cyborg pulls down the corners of his lips in disgust. "It's one thing dealing with people's trash above ground, but I wouldn't want to touch what goes underground!"

My heart pounds at the perfect segue he's provided. I fix a generous smile across my face. "You have a sophisticated sewer system on Aristozonex. I haven't seen a single sewer cover."

The cyborg looks at me with a horrified expression on his face. "You don't need to go down there, do you?"

I give an indifferent shrug. "It's our job. We work for the Inter-planetary Health Alliance. We do random checks on every planet's sewer system." I lean toward him. "You'd be surprised what's fermenting beneath cities."

The cyborg frowns. "Do you have a permit or something?"

I pull my lips into a tight line. "We're still waiting to hear back from the Sanitation Unit. They've delayed us several days already."

The cyborg grunts. "Waste of time solar trash. Sit at their desks all day and process nothing but their own garbage."

I throw a quick glance over my shoulder. "To tell you the truth, I think they're hiding something. The air samples we've taken here are disturbing."

An alarmed look passes over the cyborg's face. "I told them last month those trash vaporization chutes needed to be sterilized."

I paint on a grave expression. "I'm afraid it's a lot more serious than that. Two trash detection agents died in the past few weeks. The Sanitation Unit is trying to hush it up, but there's rumor it's a flesh-eating bacterium emanating from the sewer system." I lean conspiratorially toward the cyborg. "I don't suppose you could show us how to get down and grab a sample. It would save us several days' delay and a whole lot of grief— maybe even your life. Naturally, we would compensate you for your trouble."

The cyborg's chest heaves in and out several times as he considers the proposition. "Don't see why not. If this job's hazardous to my health, I want to know about it. My shift is over in ten minutes. Meet me at the curb."

Velkan and I wander across to a couple of nearby stalls and make a show of examining the wares. I keep one eye on the holographic timekeeper above the security gate. Exactly ten minutes later, we make our way to the curb just as the cyborg comes hobbling up. He gives us a quick nod and ducks into a waiting LevCab. Velkan and I exchange questioning looks and then climb in after him. The cyborg stares studiously out of his window, avoiding eye contact with either of us. I decide against trying to strike up a conversation. Maybe LevCab conversations are recorded, and he doesn't want to be associated with us in case we're caught, or perhaps he's always this morose after a day's work.

We ride in silence for fifteen minutes or so until the LevCab floats to a standstill on the outskirts of town. The cyborg gestures to us to pay the fare. I swipe my CipherSync and the door retracts. We disembark in an old industrial area where most of the businesses appear to be enclosed by high fences, behind which I can hear guard dogs snarling.

I look around uneasily. "Is this where the Sanitation Unit is located?"

The cyborg beckons to me with his metal finger. "Credits first. Twenty-thousand is the least I'll take."

I hesitate, pretending to be shocked by the preposterous amount, even though I would pay several hundred thousand if that's what it took to find Ghil.

The cyborg taps his CipherSync impatiently, and I transfer the credits. At the rate I'm spending them on bribes, I'll be broke before I find a buyer for the dargonite.

The cyborg peers at his wrist and then looks up, apparently satisfied. "Officially, the sewers can only be accessed by the Sanitation Unit from within their facility. But there's a backup maintenance shaft in this section of town, in case of an industrial accident."

"Great," I say, looking around. "Where is it?"

The cyborg points at a large gray building to our left. "It's in the basement of the water purification plant."

"How do we get in?" Velkan asks.

The cyborg makes an annoying clicking sound. "That's for you to figure out. My job was to bring you here. I'm not going near no flesh-eating bacteria." He turns on his heel and shuffles off into the night.

I eye the imposing fence that surrounds the water purification plant.

"There's no way we can climb that fence," Velkan says.

"If Ghil found a way in, so can we," I say a lot more confidently than I feel.

"We don't know where Ghil is," Velkan reminds me. "This is a long shot at best."

"Let's stake it out for a bit now that we're here," I say.

We conceal ourselves behind a stack of wooden crates and watch as people come and go through the main entry gate in small groups, presumably changing shifts. "Doesn't look like there's much security," I say. "All we really need is to nab some of those dingy-looking overalls and we can slip right in."

"And how do you plan on getting a hold of overalls?" Velkan asks.

I grin. "Follow a couple of workers and ask nicely."

He shakes his head. "I think I know where this is going."

"We're not going to mug them," I say in an injured tone. "I've become an expert at bribing people. We'll pay them for the overalls."

It takes a bit of persuading Velkan to go along with me, but after a while, I break his resolve. "Although I still think it's a bad idea," he says with some lingering hesitation. "They could report us to the Minders."

We stay crouched behind the crates until we spot a couple of targets around our size. They make their way out of the main gate and turn down the main street.

"Hurry!" I whisper." We have to reach them before they hail a LevCab.

I turn around to prod Velkan into action, but he's disappeared.

Chapter 31

The hairs on the back of my neck prickle. Did he take off already? How did I miss him? I jerk my head around, my eyes frantically roving every nook and cranny for any sign of Velkan. I peer across the yard at the shadowy piles of coiled pipe and stacked rebar by the main gate. Maybe he darted over there already. "Velk—"

"Sssh!" A rough, calloused hand covers my mouth and I catch the glint of a blade out of the corner of my eye. My scream comes out as a muffled yelp as I'm dragged down beneath the crates.

"It's Ghil," the voice whispers in my ear. "Velkan's here with me."

The grip of the strong hand over my mouth slackens. My muscles relax when I spot Velkan hunkered down a few feet away. I turn around slowly. Even in the dim light, I can see that Ghil's face is badly swollen, blood crusted in his hair and eyebrows. "Are you all right?" I whisper.

He gives a curt nod. "The Syndicate didn't do this. It was Crank and Sarth. They took Buir."

The words spin inside my head. My skin grows clammy. I

stare at Ghil hoping it doesn't end there; that he'll tell me she escaped or something, but the caustic pain in his eyes speaks for itself. I bite down on my lip until the metallic taste of blood fills my mouth. I can't let anything happen to Buir. The only reason she's in this mess to begin with, is because of me. "We'll go after them," I say, fiercely. "But first we have to get you to safety."

"I was trying to get down to the sewers, but there's no way inside the building," Ghil says. "Security's too tight."

"Then we'll figure something else out," I say.

Ghil shakes his head slowly. "You shouldn't have come after me. If they catch you helping me, you'll be sent to the penal colonies too."

"We're not going to leave you behind. Not after everything you've done for us."

"Trattora's right," Velkan says. "We just need to put our heads together and come up with an alternative plan."

Ghil sighs. "I already know what needs to be done. I can't run forever. The only way to end this is to undergo facial reconfiguration."

Velkan gives a somber nod. "It's worth the cost for freedom."

Ghil bows his head and traces the blade of his knife in the dirt. "I'll get my freedom back, but I'll lose a part of me. Maybe that's the price I pay for all the things I did."

"So, you're willing to go through with it if we find a dermal sculptor?" I ask.

Ghil shrugs. "I don't have enough credits to pay them."

"I don't have much left either," I say, "but I know someone who does. And I reckon he owes us a favor after setting up that meeting with Sarth and putting our lives in danger."

"What are you thinking?" Velkan asks.

"You and I will pay Stefanov a visit. If he wants his share of any more dargonite, he'll have to help us."

Ghil smirks. "The irony is that Sarth and Crank don't even realize they have our dargonite on board."

Velkan raises his brows. "They didn't find it?"

Ghil shakes his head. "They about tore that ship apart looking for it, though. They're convinced Trattora took it off the ship. They're planning to go to Cwelt and trade Buir and the other Cweltans to the Maulers in exchange for a deal on mining rights."

I swallow hard. "Then we'll intercept them before they arrive."

"It would help if we had a ship." Ghil clenches his fist in frustration.

"A ship won't do us any good if we can't take you with us. Velkan and I will go back to the pawn emporium and talk to Stefanov. Stay here until we return."

Once the coast is clear, Velkan and I slip out to the road and walk briskly to the nearest LevCab stand.

Twenty minutes later, we pull up outside the pawn emporium. A flashing holographic sign displays an end-of-season sale with discounts storewide.

"Busy," I say, eying the steady stream of customers going in and out.

"Not the best timing," Velkan acknowledges.

We make our way inside and blend in with the patrons browsing the wares. Several androids are stationed behind each counter attending customers, and Stefanov's daughter, Leeta, is assisting a customer at a jewelry display. When she spots us, she says something into her CipherSync. Minutes later, Stefanov comes striding up to us. He draws his imposing brows together. "What are you doing here?" He fixes an accusing gaze on me.

"We need to talk," I say.

Stefanov jerks his chin at Velkan. "Why's he here?"

"He's a part of this conversation," I reply. I can't help being distracted by Leeta who's obviously straining to listen in on what I'm saying. "A *private* conversation," I add, emphatically.

Stefanov throws one last disapproving look at Velkan and then leads us downstairs to his office. "As you can see, I'm extremely busy with our end-of-season sale." He closes the door behind us. "What can I help you with?"

"You have a funny way of defining help," I begin.

Stefanov narrows his eyes. "What's this about?"

"You set us up," I say. "That buyer you found us stole our ship and all the dargonite on board. She and her henchman also kidnapped one of our crew and turned in our captain, Ghil, as a fugitive."

Stefanov's face pales. He stares at me with a pinched expression on his face. "She found *me*. I should have known something was up. It was too easy."

"She's on her way to the dargonite mine as we speak," I say. "Unless we intercept her, you won't see your share of any more dargonite."

Stefanov passes a hand over his face. "I can't help with that. I don't have access to a ship."

"We'll worry about that part," Velkan says. "What we need you to do is find us a dermal sculptor willing to perform facial reconfiguration on a fugitive."

Stefanov widens his eyes. "Is your captain the fugitive who escaped today?"

I nod. "He was your buyer's right-hand man. If anyone can predict her next move, he can."

Stefanov fingers his jaw nervously. "Dermal sculptors willing to work on fugitives are rare. The risks are enormous."

"But you know of one?" I press.

He wets his lips. "I haven't spoken to her in a long time. I can't be sure the Syndicate isn't using her as an informant now. People who are caught will do anything to avoid being sent to the penal colonies."

"Contact her and ask if she can come here," I say. "We don't have much time. We need the procedure done right away."

"We can't do it here," Stefanov protests.

"Where else would we do it?" I ask. "This is as safe a place as any."

"I can't put my business in jeopardy," Stefanov says. "It's too dangerous."

"Not as dangerous as your life will become if the Minders find out about your connection to the escaped fugitive."

A nerve twitches in Stefanov's jaw. He pulls his lips into a grim line. "All right, I'll initiate contact, but I can't promise anything."

"That's not good enough." I take a step toward him. "I can promise you that if you don't deliver, your game is up. I have contacts in very high places."

Stefanov frowns. "Minder Brivardo's too deep into this to rat me out—"

"I don't care about Minder Brivardo!" I snap back. "But I do know the Syndicate Fleet Commander would be very interested to learn of your illegal dealings in dargonite—especially in light of how badly the military needs it for its new coating technology."

Stefanov's jaw drops. He scrutinizes me for a moment as if scarcely daring to believe that I could have a connection so far up on Aristozonex.

"His daughter Ayma and I go back a long way," I say.

Stefanov's face contorts with fear. "Give me an hour. I'll make some calls."

"Much better," I say. "We'll be back."

Velkan and I exit the office and ride the elevachute up.

"You scared him good," Velkan says.

"Let's just hope his dermal sculptor is still in the game and not working for the Syndicate," I say. "Otherwise, we'll all be on a transit ship to the penal colonies tonight."

The elevachute door opens and we exit on the ground floor of the pawn emporium. An android assistant presides over the jewelry counter where Stefanov's daughter, Leeta, was working earlier.

"Is Leeta here?" I ask casually. I need to find out how much she knows about Sarth and Crank, and whether she's ever seen them before. If Stefanov's lying about not knowing it was a setup, we may not be able to trust him with a dermal sculptor either.

The android obliges me with a polite smile. "You just missed her. She left in a hurry."

I raise my brows at Velkan. "Interesting timing, don't you think? Stefanov might have sent her to alert the Minders."

Velkan looks grave. "We'd better follow her and see where she's off to."

We hurry out into the street in time to spot Leeta climbing into a LevCab. I quickly hail a second one. "Follow that vehicle in front," I command, sinking back into the seat beside Velkan. I stare out the window watching the soaring high rises zip by us. "Do any of these buildings look familiar to you?" I say.

"I was just thinking the same thing," Velkan says. "We've taken this route before."

A sinking feeling comes over me when the LevCab slows to descent speed over a familiar street. I peer down at the Minder Depot below us, my heart racing. Is Stefanov about to betray us a second time?

"Park fifty feet from the other vehicle," I order the LevCab. We come to a gentle halt and I watch as Leeta climbs out and disappears around the side of the Minder Depot.

I turn to Velkan. "She's not using the main door. She's definitely up to something."

We give her a moment and then disembark and make our way down the same side of the building. At the sound of voices, we slip behind a trash vaporization unit and crouch down in the shadows. I try to still my breathing as I peer cautiously around the unit. Out of the corner of my eye I spot Leeta in conversation with someone concealed behind a half-open fire evacuation door.

"I can't make out who she's talking to," Velkan says, craning his neck. "Obviously, they don't want anyone seeing them together."

The voices grow louder. "... gave you everything I got," Leeta whines. "I need a more powerful listening device. His office is soundproofed ..."

A male voice murmurs in response. From his tone, I'm guessing he's trying to appease her, but I can't make out what he's saying. Then, a familiar figure leans out from behind the door, curls an arm around Leeta's waist and plants a kiss on her lips.

Chapter 32

I shrink back in disbelief. "Stefanov would tear him limb from limb if he knew," I whisper to Velkan. I click on the vid feed in my CipherSync and raise my wrist, panning the scene to try and get as much of Brivardo and the Minder Depot in as possible. "He's using Leeta to bug her father's office."

"Pretty shrewd on Brivardo's part, covering all his bases," Velkan replies in a hushed tone. "Making sure he always stays one step ahead of Stefanov."

"The good thing is we can use this to blackmail Brivardo," I say. "Ghil's going to need a new CipherSync, and Brivardo can make it happen."

"Now's as good a time as any to hit him up," Velkan says. "He'll be rattled to learn we saw what went down between him and Leeta."

We remain hidden in the shadows as Leeta heads back out to the main street and hails a LevCab. I check to make sure the side door to the Minder Depot is closed and then Velkan and I crawl out from behind the trash vaporization unit. "Let's make this quick," I say, leading the way around to the front of the building.

The clerk's frown deepens when I ask for Minder Brivardo. She exchanges a few words with him on her CipherSync and then buzzes Velkan and I through with a disapproving glare.

"Nice seeing you again Minder Clerk Daphnist!" I call out cheerfully as we make our way down the hallway to Brivardo's office.

Velkan throws me a skeptical look and I shrug. "I'll take a grumpy human over an android any day."

Brivardo half-rises out of his seat when we walk in, "What are you doing back here?" He narrows his eyes at Velkan. "Who is this?"

"He's one of my crew."

"You can't keep coming here," Brivardo snaps. "The clerk is beginning to suspect something's going on between us."

I give him a condescending smile. "She wouldn't be too far off the mark. I'm about the right age, aren't I, Minder Brivardo?"

A nerve twitches above his brow bone. "How dare you!"

I lean forward in my seat and click the holographic vid feed on my CipherSync. "I don't have time for games. Perhaps this will jolt you out of your short-term memory fog."

Brivardo stares at the images of himself and Leeta hovering between us like surreal ghosts of guilt. "Turn it off!" he hisses, paling before our eyes. "What do you want from me?"

"We need a new CipherSync," Velkan says.

"Now!" I add.

"Impossible." Brivardo's hand shakes as he wipes his glistening brow. "CipherSyncs can't be issued without the approval of the chief. It could take weeks."

"Forge the approval." I fix an icy gaze on him. "Either we

leave here with it, or we pay your chief a visit and inform him what it is you really do, and after that, we'll drop in on Stefanov and ask him if he recognizes anyone in our vid feed."

Brivardo taps a dispenser on his desk and snatches up a cigarette. He lights it with trembling fingers and takes a deep puff. "You found the fugitive?"

"I'm good at what I do," I reply.

He licks his lips. "He's agreed to give us the information on the mine in exchange for a new identity?"

I grin at him. "Like I said, I'm good at what I do. Now it's your turn to prove your worth."

Brivardo takes another puff of his cigarette and taps a button on his desk. A flex screen rises in front of him. "I need to hack into the chief's account first and then issue an emergency CipherSync request."

I roll my eyes. "I don't care what the steps are. Just do it."

Sweat beads on his forehead as he traces quivering fingers over the screen. "Security has been enhanced on his account recently," he says, frowning.

"Keep at it," Velkan says. "Just remember what's at stake."

Brivardo hesitates and shoots him a worried look before focusing back on the screen. The silence in the room is broken only by the sound of his heavy breathing until finally, he lets out a long shuddering sigh. "Got it!"

I straighten up in my chair. "The CipherSync?"

He looks at me with an air of irritation. "I mean I got *in.* Now I need to issue the replacement CipherSync."

I sink back and tap my fingers on the arms of the chair. As the minutes tick by, I become more and more impatient, my mind leaping through several frightening scenarios. What if Ghil got picked up while we were gone? What if Stefanov betrays us instead of finding a dermal sculptor? What if Cwelt has already succumbed to the Maulers? What if something unimaginable has happened to Buir?

"Done!" Brivardo announces in a raspy voice. He pushes his chair out and gestures to a dispenser on the wall. Right on cue, it spits out a CipherSync into the tray beneath it. Brivardo fumbles for another cigarette. "Take it and don't come back here again. It's too dangerous. Don't even contact me until you know the whereabouts of the mine."

I nod but promise him nothing as I stuff the CipherSync into my BodPak and exit the room. I've already rewarded him plenty for the information and help he's given us. I've no intention of letting him get his hands on the dargonite on Cwelt.

"Let's get back to the pawn emporium," I say to Velkan. "Hopefully Stefanov has good news for us by now."

I avoid looking in Leeta's direction when we walk by her counter. No matter how hard I try to hide it, the expression on my face would give away the fact that I know her dirty little secret. I wonder how long she's been spying on her own father and passing information to Brivardo.

Stefanov gets to his feet when we enter his office. A short woman with a narrow forehead and small eyes is seated in the chair opposite him. She fixes a sly gaze on us and instantly, I dislike her.

Stefanov gives a nervous cough and gestures at the woman. "I've found a dermal sculptor. You can address her as Doctor X. She would prefer to remain anonymous, given the circumstances."

"I have a mobile surgical unit ready and waiting inside the pawn emporium warehouse," Doctor X says in a voice that scrapes over my eardrums like a claw. "Where is the patient?"

I turn to Stefanov. "We'll need your vehicle to pick him up."

Stefanov gives a curt nod and issues a directive into his CipherSync. "It's pulling up outside. I've authorized your CipherSync to operate it."

"We'll be back within the hour," I say.

Velkan and I make our way out to the waiting vehicle and climb inside.

"I don't like her," I say.

"I didn't particularly like Doctor Azong either," Velkan says, "but she got the job done."

I let out a heavy sigh. "I suppose you're right. Dark market personalities aren't exactly endearing."

To my immense relief, Ghil is still safely tucked beneath the crates in the yard outside the water purification plant.

"We found a dermal sculptor," I say, as soon as he's safely inside Stefanov's LevAuto.

Ghil gives a grim nod, staring straight ahead. "Just need a CipherSync then."

"Already took care of it. Relax, Ghil, everything's going to be fine."

He sniffs hard. "I'm not worried about the procedure. What if none of you likes the new me?"

I give him a rueful smile. I know what he's really thinking. What if *Buir* doesn't like the new Ghil?

"We like what's on the inside," I say, gently. "That's what matters."

He runs a hand across his jaw as if touching it for the first time. "It'll be strange looking in the mirror and seeing a different man, but I'm ready to begin a new life."

We fall silent as the LevAuto ascends and picks up speed. Ghil's facial configuration procedure is only the first step. After that, we still need to figure how we're going to rescue Buir and save Cwelt from the Maulers now that we have no ship and no dargonite.

When we pull back into the pawn emporium warehouse, Doctor X and Stefanov are waiting for us at the back door of the mobile surgical unit, the side of which sports a large graphic of frontier planet timeshares with stunning backdrops of setting moons and shooting stars.

"My cover," Doctor X says, gesturing to the van with an unsettling grin. She runs a practiced eye over Ghil. "I take it this is the patient?"

"Yes," I say, peering inside the van. "Didn't you bring any assistants for such a complicated procedure?"

She fixes a stony gaze on me. "I work alone. More discreet that way."

"We can stay, in case you need some help," I offer.

"That won't be necessary. Reconfiguration is a fully computerized procedure, but it will take several hours, and it can be unpleasant to watch. It would be best if you wait upstairs with Stefanov."

She turns to Ghil and gestures to him to step inside the van.

"You got this." I splay my hand at him. "Can't wait to see your new smile."

He gives me an unexpectedly fierce hug. "As soon as this is

over, we'll find Buir," he whispers in my ear. "I promise you that."

I nod, too choked up to speak. I'm trying not to think about Buir too much. Every time I picture her at the mercy of Sarth and Crank, I fall apart inside.

Velkan and I follow Stefanov out of the warehouse and back down the basement hallway to his office.

"I have business to attend to upstairs," Stefanov says. "You can wait in here until the procedure is over if you like."

As soon as he exits the room, I turn to Velkan. "We'd better contact Ayma and let her know we won't be needing that buyer now that Sarth and Crank took off with the dargonite."

Velkan grimaces. "We need a ship instead."

I stare across at him. "Not a bad idea. Now you're the brilliant one."

"What are you talking about?"

"Ayma's father is the Syndicate Fleet Commander. If anyone has access to ships, it's him."

Velkan lets out a snort. "You think he's just going to give a warship."

"Not intentionally." I grin at him as I link to Ayma's CipherSync. "But I have an idea."

Ayma answers almost immediately. "I was beginning to think you were never going to contact me. I have a lead on a buyer, not very promising, but—"

"We're not going to need that buyer after all," I say. "Sarth and Crank kidnapped Buir and took off with the Zebulux and the dargonite."

There's a long pause before Ayma responds. "I'm sorry about

your friend. What about your captain?"

"Sarth turned Ghil in as a fugitive. He should be on a transport vessel to the penal colonies tonight, but he escaped. He's undergoing facial reconfiguration as we speak."

"A real shame Sarth managed to find you," Ayma says. "I know how desperate you were to sell that dargonite and buy your own ship to free your people."

"You can still help us." I bite my lip. "You have access to ships."

"Don't even go there," Ayma says. "You can't expect me to help you steal a ship."

"I'm not talking about stealing anything. I'm only asking you to set up a meeting with your father."

There's another long pause before she replies. "What about?"

I close my eyes and take a deep breath. "I'm going to plead for my people and ask him to send a warship to liberate Cwelt."

Ayma gasps. "It's a bold move, but it will never work. He won't commission a Syndicate warship to rescue some inconsequential fringe planet from Maulers."

"He might if he knew there was a dargonite mine there large enough to stealth coat the entire Syndicate fleet."

"You don't have proof of that," Ayma says. "I can guarantee you he won't take the word of a trader."

"I kept several nuggets of dargonite."

Ayma blows out a long breath. "All right, in that case I'll talk to him—he just walked in the door—but I can't promise anything. I'll link back in a few minutes."

She hangs up and I look across at Velkan. He shakes his head. "If this works, it will be your most brilliant move ever."

"Not quite." I lean back in Stefanov's swivel chair, a smug smile on my face. "Stealing a Syndicate warship to go after Sarth will top it."

Chapter 33

Velkan's eyes darken. He reaches across the desk and grips me by the arms. "Don't even say such a thing," he whispers in an urgent tone.

"Relax," I say. "Leeta gave the listening device to Brivardo, remember?"

The lines of disapproval deepen on Velkan's face. "There could be other bugs planted in here for all we know."

I shrug out of his grip. "She said she gave him everything she had, and I believe her. Obviously, she's besotted with him if she's willing to betray her own father."

Velkan sinks back into his chair. "You're not seriously thinking about trying to steal a ship?"

"How else are we going to pursue Sarth and rescue Buir? Anyway, we won't be stealing it, just borrowing it."

"We?"

"You, me, and Ayma."

Velkan twists his lips. "You heard what she said. She's not going to help us."

"*She's* going to make it happen. She can hack in and log a

ship out on some routine surveillance or something. We'll be back before the Fleet Commander returns."

"Why would she take a risk like that?" Velkan asks.

I stare straight at him. "Because she's one of us."

My CipherSync vibrates and lights up. "It's Ayma," I say, hitting the speaker.

"He wants to meet with you," she says.

"When?" I ask, my heart thumping wildly.

"Right away. Bring the dargonite."

I hang up and get to my feet. "Will you stay here with Ghil?"

Velkan gives a reluctant nod. "You know it could be a trap."

"Or it could mean Cwelt's liberation," I say. "We're running out of time. I can't walk away from an opportunity to save my people."

Inside the LevCab en route to the Syndicate military quadrant, I rehearse in my mind exactly what I need to say to persuade the Fleet Commander to deploy a warship to Cwelt. I finger the dargonite nuggets in my pocket and mouth my hastily thrown-together speech. I need to convince him there is enough dargonite on Cwelt to make it worth his while. I close my eyes and picture the magnificent indigo boulders and the peculiar shapes they form. My accurate description of the dargonite outcroppings on Cwelt will go a long way in convincing him that I've seen the boulders for myself.

My LevCab drops to the ground and pulls up a short distance from the main security gate outside the military quadrant. Security drones descend on me, scanning me and feeding my data into the Syndicate database. I approach the gate, but instead of being addressed by an electronic voice, a masked guard steps toward me and whisks me into a sleek LevAuto. I open my mouth to ask if he is taking me to see the Fleet Commander, but I think better of it. Wherever he's taking me, I don't have any choice in the matter, so I may as well wait it out and focus on my plea for my people.

I turn my attention to the window, keeping my eyes peeled for Ayma's gleaming glass residence. Buildings flash by below us, but none look familiar. The farther we travel, the more industrial the buildings become. My heart sinks. If this guard really is taking me to the Fleet Commander, then we must be meeting at an undisclosed location. It doesn't bode well for my safety if things don't turn out as I hope. I wonder if Ayma even knows where I am.

My suspicions are confirmed when we descend into a barricaded yard overgrown with weeds and pull around to the back of a large military hangar which has fallen into disrepair. Obviously, this meeting is strictly off the record. My stomach knots. Steel doors slide apart at our approach and the LevAuto rolls inside. I twist my hands nervously in my lap, awaiting direction. The guard says something into his CipherSync and then gestures to me to get out. I step out into the hangar and glance around, one hand protectively over my BodPak containing my remaining nuggets of dargonite and my bracelet. The guard does a quick sweep, weapon in hand. There's no sign of anyone else in the hangar. What if the real reason they brought me here is to find out where I got the dargonite and then kill me? I'm only carrying a tiny dagger that Ghil gave me for protection. Without the element of surprise, it will be next to useless against a well-trained guard.

I turn at the sound of voices wafting into the hangar. The

rolling doors open again and a heavily armed group of masked guards walks through, followed by two men in putty-colored scrubs, pushing some kind of scientific machine on a wheeled cart. I suck in my breath. Are they here for me? The guards part and a tall man in the center strides toward me, his black knee-high leather boots pounding out a forbidding chant, his cloak flapping from his shoulders, the ominous flaming planet Syndicate insignia on his stiff collar.

I stand motionless, a helpless sacrifice, like all the prey I've ever hunted. His eyes burrow into me. Instinctively, I bow, acknowledging the authority he exudes.

When I lift my head, he looks me up and down with a keen sweep of his eyes.

"I have never had reason to doubt my daughter, Ayma, before," he says, with a sardonic smile, "but when she requested that I meet with a teen trader who claims to be the sole heir of a dargonite mine on a fringe planet, I confess I hesitated."

"A prudent ruler contemplates before taking action," I say, inclining my head.

His lips tug up at the corners. "Wise words coming from a peasant woman."

"Perhaps the wisdom of elders from a primitive planet has universal application," I reply.

Something shifts in his expression, and I see the recognition in his eyes that I am someone to be taken seriously. He flexes black-gloved fingers. "You have evidence of this mine?"

I slip my hand into my pouch and pull out two of my four remaining pieces of dargonite. I open my palm and stretch it out toward him.

He signals to one of his guards who deftly retrieves the nuggets and hands them to the men in scrubs. They place them into the machine and study them through an optical scanner. One of them looks up and gives an unsmiling nod.

The Fleet Commander turns his attention back to me. "You found this dargonite on your planet?"

"Yes, there are large outcroppings there, all unmined. My people have been cut off from the trade routes for fourteen moons. We had no knowledge of the value of dargonite until recently."

"What do these outcroppings look like?"

"Breathtakingly beautiful," I say without hesitation. "Luminescent, they catch the rays of the sun and sparkle a myriad of shades. Mostly, though, they are a deep indigo, striated with feathers of primary colors." I smile. "They are smooth to the touch, and cold. Even under the sun's rays, they don't retain heat, as I'm sure your scientists already know."

The Fleet Commander folds his arms and scrutinizes me. "I'm aware of the reports of Maulers taking over the eastern arterial trade route. How long has your planet been under siege?"

"A few weeks. My people fled to the underground caves before the Maulers landed. Their supplies will last two or three months, at most."

"How did you escape?"

"I took shelter on a visiting oremongering vessel when the Maulers attacked. We had no choice but to depart when they turned their missiles on our ship." I pause to calm my breathing, drawing on everything my mother ever taught me about remaining regal in the face of pressure. "My people will perish if I don't return with help soon."

The Fleet Commander furrows his brow. "Where is your planet located?"

"Cwelt is a fringe planet near a defunct trading route in the Netherscape."

The guard on his right leans over and whispers something to the Fleet Commander. He narrows his eyes and studies me with a renewed air of skepticism.

"You were raised on this planet, Cwelt?"

I nod, unsure whether I should explain the strange circumstances of my arrival.

"I'm told Cweltans are a silver-haired people," the Commander says, his tone like steel.

"That is true." I hold my chin high. "I was brought there by traders as a young child and adopted by the chieftain."

The Commander's brows rise, and something in his face softens. "My daughter is also adopted."

He turns to the guard on his right, snapping into military mode. "Deploy the fleet tonight. We will liberate the planet and reopen the trade route."

"Thank you," I whisper, my voice choking.

"The Syndicate is not a galactic charity," he continues, in a chilly tone. "We will assume all mining rights to the dargonite in return for saving your people. I expect your full cooperation in the matter."

I breathe slowly in and out, without breaking his gaze. "The Syndicate is also not a galactic crook, Fleet Commander. Compensate Cwelt with military defenses for the mining rights and we have a deal."

He stares at me for the longest time. "You remind me so much of my daughter. You have displayed extraordinary courage in coming here and advocating for your people. Such courage merits the resources you request. If the dargonite exists, as you claim, Cwelt will emerge from this as the most well-defended planet on the fringe with a fleet unequalled in the Netherscape."

I bow my thanks, not trusting myself to speak.

The Fleet Commander turns and strides across the hangar, followed by his entourage, leaving me alone with the guard who escorted me here. He gestures to the LevAuto and I climb back inside, shaking as the adrenalin leaves my body. I desperately want to link to Ayma and talk to her, but her father will likely tell her the news himself. I'll contact her later and proposition her with the second part of my plan—going after the Zebulux.

I exit the military quadrant under the watchful gaze of the guard and hail a LevCab. Safely inside, I sink back in the seat and close my eyes. Despite all my experience as High Daughter on Cwelt, holding court with the Syndicate's most powerful military figure was a daunting prospect. I've sacrificed the dargonite to save my people, but at least I salvaged something out of the arrangement. Cwelt will be safe from future raids by Maulers or any other Galactic pirates in the Netherscape. Now it's time to focus on rescuing Buir.

Minutes later, the LevCab deposits me outside the pawn emporium. I make my way through to the back of the store without encountering either Stefanov or his daughter, and take the elevachute down to the basement.

Velkan is dozing in a chair inside Stefanov's office. He startles awake and rubs his eyelids sleepily. "Back already?"

"I've been gone for almost two hours." I plonk down on the

edge of the desk. "Do you want to hear some good news?"

Velkan straightens up, suddenly alert. "Tell me you didn't steal a ship."

I shake my head. "The Fleet Commander deployed the fleet. They depart for Cwelt tonight."

A look of astonishment mingled with admiration spreads across Velkan's face. "I didn't think he would go for it."

"He went for the mining rights." I grimace. "No surprise there. But I negotiated military defenses for Cwelt. We will finally possess our own fleet of ships. *I'll* have my own ship. You know what that means, don't you?"

A troubled expression clouds Velkan's eyes. "You still want to go to Mhakerta after what Ayma told us?"

"*Especially* after what Ayma told us. Our parents risked everything to save us. Now it's our turn to save them. This isn't the time to succumb to fear."

"I'm not scared of what we'll find on Mhakerta; I'm scared of losing you," Velkan says, his voice growing quiet.

We jerk around when the door slides open behind us. Stefanov comes into the room and stares at us, a dazed expression on his face.

"I'm afraid she's ..." He swallows hard, pulling his arched brows into pinnacles above the apprehension churning in his eyes.

"What's wrong?" I reach for his sleeve and shake him. "Is it Leeta?"

Chapter 34

My mind races to the scene in the alleyway. I should have told Stefanov what we saw. Leeta is playing a dangerous game splitting her allegiance between the two men in her life. I hope nothing has happened to her.

"It isn't Leeta," Stefanov says. "It's the doctor."

"Doctor X?" I say, a new angst niggling in my gut. "What about her?"

Stefanov frowns. "I'm sorry."

I throw an alarmed look at Velkan. Why is Stefanov apologizing to us?

Velkan gets to his feet. "Is Ghil all right?"

Stefanov runs a hand over his jaw, a grave expression on his face.

"Answer him! Where's Ghil?" I yell, jumping to my feet.

"He's in the warehouse. She ... botched the procedure."

The breath in my lungs turns to ice. Velkan and I exchange a fleeting glance and then turn and race out of the room. We tear along the musty hallway and burst through the door into the warehouse where we left Ghil.

Stefanov's LevAuto is still parked in the same spot, but the mobile surgical unit is gone. At first, I can't see any sign of Ghil anywhere. I scan the room again and then I spot what appears to be the edge of a gurney sticking out from an aisle of shipping boxes. My legs barely support me as I run toward it. I pull up short, and Velkan bumps into me from behind. We stare in disbelief at Ghil's reconfigured face—angular nose, firm jaw, smooth skin and blemish-free complexion. No trace of the crusted blood or bruises from a few short hours ago. It looks nothing like him. But he's wearing Ghil's clothes. "Ghil!" I whisper to the sleeping figure covered in an aluminum blanket.

I shake him gently and call his name again, but he doesn't respond. Stefanov's words sear my brain. *She botched the procedure.*

"No!" I whisper, scrunching the blanket in my fist.

I watch, panic-stricken, as Velkan checks for a pulse. His hand shakes as he removes it. "He's alive! Barely."

I gasp like a drowning woman who's just been rescued. Hope sears a course through me. "We'll take him to Ayma," I say, scrabbling for the rails on the gurney. "She can access the best doctors in the Aristozonex. Help me get him into Stefanov's LevAuto."

Velkan turns the gurney and pushes it forward. "I don't know if he'll make the trip."

"Stefanov will pay for this," I say, through gritted teeth. "That *doctor* probably wasn't licensed."

I feel dizzy, my breath coming in ragged spurts. How could this have happened? I wanted to help Ghil—give him back his freedom—not hurt him.

We wheel the gurney over to Stefanov's LevAuto and lift Ghil gently inside. He's so still that I fear he has passed already, but I don't dare ask Velkan to check for a pulse again. As soon as the door closes and Velkan gives the command to take us to the military quadrant, I link to Ayma and put my CipherSync on speaker. "We need your help," I say breathlessly, when she responds.

"What's wrong?"

"The doctor botched the procedure. Ghil's unconscious."

"Is the facial reconfiguration complete?" Ayma asks.

"Yes," I say. "He's unrecognizable."

"Bring him here. I'll have a team of doctors waiting in our medical wing."

I sink back against the seat in relief. I wasn't sure Ayma would agree to help us. If she's caught assisting an escaped fugitive, it could jeopardize her future career with the Syndicate military, and maybe her life. She must feel a strong connection to us if she's willing to risk everything. The bracelets have bonded us.

Velkan commands the LevAuto to attain the maximum speed and we reach the military quadrant in record time. The burly guard at the security booth is obviously expecting us. He opens the gate immediately and within seconds, Ayma's LevAuto pulls up to take us to her residence. For once, no security drones pester us. The guard singlehandedly transfers Ghil into the waiting vehicle. I've no idea what Ayma told him, but whatever he's thinking behind his mask, he's following her instructions unquestioningly.

When we reach Ayma's residence, the LevAuto glides to a stop out front. Ayma's face is strained when she appears at the front door, accompanied by two doctors wheeling a gurney. They waste no time taking Ghil from the guard's arms and whisking him away. I bite my lip, unsure if I'll ever see him again. I blame myself for what happened. I shouldn't have trusted Stefanov to find me a dermal sculptor.

Ayma ushers us inside and down the hall to her office. The burly guard at our tail takes up a position outside the door.

"They'll do everything they can," Ayma says when the door closes behind us. "I can't make any promises."

"Thank you," I say in a hoarse whisper. I toss my BodPak on the floor and sink down on a chair. "How did you explain it to the doctors?"

She gives a one-shouldered shrug. "I told them I wanted to help out a classmate's father who used a dark market doctor to save credits. They know I've got a big heart."

I flash her a grateful grin.

"If he survives, he'll need to stay here to recover," Ayma says.

I nod. "In the meantime, I have to find Buir. And I need a ship to do that."

Ayma frowns. "My private shuttle is only a small commuter vessel for getting around the Aristzone."

"That's not what I had in mind," I say. "We'll need a warship. Sarth isn't going to hand Buir over unless she has no alternative."

"My father already left for Cwelt. Anyway, he wouldn't deploy a warship to recover a stolen oremongering vessel and a kidnapped peasant from a fringe planet."

I lean toward her. "Surely he didn't take the entire fleet."

"Everything except for the stealth fighter prototype—the top secret dargonite coating technology project I hacked into."

I shrug. "Perfect."

Her eyes widen and then narrow. "You can't possibly imagine you could take the stealth fighter and pursue the Zebulux yourself?"

"I wouldn't dream of it! I'm planning on taking you and Velkan with me."

Ayma flicks me an irritated look. "You know humor in times of crises is overrated."

"I wasn't joking."

Her frown deepens. "You expect me to hack back into the military database and authorize this?"

"Exactly!"

"No!" Ayma folds her arms across her chest and stares at me defiantly.

"I only need to borrow a ship," I say. "Your father has already granted Cwelt full military defenses. I'll own my own ship after he liberates my planet. But right now, time is of the essence to save Buir."

"The Syndicate would strip me of all my privileges if they found out," Ayma says. "My father could lose his position. They might even send my parents to the penal colonies."

"That's not going to happen," Velkan says. "The Zebulux is a slow-moving and tired vessel. We could track it and reach it in a matter of hours and be back long before your father reaches Cwelt."

"If you knew Buir as I do, you wouldn't hesitate to risk everything for her," I say. "She's the most thoughtful and kind person I know. She even brought Ghil out of his crusty old shell. I've confided in her from the very first day I arrived at Cwelt.

She knows me better than anyone. And it's my fault she's in this situation. She didn't want to leave Cwelt to begin with, but the decisions I made left her with no alternative." I blink back burning tears. "Sometimes people are forced to make difficult choices—just like our birth parents did to save us."

Ayma's posture remains rigid, but her eyes soften. She presses her knuckles to her lips and ponders her decision for a few minutes. "All right," she says with a sigh. "I can log in and deploy it on a top-secret mission with only high-level clearance. The monitors will assume my father authorized it for his mission to liberate Cwelt."

"How will we get on board?" Velkan asks. "Aren't there cameras everywhere at the base?"

Ayma's lips tug up at the corners. "We won't be on the stealth fighter when it departs Aristozonex. We'll take my private shuttle and board a hundred miles out within our atmosphere. That's as far as my shuttle can go."

She sits down at her desk and studies the flex screen that automatically rises in front of her. For the next few minutes, her fingers fly furiously over the screen, her face knotted in concentration.

My stomach churns as she works. I'm placing all my confidence in her and her father to save Buir and my people on Cwelt. I hope it's not a mistake.

"All set!" Ayma gets to her feet, a resolute expression on her face. She has crossed a line and thrown in her lot with us, for better or for worse. The flex screen retracts into the desk and disappears from sight. "We can check in on Ghil via CipherSync on our way," she says.

She leads us into an elevachute that takes us up to the rooftop hangar where several sleek personal shuttles of varying sizes and colors are parked. She walks over to a scarlet shuttle and keys something into the control panel on the hull. The retractable door on the side slides open and she gestures us inside.

I look around admiringly at the plush white interior and deluxe cushioned seating—a far cry from the taped seats on the Zebulux. Hard to believe Ayma has led such a sophisticated life in the same galaxy where so many primitive planets like Cwelt still exist.

Ayma watches my reaction with amusement. "You can fly it if you want," she offers.

I slide into the pilot seat without hesitation. "It might be the first and last time I get to pilot a private Syndicate vessel."

Ayma slides into the seat next to me and keys in the coordinates where we will intercept the stealth fighter. Moments later, the entire rooftop above us opens up and retracts into the walls of the hangar, exposing the expansive evening sky. My chest tightens. I'm struck by how scared and helpless Buir must be feeling. Maybe she's looking out of a porthole on the Zebulux wondering where we are. Instinctively I splay my hand on the console in front of me. *I'm coming for you, Buir.*

Our shuttle ascends smoothly, the contented purr of a powerful engine the only sound in our ears as we depart on our pre-determined course. The sky is a burning orange, daubed with gray shadows, the filtered light highlighting streams of microscopic space debris. I implement everything Sarth taught me about flight navigation, the irony not escaping me that I'm using her knowledge now to hunt her down. Once we find her,

Sarth will have no choice but to surrender. The shields on the aging Zebulux will never withstand an attack by a stealth fighter. The only question is whether we will be in time to save Buir.

"There she is." Ayma points to the scanner. "We're right on target. Don't worry about docking. The fighter will pull us in."

She keys in a series of commands and a pair of articulated steel cables shoot toward us from the fighter. They fasten onto the hull with a sudden force that sends a shudder through the entire shuttle. Within minutes, the cables have reeled us inside an enormous hangar stocked with all forms of military hardware and racks of handheld weapons. Rolling doors clang shut behind us and heated oxygen begins pumping through the chamber. When the flashing red lights on the ceiling turn green, Ayma jumps to her feet. "We can exit now," she says.

She leads us up to the control room and then swiftly gets to work setting a navigational path to intercept the Zebulux. "We're only about twenty minutes out," she announces. "Activating cloaking mode. They'll never see us coming."

"I'm going to go look at the engine room," Velkan says, disappearing out the door.

"What's the plan once we reach the Zebulux?" I throw a worried glance at Ayma. "We can't fire at the ship with Buir on board."

"Don't worry, I can disable it if Sarth decides not to cooperate," she replies. "We'll tow them back to Aristozonex if we have to."

Velkan returns to the control room just as the Zebulux appears on the scanner. I've spent the last few minutes of our approach imagining every possible scenario and outcome, and now I'm chilled to the bone at the sight of the ship. Despite Ayma's reassurances to the contrary, this could go horribly wrong if Sarth doesn't cooperate. I know what she's capable of.

"There's a heat reading," Ayma says. "Confirming life on board."

"Let me try talking to Sarth first," I say. "I might be able to persuade her to let us send a shuttle over for Buir if we let her and Crank go free." I quell my misgivings and switch on the radio. "Sarth, do you copy? This is Trattora. I'm here under the jurisdiction of a Syndicate ship. You are ordered to surrender immediately and prepare to be boarded."

I wait for Sarth's response—a counter offer, a rebuttal, even her sarcastic laugh. But the radio remains silent.

"Try it again," Velkan says.

"Sarth, I need you to confirm that you can hear me. Your ship is being commandeered by the Syndicate. If you surrender Buir to us, we will drop the kidnapping charges against you and let you go."

After a few minutes of silence, Ayma turns to me. "Do you want me to disable the ship?"

I shake my head. "Something's wrong. It's not like Sarth to keep her big mouth shut. I need to board the Zebulux and find out what's going on."

Ayma gives a curt nod. "I'll activate a transfer shuttle. Make sure you're armed and take Velkan with you."

Velkan and I each grab a plasma laser gun from a rack in the cargo bay before climbing into the transfer shuttle.

Moments later, we attach to the airlock chamber on the Zebulux. Once we transfer into the cargo bay, I pan the area slowly, gun at the ready, searching every crevice for any sign of Sarth or Crank. My gut clenches when I spot a figure slumped like a rag doll at the wheel base of the LunaTrekker.

Chapter 35

"Buir!" I scream, darting across the floor to her.

She lifts her head groggily as I come skidding to a halt beside her. "Fetch some water!" I yell to Velkan. "Grab a canister from the LunaTrekker." I fumble to untie Buir's bound hands and then put my arm around her and help her into a more comfortable sitting position. "Are you hurt?" I ask.

She shakes her head, a lone tear rolling down her cheek. "I thought I would never see you again. They left me to die."

"Where are they?" I ask.

"Crank's warship picked them up." She throws me an apologetic look. "They found the dargonite. Sarth actually ate some of that vile mash we hid it in." She gives a weak smile. "Ghil will get a laugh out of that." Her expression freezes. She grips my arm like a vice. "They turned Ghil in. We have to rescue him before it's too late."

"Buir," I whisper. "He escaped."

She blinks, waiting for me to continue. Her eyes sweep mine like she knows I'm holding something back. "What is it?" she whispers.

I take a deep breath. "Stefanov found a dermal sculptor to perform facial reconfiguration on Ghil. Something went wrong. He … he hasn't come around from the procedure."

Buir claps a hand over her mouth. Her shoulders begin to shake but she doesn't make a sound, which makes it even more heart wrenching.

"I'm so sorry, Buir."

"Is he going to make it?" Her eyes dart to Velkan and back to me.

"The doctors are doing everything they can," I say.

Tears roll freely down her alabaster cheeks. I take her in my arms and hold her until her sobs subside.

"I brought you some water," Velkan says, kneeling beside her.

She wipes her eyes and drinks greedily before handing the canister back to Velkan. "How did you find me?"

"Ayma tracked the Zebulux in a Syndicate stealth fighter," Velkan says.

Buir's eyes widen. "The Syndicate loaned you a stealth fighter."

"Not exactly." Velkan shoots me a helpless look.

"The Fleet Commander is on his way to liberate Cwelt from the Maulers, so we availed ourselves of the opportunity to take the stealth fighter for a test run," I say. "You're going to love it. It's a prototype, built with the new dargonite coating technology that renders it invisible."

Buir arches a delicate silver brow. "I leave you for one day and you abscond with the Syndicate's top secret ship."

I give a sheepish grin, blinking back tears. "It's so good to have you back on my case."

She shakes her head and gets to her feet. "We'd better make sure we return it before the Fleet Commander gets back." She hesitates, a troubled look clouding her eyes again. "And I need to be there for Ghil."

I glance around the cargo bay one more time and then lead Buir across to the transfer shuttle where Velkan is already waiting.

"This could well be the last time you set eyes on the Zebulux," I say to Velkan as we climb aboard. "Any regrets?"

He grimaces. "None."

I fire up the shuttle and fasten my harness. "She's somebody's salvage now," I say as we lift off and exit the dock.

Back on the stealth fighter, I introduce Buir and Ayma.

"I remember seeing you at the EduPlex." Ayma runs an admiring eye over Buir's waist-length silver white hair. "Trattora speaks highly of your friendship."

"I appreciate everything you've done," Buir replies. "Do you have any more news on Ghil?"

"I linked to the doctors for an update on his condition about ten minutes ago," Ayma replies. "He's out of surgery. It's touch and go."

A pained expression flits across Buir's face. "Please, hurry. I need to be with him."

"It's going to be all right," I say, escorting her to an empty seat. "Ghil is strong. He'll pull through."

Ayma settles into the pilot's seat. As she engages the thrusters, her CipherSync lights up. She looks up sharply. "It's my father!"

My breath catches in my throat. "Is there any way he could have found out we took the fighter?"

"I don't think so. I'd better respond." She activates her CipherSync and puts it on speaker. "Father! Are you at Cwelt already?"

"I'm afraid we've encountered unexpectedly fierce resistance from Maulers stationed along the route. The fight to reach Cwelt, let alone liberate it, could be prolonged."

"How long do you estimate?"

"Several weeks at a minimum. The Maulers' ships are inferior, but guerrilla tactics will drag out the fight. Your mother has been called in to head up an emergency war advisory council."

"Don't worry about me, Father."

"I always worry about you." The Fleet Commander clears his throat. "It might be difficult to reach me until the Maulers have been subdued. I'll link to you as soon as I have news of victory."

The line crackles and cuts out.

I throw a quick glance back at Buir curled up in the seat behind us, eyes closed. I turn to Ayma, my heart beating rapidly. "This is our chance," I whisper. "With the fleet gone that long, we'll have time to chart a course to Mhakerta. Maybe the stealth fighter can pass undetected through Preeminence's air defense system."

Ayma rubs her brow, studying me for a moment. "If I could get through undetected, I could hack into the main neural framework and find out more about how Preeminence operates."

"So, you'll do it?"

She drums her fingers on the console. "If our birth parents are trapped by some despotic AI system, I'm willing to risk entering Mhakerta's airspace. I've been wanting to see the inside of that framework for years."

I breathe out a long sigh of relief as I slide back into the co-pilot's seat. "Thank you."

Ayma locks eyes with me. "Don't thank me yet. I don't know what we're getting into, and I'm not sure I can get us back out of it."

As we approach Aristozonex, Ayma activates the ship's cloaking technology again. "We'll take Buir back down on my personal shuttle. I'll tell the doctors she's Ghil's daughter. They can both stay here until we return, unless you want Buir to come with us?"

I shake my head. "She's been through enough already. And someone needs to stay with Ghil."

"I realize you and Buir are close, but we need to make this quick." Ayma pins a penetrating gaze on me. "My father may end up driving the Maulers out more quickly than he estimates. The stealth fighter needs to be back before the fleet returns, or there will be serious repercussions."

I know what she's trying to tell me; that there's no time for prolonged farewells and tears, even though there's a chance I may never see Buir again. But this isn't her cause to fight. What happens next is about Ayma and Velkan and me joining forces to find out what transpired on Mhakerta fourteen moons ago.

We transfer into Ayma's personal shuttle and make the short flight back to her rooftop hangar. She leads us back downstairs to the medical suite where Ghil lies motionless, connected to a dizzying array of machines.

Buir brushes past the doctors huddled around the monitors and makes her way to Ghil's bedside. She takes his hand and strokes it gently, her face pinched with grief. I turn away, my stomach knotting. Ghil promised he would find her again, but in the end, she found him.

I turn to one of the doctors. "How is he doing?"

"We have temporarily induced stasis in an attempt not to weaken his heart any further. It's a waiting game for now."

"Make sure his daughter has everything she needs," Ayma instructs him. "I have business to attend to and will be unavailable for the next several days."

The doctor bows his head and returns to the monitors.

"We should go," Velkan says. "Every minute we delay increases the risk of being discovered."

I nod. "Tell Buir we're going to return the fighter. I can't lie to her, not even to keep her safe."

I watch him walk over to Buir and say something to her.

She looks up and half rises out of her seat.

I steel myself for her parting words, but she's too broken to give me any of her sensible reminders and instead nods and sits back down. She flicks her shimmering hair over one shoulder and swats at a tear that dangles from the end of her nose.

I splay my hand good-bye one last time. It breaks my heart to know that if Ghil doesn't make it, she'll have to face his death alone. But I'm glad for her sake that she'll be someplace safe while we're gone.

Ayma arches a questioning brow at me and I nod. Velkan gives my arm a comforting squeeze as I turn away. I walk with heavy footsteps out of the room, afraid if I look back at Buir's tear-stained face, I won't be able to leave.

Inside Ayma's shuttle, I slump wearily into my seat. There's a hole in my heart at the thought of leaving Buir behind that makes me feel number than I thought possible. But it wouldn't be fair to ask her to participate in the enormous risk we're about to take by entering Preeminence's airspace. My job is to protect my people, and so far, I haven't done a good job of it. Meldus' death still weighs heavy on my conscience.

The shuttle takes off from the rooftop, veers left, and climbs quickly to the navigational path Ayma has set back to the stealth fighter. I sit, lost in my thoughts, for the duration of the flight. Twenty minutes later, we glide effortlessly into the fighter's cargo bay and wait for the green light signaling it is safe to disembark.

"Do you want to pilot?" Ayma asks once we reach the control room. "It might take your mind off things for a bit."

I tweak a grateful smile. "Thanks, but I'm too distracted. I need some time to process everything."

She nods and flicks on the navigation lights.

"Anyone hungry?" Velkan asks. "We haven't eaten all day."

My eyes immediately well up with tears. Buir was always the one to think about stuff like that. "I have a few extra energy bars," I say, sniffing hard as I look around for my BodPak. I peer under my seat, and glance around the control room, frowning. "I must have set my BodPak down somewhere during all the confusion."

"There are probably emergency provisions on board," Ayma says. She turns her attention back to the console. "I'll plug in our coordinates if someone wants to scrounge for food."

"I'll go," Velkan offers.

He returns a few minutes later with several packets of snack food and divides them up between us. I rip mine open, salivating at the smell. I'm just about to dig in when the riveted metal doors to the control room slide open again.

I turn in my seat and widen my eyes in horror at the Syndicate soldier towering in the doorway, black, leather-clad legs astride, his imposing frame blocking our only escape route. He steps toward us, gripping a plasma gun, his three-quarter length military coat flapping behind him. My snack pack falls from my hand, the contents spilling all over the floor. I crane my neck to see how many more are behind him. We can't possibly fight Syndicate soldiers. My throat constricts with fear. How did they find us? And how did they get on board?

Velkan moves silently to my side, his fists clenched.

Ayma springs to her feet. "What are *you* doing here?"

I turn to her in astonishment. She's talking to the soldier as if she knows him.

He meets Ayma's gaze briefly before inspecting Velkan and me with unabashed curiosity. "I could ask you the same thing. It's not every day the Fleet Commander's daughter steals a stealth fighter."

Ayma jerks her head toward the door. "Who else is with you?"

"I came alone," he replies calmly. His lips tug upward in an apologetic smile. "I overheard your plan and snuck on board before you deployed the launch sequence."

Ayma glares at him. "I know you think it's your duty to protect me, Phin, but you don't belong here."

"I'm not here to protect you." He reaches inside his coat, pulls out my BodPak, and tosses it to me. "I'm here to return this."

"Where did you find it?" I ask, frowning.

"You left it behind in Ayma's office."

I look at him more closely and realize it's the guard who

carried Ghil inside for us. I narrow my eyes at him. "What do you want?"

He walks toward me, slow, deliberate steps, his boots clipping the metal floor.

Velkan tenses, and I lay a restraining hand on his arm while keeping a close eye on the plasma gun in the soldier's hand.

He comes to a halt directly in front of me and holds out a small leather pouch.

I eye it suspiciously, a disturbing image of a bloodied finger flashing before my eyes. "What's this?"

"Open it," he insists, pressing it into my hand.

I tug the cord securing the neck of the pouch, tip the contents into the palm of my hand, and suck in a silent breath. *A perfect match to the other three.*

"Whatever mission you're on," Phin says. "I'm a part of it too."

END OF BOOK ONE

Jump on board my VIP READER CLUB and I'll gift you my Sci-fi Dystopian Thriller Story *When I Find You*.
Type this link into your browser
https://normahinkens.com/find-reader-bonus/

Reviews are my tip jar! Please be generous!
Your help in spreading the word is invaluable.
THANK YOU for leaving a review on Girl of Fire.

BIO

Award-winning Indie author Norma Hinkens writes Pretty Gritty Fiction at a pace that will leave you slack-jawed. She's also a travel junkie, legend lover, and idea wrangler, in no particular order. She grew up in Ireland, land of make-believe and the original little green man.

Connect with her on Facebook for funnies, giveaways, cool stuff & more!

https://www.facebook.com/NormaHinkensAuthor/